UNEARTHLY DESIRES

'You've been a naughty boy,' I said, amazed by the ease with which I'd fallen into the role of schoolteacher punishing a naughty pupil. 'And naughty boys need their bare bottoms spanking hard.'

'I won't do it again, miss,' he said as I spanked his glowing buttocks harder.

'You'd better not,' I returned. 'If you do, you'll get the cane.'

Repeatedly spanking the fiery flesh of his naked bottom, I realised that my clitoris was again calling for attention. My panties soaking up my juices of lust, my libido rising fast, I wondered what on earth was happening to me. I'd masturbated in my bed the previous night and was now spanking a man I'd never met before – what had I become?

By the same author:

TASTING CANDY
DEPTHS OF DEPRAVATION

UNEARTHLY DESIRES

Ray Gordon

This book is a work of fiction.
In real life, make sure you practise safe, sane consensual sex.

First published in 2006 by
Nexus
Thames Wharf Studios
Rainville Road
London W6 9HA

www.nexus-books.co.uk

Typeset by TW Typesetting, Plymouth, Devon

Printed and bound by
CPI Bookmarque, Croydon, CR0 4TD

ISBN 0 352 34036 3
ISBN 9 780352 340368

One

The day I moved into Juniper House I had no idea of the changes that lay ahead of me. I had no idea of the horrors – or the immense sexual gratification – that I was to experience. Although I was in my early twenties and had had several boyfriends, I was naive and sexually inexperienced. The ease with which I slipped into the mire of crude sex shocked me. But I had no power to fight the lure of degrading sexual acts, perverse sexual acts. On reflection, I should have realised that something was wrong on that fateful day when I went to view the house. Had I known then what I know now . . .

I'd wandered into the estate agent's office and had been drawn to Juniper House immediately. The young man behind the desk didn't seem interested in me until I told him that I had cash. He looked me up and down, obviously wondering how a girl of my age had managed to raise four hundred thousand pounds. My appearance reflected the truth – I was far from the affluent type. I was wearing the red miniskirt that Sally, my best friend, had given me. She'd also donated the white T-shirt. My long blonde hair was tousled, hanging in rats' tails over my shoulders. I'd run out of shampoo and couldn't afford to put money into the electricity meter for hot water.

1

No doubt humouring me, the agent opened a filing cabinet and passed me the details of Juniper House. I'd barely glanced at the sheet of A4 paper before making an offer. He frowned and stifled a snigger. He suggested that I view the property first and then he drove me out into the country. I'd always loved the countryside, and it was nice to get away from the noise and grime of the city for a while and breathe in the fresh air. Set on the outskirts of an idyllic country village, the house was far removed from the rented flat I'd been used to, far removed from the traffic and diesel fumes of the city. I'd never dreamed that I'd own property, let alone a beautiful home surrounded by wonderful gardens.

Dressed as I was in my scruffy clothes, I wondered again whether the estate agent really believed that I had any money. He probably saw this as an opportunity to get out of the office for a while. He must have thought me a time-waster but had decided to enjoy the country air for an hour or so. I wasn't interested in his thoughts. I wasn't interested in him. He was simply the middleman. My interest lay in Juniper House. Climbing the steps to the front door, I instinctively knew that this was to be my home, and I repeated my offer.

'I don't wish to be rude,' he said, opening the door and ushering me into the large hallway. 'But four hundred thousand is a lot of money.'

'It is,' I agreed, cocking my head to one side and smiling at him. I knew what he was getting at as he looked me up and down again. 'It's far too much. That's why I'm offering three-eighty.'

'The place is furnished,' he said, ignoring my offer and leading me into the lounge. 'The old lady died and the son lives abroad. He's not interested in the furniture or his mother's personal belongings. All he wants is the money.'

'It's like the *Marie Celeste*,' I breathed, noticing a mouldy teacup and a plate of decaying biscuits on a small table by an armchair. 'It's uncanny.'

'The son wouldn't pay to have the place cleaned up,' he enlightened me, waving his hand at a pile of magazines strewn over the sofa. 'And he's not open to offers. He wants the whole four hundred thousand.'

'I'll take it,' I blurted out. 'What do I have to do? Will you accept a cheque or . . .'

'Er . . . you'll need a solicitor,' he replied, somewhat bemused. 'We'll go back to the office and start the ball rolling.'

The sale went through quickly. Within two weeks I'd moved into Juniper House and had begun the job of cleaning up. Gazing across the huge expanse of the lawn as I cleaned the lounge windows I couldn't believe that all this was mine. There were flower borders and shrubs and statuettes. A wooden bench was set on a paved area beneath an old oak tree, and I knew that I'd discovered paradise. I felt as though I was dreaming as I recalled my small flat. No money, behind with the rent, no job, no prospects . . . From lowly tenant to lady of the manor: I couldn't believe the change.

But the change hadn't been down to me. It wasn't as if I'd earned the money or won the lottery. Four hundred thousand pounds. The money was down to a mistake made by my bank. When I'd contacted them, they'd insisted that my statement was correct. I wrote to the manager, explaining that there'd been a mistake, and he sent me another statement. Four hundred thousand pounds in credit. I then went to see the manager, and he again confirmed the balance. I wasn't going to argue any more. Before he'd had a chance to change his mind, I'd bought Juniper House.

Having cleaned the lounge and the kitchen, I went upstairs to the large room at the front of the house. It was bright and airy, with beautiful countryside views, and I decided that this was to be my bedroom. It had also been the old lady's bedroom. The bed was unmade and there was another mouldy cup and a bottle of pills on the bedside table. For some reason I felt a shudder run up my spine as I noticed that the alarm clock had stopped at two-thirty, and I was reminded again of the *Marie Celeste*. It was like moving into an inhabited house, I mused as I made up the bed with my own sheets and quilt. I half expected the old lady to appear in the doorway and ask me what I was doing in her room. But she was in some other world, an unseen world, and this was my room now.

After a day of cleaning I was exhausted and decided to have an early night. Although I was very comfortable as I lay in the huge bed, I felt acutely alone. I'd been alone in my flat, but there'd always been neighbours banging around and music emanating from somewhere or other. I'd been surrounded by life – but now? Out in the country, alone in a huge house ... But, as I drifted in and out of sleep, I felt that I wasn't alone. Faces loomed from the darkness, the pale faces of sad young girls. Was I dreaming?

My hand between my thighs, my fingers toying within the valley of my puffy sex lips, I felt sexually alive as never before. My clitoris was solid, my juices of desire flowing freely between my swelling labia. Staring into the darkness as I massaged the sensitive bulb of my clitoris, I couldn't understand why I felt so aroused. When I'd been in my flat, worry and financial troubles had quashed my libido, virtually killed it. I'd rarely thought about sex and had never felt the need to masturbate. Perhaps, now that I owned a lovely house, I was relaxed and my sexual desires were free to surface.

Raising my leg and slipping my free hand beneath my thigh, I drove two fingers into the very wet sheath of my tight vagina. Massaging the solid nub of my clitoris, fingering my contracting pussy, I was surprised by the uncharacteristic thoughts flooding my mind. Two men attending my feminine needs, two erect penises, one driving deep into my hungry pussy and the other bloating my mouth ... Sperm jetted and bathed my tongue, sperm filled my contracting pussy and overflowed and sprayed my inner thighs as I was fucked senseless. Images of spanking and naked-bottom caning loomed in my mind. A leather belt cracking loudly across the tensed orbs of my bottom, a solid penis shafting my hot vagina and spunking my cervix ... Where were these strange thoughts and images coming from? I mused dreamily as I neared my orgasm.

Listening to the squelching of my sex juices as I pistoned my vagina with my fingers, I arched my back and whimpered as the birth of my orgasm stirred deep within my contracting womb. More images loomed in my mind: a purple knob pumping creamy sperm into my thirsty mouth, a finger entering the tight duct of my hot rectum ... Never had I thought about my bottom in terms of sex, never had I dreamed of anyone fingering me there. Where *were* these weird notions coming from?

My naked body shaking violently with the most powerful orgasm I'd ever experienced, I cried out and squirmed and writhed in the bed. Again and again, shock waves of pure sexual ecstasy crashed through me, reaching every nerve ending, tightening every muscle. My firm breasts heaving, my eyes rolling, I fingered my vagina faster and massaged my clitoris harder, sustaining my incredible pleasure. The bed rocked and creaked, my gasps of pleasure resounded around the room, and darkness shrouded my illicit act. Again, lewd images flooded my mind. A solid penis entering the tight sheath of my rectum, two swollen knobs bloating my mouth . . .

Finally drifting down from my self-induced coming, I lay quivering and panting for breath beneath my quilt. I had no idea what had happened to me, why my mind had been riddled with thoughts and images of obscene and crude sex. Perhaps it was because my mind was free at last. Perhaps my libido had slipped its chains of restraint and was now free to soar out of control. Slipping into sleep, I dreamed my dreams of illicit sexual acts, two men attending my needs and bringing me massive orgasms. My dreams worried me – and comforted me.

After a good night's sleep, I sat in the kitchen sipping coffee and planning my day. Putting the events of the previous night behind me, I decided to do some shopping. I then realised that I had very little money. It hadn't occurred to me at the time, but spending all my money on the house had left me broke. The stark reality hit me: I was back where I'd started. No money, no job . . . Worse still, I now had a huge house to run and maintain.

I knew nothing about antiques but I was sure that several pieces of the old lady's furniture were worth something. There was a roll-top bureau and a glass-fronted cabinet that must each have been well over one hundred years old. Examining an old vase, I didn't like the idea of selling the furniture, but I had no choice. The vase alone might be worth a fortune, I mused, recalling an antiques programme that I'd seen on television. There were several oil paintings adorning the walls. Were they worth anything? Desperate for cash, I was going to have to sell something.

The first antique dealer I contacted didn't even bother to turn up. He'd seemed keen enough when I'd phoned and described what I had for sale but, for some reason, he must have changed his mind. The second dealer did arrive, though. He was old, with thinning grey hair, and I thought he was an antique himself. He looked at the furniture, made what I thought to be a reasonable offer, and said that he'd arrange payment and collection. That was the last I heard from him.

Becoming desperately anxious over my lack of cash, I decided to take in lodgers. The house was huge, with several rooms ideally suited for letting, and I reckoned that I could make enough money to survive. One young man responded to the advert I'd put in the local post-office window and had seemed very keen when he'd phoned me. But, once he'd seen the room, he couldn't escape fast enough. Without a word, he hurried down the stairs and fled the house. Had he seen a ghost?

A middle-aged woman turned up and said that she liked the room very much. She worked in London and reckoned that she could easily commute from the village railway station. She seemed pleasant enough and we got on well together. When she offered to help me with the upkeep of the garden I knew that she'd be an ideal tenant. We were chatting over coffee about the rent and her moving in when, inexplicably, she grabbed her handbag and fled the house.

* * *

Sitting in the lounge one evening, I began piecing things together. The vast amount of money in my bank account, the way I'd been drawn to Juniper House, the quick sale ... Everything had gone so smoothly. I'd instinctively known that the house was to be mine. It was as if it was meant to be. So why had everything gone wrong? I'd been unable to sell the furniture, unable to find a lodger ... Although I owned a beautiful house, I was worse off than I'd ever been. The bills had started rolling in, I had no food to speak of, and I was stony-broke.

Trying to free my mind of worry and relax on the sofa, I was pondering on selling the house when I became acutely aware of my clitoris. I'd not been thinking about sex, but my clitoris was swelling between my puffy vulval lips, my juices of desire flowing from my sex crack. This had nothing to do with my being relaxed. Worrying about the lack of money and what the future held, I was far from relaxed. I'd been considering having the phone cut off because I couldn't afford to pay the bill, and I was reminded of the harsh times back in my flat. But, despite my anxiety, my libido was soaring out of control.

Squeezing and kneading the firm mounds of my breasts, tweaking my erect nipples, I was about to slip my blouse and bra off and caress the sensitive teats of my breasts when the front doorbell rang. Running my fingers through my long blonde hair, trying to make myself look presentable, I pushed all thought of sex out of my mind as I dashed into the hall. Had one of the would-be lodgers come back? I wondered, opening the front door.

'Yes?' I said, smiling at a middle-aged man standing there.

'Sorry I'm late,' he said, looking at his watch. 'I

8

had trouble getting away. Are you still able to accommodate me?'

'Accommodate you?' I murmured, frowning at him. 'Ah, the room. I'm sorry, I wasn't thinking.'

Dressed in smart black trousers and a crisp white shirt, he was well turned out, probably a business-man. With his dark hair swept back from his forehead, he was also pretty good-looking. He'd make a good lodger, I decided, hoping that he'd like the room at the back of the house. Reckoning that he wasn't short of money, I was sure that I wouldn't have trouble with his rent. And I doubted that he'd throw wild parties. But he seemed confused as he gazed at me and I wondered whether he'd already had a change of mind. Was he too going to run off without a word of explanation?

'You *have* come about a room?' I asked him.

'I want to play another game this week,' he chuckled, walking past me into the hall. 'You're my teacher, and I've been a naughty schoolboy.'

'What?' I breathed, my eyes widening as he marched into the lounge. What the hell was he talking about?

'I've been a naughty schoolboy and I need a good spanking,' he announced matter-of-factly, grinning at me as I followed him into the lounge. 'Money up front, as always.'

Watching him open his wallet and place fifty pounds on the coffee table, I couldn't believe that this was happening. 'There's been some mistake,' I said, forcing a smile. 'I don't know what –'

I stared in stunned silence as he lowered his trousers and leaned over the back of an armchair. Who the hell *was* this man? What on earth did he think he was doing? To walk into my home and drop his trousers . . . In my confusion, I began to wonder whether *I* was the one who'd made a mistake and was in the wrong house. Was this some kind of television stunt? Would a celebrity walk into the room and announce that I'd been made a fool of? Dragging my stare away from the man's naked buttocks, I gazed at the cash lying on the table. I didn't know him from Adam but he obviously thought that I was a prostitute. Had the estate agent suggested that I might be easy game? I wondered. I doubted that very much. Had the man seen me in the village, discovered where I lived and thought he'd try his luck? I didn't know what to think. But I knew that I had to throw him out.

'What are you waiting for?' he asked me.

'When were you last here?' I breathed.

'Last week,' he replied. 'Have you lost your memory?'

'No, no,' I murmured, trying to understand what was going on. 'It's just that . . .'

'We've played the naughty-schoolboy game before, so what's the problem?'

'Nothing,' I replied, eyeing the cash again.

Fifty pounds in return for spanking this man's naked bottom? Easy money, I mused. But I wasn't a prostitute and had no intention of becoming one. There again, if a spanking was all he wanted, and he called round once a week . . . I hadn't eaten properly for several days and was in dire need of a decent meal. Fifty pounds? No one would know what I'd done, I thought as I stood behind him. It would be my secret, my dirty little secret. Besides, where was the harm in spanking his bottom? It wasn't as if I was going to have sex with him. The more I thought about spanking him – and the more I thought about food – the more I convinced myself that I should comply with his crude request. His mistake could well become my gain.

10

Raising my hand, I brought my palm down across the tensed flesh of his pale buttocks with a loud slap. He let out a gasp and said that he'd been a naughty boy and should be spanked harder. He was weird, obviously some sort of pervert, but I reckoned that he was harmless enough. He probably had a wife and kids at home, I reflected, bringing my hand down again across his naked buttocks. He wouldn't try to force himself upon me, I was sure. All he wanted was to live out his fantasy. And all I wanted, all I needed, was a decent meal.

Spanking him harder, I wondered again who the hell he was. And who *he* thought *I* was. He couldn't have known me, I mused. He was obviously mistaking me for someone else – but who? He couldn't have been to the house to receive a spanking from the old lady. Or could he? Even if she had been a prostitute, the man couldn't have mistaken me for her. Did I have a double? In my confusion I wondered whether I was one of a pair of twins and my mother hadn't told me about my sister. Was I going mad? The man had obviously been to the house before and thought that he'd met me. Whatever the confusion, whatever the mistake, I was fifty pounds the richer.

'You've been a naughty boy,' I said, amazed by the ease with which I'd fallen into the role of a schoolteacher punishing a naughty pupil. 'And naughty boys need their bare bottoms spanking hard.'

'I won't do it again, miss,' he said as I spanked his glowing buttocks harder.

'You'd better not,' I snapped. 'If you do, you'll get the cane.'

Repeatedly spanking the fiery flesh of his naked bottom, I realised that my clitoris was calling again for attention. My panties soaking up my juices of lust, my libido rising fast, I wondered what on earth

11

was happening to me. I'd masturbated in my bed the previous night and now I was spanking a man I'd never met before. And I'd taken cash in return. What had I become? My clitoris solid, my pussy milk flowing in torrents into the crotch of my panties, my mind was again riddled with thoughts of crude sex. Had I somehow woken my latent desires? Or had I gone completely mad? I'd had several boyfriends but had only indulged in straight sex with them. Never had I dreamed of spanking a man's bare bottom.

The loud slaps resounded around the room. Not only was I losing control of myself, but I was enjoying the game immensely. Was the thought of the cash driving me on? Was the thought of enjoying a decent meal compelling me to commit the lewd act? Noticing the man's heavy balls swinging between his parted thighs, I imagined that his cock was as hard as rock. It had been several months since I'd last enjoyed the feel of a solid penis driving deep into my pussy, and I felt an overwhelming desire to . . . what the hell was I thinking? I wondered. What the hell was I becoming? There was no way I was going to have sex with a stranger. And to take cash in return for . . . maybe I *was* a prostitute.

'That's enough,' I finally said, trying to get a grip on myself as I gazed at his crimsoned buttocks.

'What about the leather belt?' he asked me. 'You usually give me the strap when I've been naughty.'

'The strap?' I echoed. Was this a dream?

'You *have* lost your memory,' he chuckled. 'I'm talking about the leather strap you keep in that cupboard,' he added, pointing to the sideboard.

Opening its door, I rummaged through the cupboard and pulled out a leather belt. How did he know it was there? Had I really lost my memory? Overcome with confusion, I wrapped the end of the belt around my hand and stood behind the man again. It wasn't the money which was driving me on, I knew. It wasn't even the thought of a decent meal. But *something* was urging me to commit the indecent act. Something – or someone?

Bringing the leather belt down across the man's twitching behind with a loud crack, I felt my womb convulse with sexual excitement. Again, in my rising wickedness, I brought the belt down with a deafening thwack. The man's buttocks were now glowing a fire-red: I lost control completely and repeatedly lashed the raw flesh of his quivering bottom. Images of his solid cock loomed in the confusion of my mind. His swollen knob entering my tight pussy, his shaft opening me to capacity, his spunk bathing my ripe cervix as he fucked me. Again and again I flailed his bum cheeks, the cracking of the belt echoing around the room as my arousal soared out of control.

'That's enough,' he finally gasped.

'But you've been a very naughty little boy,' I replied, bringing the belt down again. 'You've been wanking.' The shocking words tumbling from my lips, I couldn't understand why I was saying such things. 'You were caught wanking in the school toilets, and now you'll have to be punished most severely.'

'No, no more,' he breathed, hauling his body upright and turning to face me.

'Why are you stiff?' I asked him, gazing in awe at his magnificent penis standing to attention above his rolling balls. My vagina tightened, yearning to hug the sheer girth of his beautiful cock. 'You're not going to wank again, are you?' I asked him.

'No, miss.'

'Show me how you wank,' I ordered him, shocked again by my crude words. 'Show me what you did to deserve the leather belt.'

Grabbing his solid cock, the man breathed deeply as he ran his hand up and down the veined shaft. Watching his purple knob appear and disappear as he moved his foreskin up and down, I once more felt my clitoris swelling and my juices of arousal seeping into the tight crotch of my wet panties. His full balls jerked, bouncing up and down as he wanked, and he leaned against the back of the armchair to steady his trembling body. I'd never seen a man masturbate, and I watched in expectation, waiting excitedly for his sperm to jet from his bulbous knob.

Wondering again what had happened to me, pondering on my uncharacteristic thoughts, my lewd behaviour, I knew that something was influencing me. I'd never met this man before, and yet I'd spanked him, lashed his naked buttocks with a leather belt, and was now watching him wank and eagerly awaiting his spunk. His balls bounced faster as he increased his wanking motion. I knelt on the floor and focused on his purple knob. Mentally urging him to come, to shoot his orgasmic liquid over the carpet, I only just managed to restrain myself from grabbing his cock and finishing the job for him.

Piecing things together, I was sure that the money and the house were meant to be. It was as if the whole episode had been orchestrated. When I'd left the bank I'd been drawn into the estate agent's office. Juniper House was four hundred thousand, the exact amount that had miraculously appeared in my bank account. And now a man I'd never seen before had turned up and offered me money to spank him. Normally I would have sent him packing, probably called the police. But this wasn't 'normally'. This was completely *ab*normal. Not only had I spanked him, thrashed his naked buttocks with the leather belt, but I'd ordered him to wank.

The man's body crumpled as his sperm jetted from his swollen knob, splattering over the carpet, and I was tempted to take his cock into my mouth and drink his orgasmic cream. What the hell was I thinking? I wondered again. I'd never been into oral sex – the very idea had revolted me. But now? Licking my lips as I watched a long strand of spunk hanging from his hand, I was engulfed by an overwhelming desire to suck his beautiful knob into my wet mouth and swallow his creamy sperm. Rising to my feet as he brought out the last of his orgasmic liquid, I tried to come to my senses. I was thinking like a common whore. I'd behaved like a slut.

'God, I needed that,' he gasped, finally tugging his trousers up and concealing his sperm-dripping penis. 'I'll see you next week. And I'll try not to be late.'

'Yes, that's fine,' I replied abstractedly as he walked into the hall. A thousand questions battering my tormented mind, I followed him to the front door and offered him a smile. 'Is there anything else I can do for you?' I asked him stupidly. 'I mean, do you want more than –.'

'You know what I like,' the man cut in. 'A good spanking, and then a wank while you watch. I'll see you next week, Alison.'

Alison? The front door closed and he'd gone. And I was in a state of shock. How did he know my name? Holding my hand to my head, I felt a bolt of fear course through me. More confused than ever, I didn't know what to think. Had I lost my memory? I couldn't have. I'd only moved into the house a few days previously. The house had been empty until I'd moved in, so . . . Again holding my head as I returned to the lounge, I felt dizzy in my confusion. He knew me, he knew my name, he knew where the leather belt was . . . Grabbing the money from the table, I clutched the notes in my hand. They were real. I hadn't been dreaming.

Awash with guilt and remorse for what I'd done, I flopped onto the sofa. I no longer felt hungry – I was too bewildered to eat. Wishing that I'd questioned the man, asked him who he was, where he lived and how he knew me, I decided not to see him again. I wouldn't answer the door the next time he called. I wasn't a prostitute. No matter how broke I was, no matter how much money he offered me, I wasn't going to turn to prostitution in order to survive.

The following day I walked into the village and enjoyed a full English breakfast at a small café. Then I began looking for work. The local shops had nothing to offer, and I ended up asking in the village pub. Bar work, cleaning . . . I'd do anything to bring in some cash. Nothing. At my wit's end, I was about to go home when I noticed a small antiques shop. My furniture *must* be saleable, I felt sure as I entered the shop and looked around. Although the man who'd viewed the bureau and cabinet hadn't come back he'd offered me two hundred pounds. And the oil paintings must have been worth something.

'Sorry,' the man behind the counter said. 'I'm not buying in at the moment.'

'You could at least take a look,' I sighed. 'I only live up the lane, at Juniper House.'

'Juniper House?' he echoed, frowning at me. 'You've bought the place?'

'Yes, and I want to sell some of the furniture.'

'I didn't know the place had sold. How long have you been there?'

'Not long. Look, I need some money. I'll take whatever you offer me.'

'I have no room at the moment. As it is, I have far

16

too much stock. What do you intend to do with the house?'

'Live in it,' I snapped, leaving the shop.

I hadn't meant to be rude to the shopkeeper but I was becoming desperate. I'd spent the fifty pounds, my illicit earnings, on shopping, and was wondering how long the food would last. Lugging the carrier bags home, I dumped them on the kitchen table and made myself a cup of coffee. The situation was ridiculous, I mused, taking my coffee into the lounge. I owned a huge house worth nearly half a million pounds, and yet I was completely broke. At least I'd enjoyed a decent breakfast and now had enough food to last for several days. But what then?

Sipping my coffee, I pondered again on the possibility that the whole thing had been orchestrated. If that was the case, if there was a plan, then what was the next stage? I was going crazy, I knew. Of course there was no plan. The bank had made a mistake with my account, and I'd spent every penny on Juniper House. I'd been stupid with the money, it was as simple as that. But my stupidity didn't explain away the man who'd paid me to spank him. He knew my name, he knew where the belt was . . . And I hadn't even thought to ask his name. I could have taken his name and phone number, I reflected. I could have said that I'd lost my address book and needed his name and number. But I'd been confused and unable to think straight. Confused – and sexually aroused as never before.

After two days of travelling around the surrounding towns and villages looking for a job, I'd given up all hope of finding work. It seemed that everything was against me. I was too young or the post had just been filled or times were hard and businesses were downsizing . . . Wondering where my next meal was coming from, I knew that I had to sell the house. If I bought another place for half the price, I'd have a home and two hundred thousand in cash. I rang the estate agent, sure that he'd be able to sell the property.

'I don't know,' he sighed. 'It looks as if there's a property crash on the way.'

'You could at least try,' I said irritably.

'I'll put it on the books, but I can't promise anything. Aren't you happy there?'

'I'm broke,' I confessed. 'I can't find work and . . . I can't even let a couple of rooms.'

'You want lodgers?'

'Yes, I do. Can you help?'

'Possibly. Have you considered bed and breakfast?'

'No, but it sounds good.'

'It's the right time of year for holidaymakers. And your location is pretty good as a base. There are walks, country pubs, the steam museum at –'

'OK,' I cut in. 'Let's go for it.'

'I'll get back to you. I'll check with our other offices and let you know.'

Bed and breakfast was a pretty good idea. Since I was not too bad at cooking, I could also offer evening meals at extra cost. Feeling elated by the idea, I managed to push all thoughts of my male visitor to the back of my mind and get on with cleaning the house. There was plenty of space for parking, the rooms were large and airy, and the dining room would easily accommodate two if not three families. Once I had regular holidaymakers and word got round, I'd be fully booked for the following year. All I had to do in the meantime was survive.

Two days had passed since I'd spoken to the estate agent but it felt like two weeks. What was he doing?

18

Had he made any inquiries? He'd been right about Juniper House being ideally located for bed and breakfast, and I pondered on the idea of placing an advert in a national newspaper. The idea was good, except I couldn't afford to pay for an ad. Trying to take my mind off my worries, I decided to clear out the old lady's bureau. Sorting through a pile of papers, I happened to find a letter addressed to her. It was from her son, and contained nothing of interest – apart from one thing. It was addressed to Alison Beaty. Alison? I pondered anxiously. This was uncanny. We shared the same Christian name.

Two

I'd just finished my meal one evening – beans on one piece of toast – when the doorbell rang. Hoping that it was good news, I wondered whether my friend Sally had come to visit me. I needed to talk to her, spend some time with her. Cut off in my huge country house, I was beginning to feel acutely lonely. Sally had promised to come down from London and stay for a few days, but I'd heard nothing from her. Had my phone been cut off?

'Hello,' I said cheerily, finding a young man on the doorstep. Had he come to look the place over? Had the estate agent sent him? 'Please come in.'

'What do you offer?' he asked, walking into the hall and looking me up and down.

I immediately knew that he wasn't interested in bed and breakfast. Bed, maybe, but not breakfast. 'Offer?' I echoed, my stomach churning. This couldn't be happening again. 'What do you mean?'

'What services do you offer? And how much?'

'What are you into?' I asked him, immediately wishing I hadn't.

'How about a hand job?' he said unashamedly.

I wanted to tell him to leave, but I couldn't. As hard as I tried to order him to go, my thoughts just wouldn't turn into words. Wandering into the lounge,

I knew instinctively that he'd become a regular client. I didn't want to get into prostitution, I didn't want . . . Fifty pounds? Was that a fair price for a hand job? He followed me and stood in the middle of the room. He wasn't bad-looking, but did I want to wank off a total stranger? The thought of cash – and food – was enticing. But something else was motivating me, urging me to commit the illicit act. Where had he come from? Who had sent him? Was this all part of an unfolding plan? If so, who was behind it? And why?

'So, how much for a hand job?' he asked, making himself comfortable in the armchair.

'Er . . . I normally charge fifty,' I replied, watching closely for his reaction. 'May I ask who sent you?'

'I'd rather not say.'

'Will you at least tell me where you live? Are you from the village?'

'Why all these questions?' he asked. 'I'm a married man, and I'd rather you knew nothing about me.'

'Yes, I realise that discretion is . . . But I would like to know who recommended me.'

'It was a chap in the pub. Will you accept forty?'

'As it's your first time, yes. Money up front, of course.'

'It's not my first time,' he breathed, smiling at me. 'I was here last year. You obviously don't remember me.'

'Last year? But I thought a man in the pub had recommended –'

'That's right. But it was last year.'

Taking some notes from his jacket pocket and tossing them onto the coffee table, the young man unbuckled his belt and tugged his trousers down to his ankles. Last year? I mused. This was crazy. *I* was crazy. I'd either lost my memory or . . . *Was* I crazy? Had I lived here in the past? Wondering whether I'd

21

lived at Juniper House in a previous life, I thought that I might be dead. I'd seen some ridiculous film on television about people not accepting that they were dead. Was I in the spirit world? Was this heaven? Or hell?

Watching as my visitor's stiffening cock rose from the soft flesh of his scrotum and finally stood to attention, I knew that I was alive and kicking. I also felt instinctively that this was right. I needed money, he needed relief, so what was the problem? There was no problem, other than the fact that I didn't want to become a common prostitute. *Prostitute*. The word conjured up images of miniskirted sluts hanging around on street corners. Picked up by dirty old men in cars, they offered blow jobs and . . . That wasn't for me. Gazing at my would-be client, I knew that there had to be an explanation. This was the second man who knew me, the second man who not only believed that I was a prostitute but who had been to the house before.

A prostitute. The word wouldn't leave my thoughts. A common prostitute. I was far from common, I mused. Stony broke, but certainly not common. It wasn't as if I was offering him a blow job or full sex, I consoled myself. Giving the odd hand job or spanking could hardly label me a prostitute. A chap in the pub? I reflected. Did he mean the pub in the village? I dared not ask him any more questions. I needed his money, and the last thing I wanted to do was frighten him off. But a few tentative questions in the pub later that evening might prove enlightening.

I finally settled at his feet (he'd seated himself in an armchair) and scrutinised his beautiful organ. His shaft was broad and long, his purple knob peeping at me through the opening in his fleshy foreskin. His full balls heaved and rolled, and my clitoris swelled and my juices of desire flowed into my already wet panties. I hadn't felt so horny for a long time and I had difficulty controlling myself. To have taken his knob into my wet mouth and sucked gently . . . Again wondering where my lewd thoughts were coming from, I tried not to think about sex. This was business, I reminded myself. I was doing this for cash, not for sexual enjoyment.

Tickling his scrotum with my fingernails, I felt my stomach somersault as I imagined his solid penis entering my tight vagina. Shafting me, in out, in out, fucking me, spunking me . . . I *was* a prostitute. Pondering again on the word, I wondered what had changed me. I'd never considered myself a prude, but I'd not had a great deal of sexual experience. I'd enjoyed the closeness of lovemaking with one or two boyfriends, but I'd never actually craved sex. Until now. And I'd certainly never dreamed of offering to wank a man to orgasm in return for cash. Hard, cold sex. What had I become? A prostitute.

Grabbing the warm shaft of the young man's rock-hard cock, I moved my hand slowly up and down its length. I felt that I wanted to pleasure him properly, expertly. If he was to come back for more . . . Was that what I wanted? Several men visiting me regularly for hand jobs – was that what I wanted? I didn't know what I wanted as I wanked his beautiful organ, rolling his foreskin back and forth over the purple globe of his succulent knob. There *was* one thing, I reflected. I wanted answers. I wanted to know who these men were, and who they thought I was.

'You have a beautiful cock,' I breathed huskily, running my thumb over the glistening surface of his purple knob. Where were these words coming from? 'Hard, long . . . I hope you're going to pump out a lot of spunk for me.'

'Yes, I will,' he gasped, his eyes rolling as I fondled his heavy balls with my free hand and continued to massage his swollen glans.

'When did you last come?'

'I don't know. A few days ago, I suppose.'

'Does your wife wank you?' I felt wicked, dirty. 'Does she wank your hard cock and watch your spunk shoot out?'

'No, no, she doesn't.'

'Then it's just as well that you have me to look after your needs.'

Losing myself in my arousal as I wanked his solid penis, I reminded myself again that this was business. No matter how much I wanted to suck on his beautiful knob and drink his fresh spunk, no matter how I yearned to feel his hard cock stretching open my tight pussy, this was purely a business arrangement. Forty pounds, food and drink ... But what about the bills? I'd need several hundred a month coming in to survive properly. There was only one way to bring in more cash. Get more clients.

'God, don't stop,' the young man gasped. 'I'm nearly there.'

'You're a naughty boy,' I said with a giggle, longing for his spunk to shoot from his knob-slit and bathe my hand. 'You must come here every week and allow me to wank you.'

'Yes, yes, I will.'

'I want you to come all over my hand. Be a good boy and spunk all over my hand.'

I reckoned that I was enjoying myself as much as he was as his cock swelled and his glans turned deep purple. His creamy sperm jetted from his throbbing knob as he gasped and writhed in the armchair. The feel of his male cream flowing over my fingers as I continued my wanking motions sent my libido to frightening heights – I had to fight desperately to stop myself from taking his cock into my mouth and drinking his gushing spunk. What the hell was coaxing me? I wondered as I gazed at his spunk running over my hand and landing on his bouncing balls. What was driving me on?

Massaging his orgasmic cream into his scrotum with my free hand, I knew that I'd soon be going further with my clients. Cocksucking, spunk swallowing . . . Would I have full-blown sex? I mused as my clitoris again called for attention. His sperm flow finally slowed and I released his cock and wiped my hand on my T-shirt. This was extremely easy money, I thought, rising to my feet and grabbing the cash as my client recovered from his coming. Forty pounds for a few minutes' work? I'd only need to attend a couple of cocks each day and I'd be rich. What should I charge for full sex?

'Would you like to call each week?' I asked my young visitor as he pulled his trousers up and moved to the door.

'Every Wednesday,' he replied. 'I'm in the area every Wednesday, if that suits you?'

'That suits me fine. In case something crops up, do you have a phone number I could call you on?'

'Er . . . no, no, I haven't.'

'Not to worry. Until next week, then.'

As he left, I thought about following him. But with my luck he'd see me and I'd lose him as a regular client. How many more men would turn up on my doorstep? I wondered as I grabbed my jacket. How many more men would come to me for my sexual services? It was strange how everything was falling into place, and I couldn't help but wonder again whether this was being orchestrated. There was coincidence, and there was .... What? Sharing the same Christian name as the old lady was uncanny. Was it purely coincidence?

I left the house, walked down the lane to the village pub and decided to sit in a secluded corner. If anyone thought that they recognised me, if someone wanted to speak to me, they'd come and join me. If a client I'd never seen before approached me, should I make out that I knew him? How I should react, I had no idea. But I felt that I'd get some answers by visiting the pub. And, if not, then at least I'd enjoy an hour or so away from the house.

The pub was quiet with only three or four people standing at the bar, but I recognised one of them. He was the antiques dealer I'd been rude to. He acknowledged me with a smile and a nod as I bought myself a vodka and lime. Had he been to Juniper House? I wondered, taking a seat at a corner table. Had he known the old lady? More to the point, was he a client? I needed answers.

'I'm sorry I couldn't help with your furniture,' he said as he approached, bringing his beer with him.

'And I'm sorry I was rude to you,' I replied. 'I was in a bit of a state and . . . I'm Alison, by the way.'

'Jim, Jim Burrows. Have you settled into the house?'

'Just about. What with the old lady's belongings everywhere, there's still quite a lot to do. Did you know her?'

'I didn't really know her, but I've met her several times over the years. I've lived in the village all my life.'

'What did she do? I mean, did she have many friends or visitors?'

'I've no idea,' he murmured pensively as he sat opposite me and placed his drink on the table. 'She never married. She had a son, but he went off abroad somewhere. She was very secretive, by all accounts.'

'Oh?'

'She kept herself to herself. Rumour has it that in her younger days she was quite a one for the men. Mind you, in a village like this, rumours are rife.'

He was a nice man, and I felt guilty about having been rude to him. Dressed in a tweed jacket and wearing a cravat, he looked like an antiques dealer. Reckoning him to be in his sixties, I thought he was warm and friendly and I hoped to get to know him. But he didn't seem to know a great deal about the old lady. I'd gone to the pub in the hope of finding some answers, not making small talk with an ageing man. But since he'd lived in the village all his life I'd have thought that he'd have known something about the old lady. Perhaps he did and was keeping quiet. Persisting with my questioning, I asked him whether he'd ever been up to the house.

'No, no,' he replied, finishing his beer. 'I don't know of anyone who's been there. I don't usually listen to local gossip, but it seems that she had many affairs. Apparently, she was a man-eater.'

'Jim, I know this is going to sound odd,' I breathed, leaning forward across the table. 'But was she a prostitute?'

'I have no idea,' he replied, chuckling. 'Why do you ask?'

'It was a rumour I heard.'

'Perhaps she was, and that's why she was so secretive. Changing the subject, I'd like to look at the furniture. I'll at least value it for you and, once I've moved some stock, I might be in a position to buy.'

'That's nice of you. My finances aren't quite so bad now, but I'd like to sell one or two items. When would you be able to take a look?'

'Now, if that's OK?'

'Oh, er . . . yes, yes – that's fine,' I said, finishing my drink.

As we left the pub and walked along the lane I wondered whether Jim was married. I thought that it might be nice to become friends with him. I was an outsider and, seeing as he'd lived in the village all his life, I thought that he might introduce me to other villagers. I didn't want to be known just as *that girl in the big house*. I'd far rather get to know some of the locals and possibly make a few friends. But, like the old lady, I was going to have to keep some secrets. Dirty secrets.

'You live alone?' Jim asked me as we climbed the steps and I opened the front door.

'Yes, I do. It's silly, isn't it? A huge house like this, and I live here alone.'

'I have a small cottage,' he said as I led him into the lounge. 'I live alone, but I have the shop to keep me busy.'

'I suppose I keep myself busy,' I said. Busy with clients?

'This is an amazing place, Alison,' he breathed, looking about the room. 'As I said, I've never been here before. I wonder where the lady acquired the furniture? Some of it's pretty old.'

'I don't know. But I'm glad it was left here. I didn't bring anything from my flat in the way of furniture because it was all junk. Would you like a cup of coffee?'

'No, I'm fine, thanks. That bureau looks interesting. May I?'

'Yes, carry on,' I said, sitting on the sofa. 'Hopefully, you'll tell me that it's worth thousands. As you've probably gathered, I'm stony-broke. I've been trying to let a room to get some money in, but no one's interested.'

'I suppose you're cut off out here in the country. Had you been in town it might have been easier.'

As Jim examined the bureau, I felt an overwhelming desire to run my hand up and down his cock and bring out his sperm. I hadn't even been thinking about sex, and yet my arousal was rocketing. Desperate as I was to feel the hardness of his manhood in my hand, I dared not let him discover that I was a prostitute. If word got around the village ... Was that why the old lady had been secretive? I wondered again. Had she been a prostitute?

Jim hadn't turned up unannounced and asked me what I had to offer, unlike the other men. There'd been nothing peculiar or mysterious about our meeting. So why was my mind riddled with thoughts of wanking his hard cock and watching his sperm jet from his purple knob? I'd been going through a massive change since I'd moved into the house, that was for sure. From a shy and almost prudish girl to a prostitute, the transformation was incredible. But why had I changed? Why this fascination, this obsession, with sex?

Whatever had changed me, I had to have Jim's cock. The thought of stroking his full balls, the feel of his sperm flooding over my hand as I wanked him . . . But I could hardly ask him whether he wanted a hand job. Pulling my short skirt up and parting my thighs a little, I hoped that he'd spy my tight panties and get the message. As I lay back on the sofa, I knew that he'd think me a slut, but I couldn't help myself. I'd had no thoughts about sex when I'd invited Jim to the house. I'd hoped that we'd become friends, nothing more. He was in his sixties, I reminded myself. I was in my early twenties. He was far too old for me. Parting my thighs further, I wondered what the hell I was playing at as he turned and gazed at the crotch of my tight panties.

'It's worth around five hundred,' he said, unable to take his eyes off my panties.

'What is?' I asked stupidly.

'The bureau. What I'll do, if it's all right with you, is give you five hundred and pick it up once I've made some room in the shop.'

'Five hundred?' I breathed. 'That will certainly help my finances.'

'Call into the shop tomorrow and I'll give you the cash. Right, I'd better be going.'

'Don't go yet,' I said huskily. 'I get very lonely, Jim. Come and sit with me for a while.'

Resting my hand on his knee as he sat beside me, I felt that I wasn't in control. Something, or someone, seemed to be influencing me, urging me on. Moving my hand up his thigh, I squeezed the crotch of his trousers and told him how much I liked him. He smiled at me, but obviously didn't know what to say. He must have thought this was his lucky day, I mused. A girl in her early twenties coming on strong, grabbing his crotch . . . He also must have thought me a whore.

'I'm sorry,' I breathed guiltily. 'I don't know what's come over me. I don't normally –'

'You don't have to explain,' he cut in. 'I too get very lonely, Alison.'

Unzipping his trousers, I hauled out his solid penis and ran my hand up and down its length. He breathed deeply, reclining on the sofa and closing his eyes as I massaged his swollen knob through his fleshy foreskin. A terrible thought occurred to me as I masturbated him. He was older than my father. Perhaps, when I'd met him in the pub, I'd looked upon him as a father figure. But not now. I was wanking a man in his sixties, waiting for his spunk to gush from his throbbing knob and splatter my hand. What must he have thought of me? What the hell did I think of myself now that I was a prostitute? Had I lost all self-esteem?

I had to stop worrying, I decided. So Jim was older than my father. So what? Did age really matter? I wasn't doing this for money, he wasn't a client. We were friends, and I hoped that we'd see more of each other. I hadn't seen my father for several years, and my mother had never been interested in me. I needed a friend, a male friend. A father figure, and a lover. Would we become lovers? I was a prostitute. If Jim discovered the shocking truth . . . No one would ever learn of my secret life, my dirty life.

'Is that all right for you?' I asked him, increasing my wanking rhythm.

'God, yes,' he murmured. 'It's been so long since . . .'

'You won't have to wait in the future, Jim. You have me now.'

'But I'm an old man and you're a young girl. Why the interest in me?'

'Because I like you very much. Now stop talking and relax.'

Leaning forward, I fully retracted Jim's foreskin and sucked his purple globe into my hot mouth. I'd lost control, I knew as I probed his knob-slit with my wet tongue. This wasn't me, this wasn't my doing. Never had I dreamed of sucking a man's cock. The very notion of sucking and licking a man's knob had always revolted me. But now I was loving every minute of it. The salty taste, the smoothness of his glans beneath my sweeping tongue, the feel of his hard shaft between my full lips . . . Now I was desperate to taste fresh sperm.

'You're amazing,' Jim breathed as he clutched my head. 'I'm coming . . . God, I'm coming.'

His sperm gushed, flooding my mouth and filling my cheeks. I savoured the heady taste of his male cream before swallowing hard. My mouth overflowing, I listened to his low moans of pleasure as he rocked his hips and fucked my mouth as if it were my vagina. I couldn't think why I'd been against cocksucking in the past, so revolted by the thought of drinking spunk. I loved the taste of spunk, the feel of a knob throbbing in orgasm against my snaking tongue. His solid shaft twitching, his sperm pumping in spurts from his ballooning knob, he breathed heavily and trembled as I continued to drink from his fountainhead. Repeatedly swallowing his spunk and wanking his shaft to sustain his orgasm, I sucked hard on his beautiful knob until his balls had drained and he shuddered his last orgasmic shudder.

'All right?' I asked him, slipping his deflating cock out of my mouth and licking my sperm-glossed lips.

'God, yes,' Jim managed to gasp. 'You're incredible, Alison. I thought I was only going to value your furniture, not enjoy the pleasure of your pretty mouth.' Zipping his trousers, he looked me in the eye and smiled. 'I suppose you have several men friends?' he asked me dolefully.

'I don't have any men friends,' I lied. No, it wasn't a lie. I had clients, not friends. 'I'm new here, so I have no friends.'

'Alison, would you like to see me again? I mean, we could have a drink in the pub or –'

'I'd like very much to see you again, Jim,' I cut in. 'I've had a nice evening. It makes a change from sitting here alone.'

'And my evening has been . . . how shall I put it? Most enjoyable. You asked me whether the old lady who lived here was a prostitute. What have you heard about her?'

'It was something the estate agent said. I can't remember his exact words, but he said something about the old lady having clients visit her.'

'About forty years ago there was a rumour going around the village. It seems that she had several male friends, and some of the locals thought that she might be charging them for sex.'

'Why didn't you tell me this before?'

'I'd forgotten about it. Forty years is a long time, Alison. Besides, it was only a rumour.'

'Do you know anything else about her?'

'No, not really. When she was young, she was extremely attractive. Actually, she looked very much like you. Long blonde hair, fresh face, big blue eyes . . . You could be her double.'

My heart racing, I clasped my hands together to stop them trembling. Her double? We shared the same Christian name, she looked like me . . . What the hell was going on? I wondered as Jim examined the roll-top bureau again. The clients who'd visited the house forty years ago would be old men now. How come younger men were mistaking me for the old lady? Feeling anxious and fearful, I saw Jim to the front door and arranged to meet him in the pub the following evening. I would have asked him to stay a little longer, offered him some coffee, but I had some serious thinking to do. After watching him walk down the drive to the lane, I closed the door and went back into the lounge. My evening had been ruined. I'd so much enjoyed sucking Jim's cock, drinking his sperm and . . . Now my thoughts had turned back to the old lady.

Sifting through the piles of papers in the bureau, I was hoping to find something, anything that would throw some light on the incredible situation. There was nothing, apart from an old piece of blotting paper with the word *séance* on it, back to front in blue ink. Had she been playing around with the occult? I wondered. Was she now coming back and haunting me? If she was influencing me, that still didn't explain the male visitors. Feeling more confused than ever, I rummaged through the papers at the back of the bureau and discovered a key with a label attached.

'Den,' I breathed, sure that the word didn't refer to a man's name. 'Sex den?' I'd been into every room in the house, checked every nook and cranny. Had I missed something? Clutching the key, I wandered into the hall. 'Den,' I breathed again, sure that there was a secret room somewhere in the house. Was there a concealed door or panel somewhere? I wondered. Having no idea where to begin my search, I was about to climb the stairs when the front doorbell rang. Almost jumping out of my skin, I wondered whether Jim had come back. Did he want the pleasure of my mouth again?

'Sally,' I exclaimed, beaming as I opened the door. 'It's great to see you.'

'Sorry I didn't phone,' she said, dumping her suitcase on the hall floor. 'I lost your number and had no way of contacting you.'

'That doesn't matter. It really is good to see you. Come into the lounge.'

'God,' she murmured, following me in and flopping onto the sofa. 'This is an amazing house. I still find it hard to believe that you got all that money for nothing.'

'So do I. I'll have to show you round later. Did you drive down or get the train?'

'I got the train, and then a taxi from the station. The taxi driver was weird. He asked me whether I intended to work at Juniper House.'

'Work here?'

'He was a randy old man. He kept looking at my legs and grinning. I wish I'd worn jeans instead of a short skirt. I asked him what he meant and he said that he didn't realise Juniper House was back in business.'

'Back in business?' I echoed. *Prostitute, brothel*. 'I have no idea what he meant by that. Anyway, I'm so glad you came.'

'Don't you get lonely here? A massive house all to yourself, stuck out in the country . . . you must get very lonely.'

'No, not at all. I've made one or two friends. In fact, one of them has only just left.'

'Men?' she said, with an impish giggle. 'Talking of which, I bumped into Charlie the other day. He said that he's split up with Julia again and . . .'

As Sally rambled on, I pondered on the taxi driver's words. Back in business. Why would he think that Sally intended to work at Juniper House? Putting two and two together, I knew exactly what he was talking about. The house had been a brothel, and he thought that the business was up and running again and Sally was going to work as one of the girls. Surely, if the house had been a brothel, the villagers would have known about it? Was the taxi driver a local man? He obviously knew something about Juniper House.

Eyeing Sally's slender legs as she updated me with the gossip, I thought how attractive she was. It was no wonder that the taxi driver had eyed her long legs. In her late teens, with long black hair and huge dark eyes, she was slim and beautiful. I wouldn't be able to entertain my male callers with Sally around, I decided. She'd probably only stay for a few days. My business would have to close for a while. Business? I had to accept what I now believed to be a fact. I'd bought a house that had been a brothel. And I was rekindling that business.

'You've certainly moved on,' Sally said, breaking into my reverie. 'From a poxy little flat to a country mansion . . .'

'It's not a mansion,' I replied with a laugh.

'It *looks* like a mansion. How the hell are you going to keep the garden looking nice? It'll take you hours just to mow the lawn. You'll have to get a gardener, Alison. A fit young man with a bronzed muscular body and –'

'There's a problem,' I cut in. 'I don't have any money. I spent every penny on this place, and now I'm broke.'

'You could get a job. What you want to do is . . .'

Again allowing Sally to ramble on, I gazed at her nipples pressing through the thin material of her blouse. Her breasts were small, but firm and well rounded. Lowering my gaze to her naked thighs, I imagined the tight crack of her pussy. Was she wet? What did her inner folds taste like? What the hell was I thinking? I wondered anxiously. I'd never looked at Sally with sex in mind, but now . . . Something was influencing me, I knew as images of her naked body loomed in my mind. Lesbian tendencies? Perhaps I was a latent lesbian? I'd never had lesbian tendencies. There again, I'd never dreamed of working as a prostitute.

'I haven't made up a bed,' I said, interrupting her.

'That's OK. We'll do what we used to do after our nights out. I'll share your bed. Do you remember that time when those lads came back with us and accused us of being lesbians because we shared a bed?'

'Yes, I do,' I murmured pensively. *Lesbians. Lesbian sex. Girl on girl.*

'And, to get rid of them, you said that they were right: we *were* lesbian lovers.'

'Yes, I remember.' I didn't want to talk about

lesbians. 'Look, I haven't got any drink in. Would you like a coffee or . . .'

'Wait there,' she said, leaping to her feet. 'I have supplies in my suitcase.'

'Supplies?'

'Vodka,' she called from the hall.

'Oh, right. I have nothing to go with it, Sally. No orange or –'

'I've come prepared.' She giggled as she returned clutching two bottles. 'Vodka, and tonic.'

We sat drinking for a couple of hours, and all I could think about was lesbian sex. The more the alcohol affected me, the more I thought about Sally's young body. Her tits would be hard, her nipples ripe for sucking. How tight was her pussy? How wet was she? Would she enjoy having another girl massage her clitoris to orgasm? Or a female tongue lapping between her fleshy sex lips? What did she taste like?

'Time for bed,' I said, finishing my vodka and rising to my feet. 'I'll show you around the house tomorrow.'

'Lead the way,' she said, obviously worse the wear for drink.

Leading Sally up to my room, I knew that I wouldn't be able to control myself. She was young, fresh, alluring . . . The fragrance of her perfume filled my nostrils as I watched her undress, and I knew that I had to have her. Sitting on the edge of the bed and admiring her curvaceous body as she stripped down to her underwear, I was gripped by an overwhelming desire to hold her in my arms. I wanted to kiss her, love her, touch her, feel her . . . Was the old lady nearby? Was she trying to influence me?

Sally seemed to be oblivious to me as I gazed at the small indent of her navel adorning the smooth flesh of her stomach. She knew nothing of my lewd thoughts, my lesbian thoughts, as I eyed the ripe teats of her nipples pressing through her small bra. Her white cotton panties were bulging with her full sex lips, and I could see her crack clearly defined by the tight material. Licking my lips, I felt my womb contract as I imagined running my tongue up and down her moist valley of desire.

Stripping down to my bra and panties, I climbed into the bed and lay next to Sally. Inhaling the heady scent of her perfume, I could feel the warmth of her young body as she breathed deeply. She was sleeping, I knew as I turned on my side and faced her. *Sleeping beauty*. Running my fingertips up her inner thigh, I tentatively kneaded the swell of her panties. She was beautiful, sensual . . . I could feel the valley of her vulva, the puffy hillocks of her outer labia rising either side of her sweet crack. I had to stop myself. I had to take control of my inner desires and . . . My inner desires? Or the old lady's inner desires?

Retracting my hand, I fought against the powerful urge to pull Sally's panties down and slip my finger deep into the wet heat of her vagina. *Touch her*. I could hear whispers in the room. *Feel her, caress her*. Were the whispers in my head? Was I going mad? Leaping out of the bed, I left Sally sleeping and went down to the lounge. The only way I could stop myself from committing an act of lesbian sex was to keep away from Sally. It was a warm night, and the sofa was comfortable enough. And Sally was safe enough.

Three

I woke to the sun streaming in through the lounge window. It was going to be a hot day. It had almost been a hot night, a night of hot lesbian sex. I'd have to make up a bed in one of the spare rooms, I decided as sleep left me. I couldn't risk sharing a bed with Sally, and I didn't want to sleep on the sofa again. Lying next to her young body in bed . . . I knew that I couldn't trust myself. I knew that I'd touch her, feel her, caress her and . . . Hearing her banging about in the kitchen, I clambered off the sofa. I had to stop thinking about sex, I mused as I joined her and filled the kettle. I wished that she'd got dressed rather than come down to breakfast in her bra and panties. I should have dressed, too. I had to stop thinking about lesbian sex.

'I slept on the sofa,' I said. 'There was no room in the bed.'

'There was plenty of room,' Sally retorted. 'I slept perfectly. Apart from a weird dream.'

'Perhaps it was the heat,' I murmured, pouring two cups of coffee. 'I was tossing and turning, and finally went to the lounge. What was your dream?'

'About lesbian sex,' she replied nonchalantly. 'It was probably because we mentioned lesbians last night.'

'Tell me about it,' I said, gazing longingly at the firm mounds of her breasts straining against her skimpy bra. 'What happened?'

'I was in bed with another girl, and she stroked my pussy lips. And then she fingered me.'

'Who was the girl?'

'God knows. I've had plenty of dreams about lads with big cocks, but I've never dreamed about having sex with another girl. It was quite exciting, sexually stimulating. So, what are we going to do today? How about starting with a tour of the house after breakfast?'

'Yes, of course.'

The air turned chilly and I felt that something or someone was nearby. Whatever it was, I definitely sensed what I can only describe as a presence. Gazing at Sally across the table, I realised that she wasn't moving. As if frozen in time, like a scene in a photograph, she remained perfectly still. Her expression was blank and her eyes were glazed over as if she was hypnotised. I had no feeling of fear as I moved around the table and asked her whether she was all right. Only a sense of great power. Sexual power.

Stroking her long black hair, I moved my hand down and squeezed the mounds of her firm breasts through the silky material of her bra. She said nothing, did nothing, as I encircled the outline of her nipples with my fingertip. I could smell the perfume of her hair, feel the warmth of her young body as I tentatively lifted her bra clear of her firm breasts. Why was I doing this? I wondered, tweaking each ripe nipple in turn. If this was the old lady influencing me ... It wasn't possible, was it? How had she hypnotised Sally?

Squeezing her small breasts, feeling the firmness of her youthful mammary spheres, I leaned over and sucked her ripe nipple into my hot mouth. A pang of excitement coursing through me, my clitoris swelling, my womb contracting, I mouthed and suckled fervently on each nipple in turn. I'd never dreamed of doing this to another girl. I'd never imagined doing anything sexual to another girl. But the feel of her erect nipple in my mouth, the sensitive protrusion pressing against my wet tongue ... I sucked hard, rhythmically squeezing and kneading her firm breast and imagining that I was drinking her milk. Slurping, sucking, mouthing, I finally moved to her other breast and bit on the brown bud of her nipple. Losing myself in my lesbian desire, I ran my fingers over the smooth plateau of her stomach to her tight panties. I wanted her, needed her ...

I stepped back and moved to the door as Sally stirred. I dashed into the lounge and sat at the bureau. She'd obviously wonder why her bra was pulled up, why her milk teats were wet and fully erect, and I didn't want her asking me awkward questions. Sifting through some papers as she wandered into the room, my heart racing, my hands trembling, I made out that I hadn't noticed her. If she suspected me ... But how could she? I was safe enough, I was sure as she asked me what I was doing.

'Just going through some papers,' I said, turning my head and smiling at her.

'I didn't see you leave the kitchen.'

'Didn't you?' I murmured nonchalantly. 'Ah, there it is. I was looking for the phone bill. Anyway, are you ready for a tour of the house?'

'Did you notice my bra?' she asked, standing by my side.

'Your bra? What about it?'

'Er ... nothing. OK, let's look around the house.'

Following her upstairs, I eyed the firm cheeks of her bottom, the bulge of her tight panties nestling

41

between her shapely thighs. I had to stop thinking about sex, I thought for the umpteenth time as we went into the back bedroom. But she was beautiful, her skin unblemished in youth, her curves and mounds so inviting. Oblivious to my lewd thoughts of lesbian sex, she looked around the room and commented on the vase of flowers on the table by the antique bed. I said that I'd wanted to let the room and told her how my would-be tenants had fled the house.

'How odd,' she breathed, sitting on the edge of the bed as I finished my story. 'It's a lovely room. I wonder why . . . Perhaps it is haunted.'

'What makes you say that?' I asked, frowning at her.

'I was only joking.' She tossed her long black hair over her shoulder and giggled. 'Perhaps they saw a ghost and ran off.'

'Hardly,' I replied. 'There are three spare rooms. They're all large and airy and would bring in some decent money. If I could find some tenants, that is. I've also considered bed and breakfast.'

'There's money in that, Alison,' she said enthusiastically. 'My aunt runs a B-and-B down in Devon, and she's loaded. All you'd have to do for breakfast would be to chuck a few eggs and some bacon into a frying pan. A bit of toast and fresh orange juice . . . and clean sheets on the beds, of course.'

'Talking of which, I'll make up the bed for you later.'

'I'd rather share your bed,' she said softly, her huge dark eyes staring into mine.

'Sally, I can't sleep squashed up like that. I know it's a double bed but . . .' My words tailed off as Sally reclined on the bed as if she'd fallen asleep. I shook her leg. 'Sally,' I said. 'Sally, what's the matter?'

Remaining perfectly still, she breathed deeply as if under hypnosis again. I was sure that this was the old lady's doing as the air turned chilly again. How or why this was happening, I had no idea. Did the old lady want me to indulge in lesbian sex with Sally? A ghost? I mused, recalling Sally's words. I felt no fear or concern as I eyed the bulge of Sally's panties. On her back with her feet on the floor and her legs apart, her young body was so alluring, so incredibly inviting.

This couldn't be the old lady's doing, I decided, changing my mind. There was no such thing as ghosts. Mulling over the recent events, the male visitors, the man knowing where the leather strap was kept, I reckoned that I'd let my imagination run away with me. The notion of living in a haunted house had gripped me, intrigued me. In a way, I'd *wanted* to think that the house was haunted. The idea was exciting, but there was bound to be a perfectly normal explanation.

Reckoning that Sally had fainted, I shook her leg again. Settling on the floor between her feet, I wondered whether she was feigning unconsciousness in the hope that I'd touch and caress her. Was she a lesbian? I mused, running my fingertips over the swell of her tight panties. More to the point, was *I* a lesbian? During my early teens I'd had a crush on a girl at school. But that was all part of growing up, hormones going wild. She was a year above me, and I used to gaze at her in the playground. It was a silly crush and had nothing to do with lesbian sex.

Not believing that the old lady was responsible for Sally's peculiar state, I convinced myself that Sally was playing games. It was quite exciting, sexually stimulating. Recalling her talking about her lesbian dream, I was sure that she was faking. In the three years I'd known her, she'd never had a relationship with a man lasting more than a week or so. Was *she* a lesbian? There was one way to find out, I thought, pulling the crotch of her panties aside and exposing the full lips of her pussy.

'Is this what you want?' I asked her, stroking the firm cushions of her outer labia. Caressing the pink folds of her inner lips that protruded invitingly from her moist sex valley, I thought of slipping a finger deep into her teenage pussy. She'd be hot, tight and very wet. I thought it strange that not only was I desperate to indulge in lesbian sex but all my feelings of guilt had melted. Right, wrong, normal, abnormal ... Perhaps my inhibitions had gone because I thought Sally was feigning sleep or whatever. But why did I feel such strong lesbian desires? Perhaps I'd always harboured deep-seated lesbian tendencies.

'You don't have to pretend,' I said, with a giggle. Sally remained silent and motionless as I leaned forward and kissed the warm flesh of her outer lips. Tentatively pushing my tongue out, I tasted her sex crack. Sweet, bitter, tangy ... Breathing in the heady scent of her black pubic curls, I felt my womb contract and my clitoris swell as my libido soared out of control. Repeatedly running my tongue up and down her pink crack, savouring the taste of her most private place, I finally parted her fleshy lips with my thumbs and licked the creamy-wet cone of flesh surrounding the entrance to her young pussy. She was beautiful, warm, wet ... Perhaps I *would* share my bed with her, I thought as I lapped up her flowing pussy milk.

Peeling the fleshy lips of her vagina wider apart, exposing the solid bulb of her pink clitoris, I swept my wet tongue over its sensitive tip. My own clitoris was calling for my intimate attention and I wondered

44

whether Sally would like to reciprocate and tongue me to a massive orgasm. Sixty-nine? I mused, picturing our naked bodies entwined in lesbian lust on the bed, our tongues lapping at each other's sex holes. Tongues tonguing, fingers fingering . . . Lesbian lust.

Pushing my tongue into the hot sheath of her vagina, I lapped up her sticky sex cream, sucked out her juices of desire and drank from her teenage body. The solid nub of her clitoris pressing hard against my nose, her juices of desire streaming from her open sex hole, I was sure that she was feigning unconsciousness. Would she be able to remain silent when she reached her orgasm? I wondered. Or would she writhe on the bed and cry out as her lesbian pleasure exploded within my hot mouth?

Moving up her gaping valley and sucking her ripe clitoris into my mouth, I drove a finger deep into the tight sheath of Sally's young vagina. She was wet, hot, tight . . . She was going to come, I knew as her teenage body began to tremble. Driving a second finger into her contracting pussy, I massaged her creamy-wet inner flesh and repeatedly swept my tongue over the hard nub of her clitoris. She was almost there. Her stomach rising and falling jerkily, her milk flooding my fingers, her clitoris inflating . . . Trembling, breathing heavily, she was almost there.

Sally came with a shudder and an incredible gush of pussy milk. Sustaining her orgasm, I pistoned her contracting vagina and sucked and licked her pulsating clitoris. Since I'd moved into the house, I'd wanked two men, sucked off another, and was now indulging in lesbian sex. I was happy, I thought as Sally's vaginal muscles gripped my thrusting fingers. After years of searching for something, years of struggling to survive, I'd found my niche in life. Sally would definitely be sharing my bed with me, I decided as she let out a gasp of pleasure and pumped out another gush of sex milk.

Wondering whether she'd like to move in permanently, I imagined her entertaining my clients. Between us we could earn a small fortune. Putting on lesbian shows, giving double blow jobs ... We'd make a good team, I mused as I sucked out the last ripples of pleasure from her clitoris. But she lived at home with her parents, and her father was very strict. There was no way he'd allow Sally to live with me. There again, he'd have to allow his little girl to fly the nest at some stage. Easing my fingers out of her drenched pussy, I moved down and drank the warm milk flowing from her inflamed hole. Creamy, lubricious ... My lips locked to the pink flesh surrounding her love hole and I tongued her hard. She tasted heavenly, and I knew that I was hooked on lesbian sex.

'What's happening?' Sally murmured, her head lolling from side to side. I covered her beautiful pussy with her panties, leaped to my feet and dashed out of the room. I wanted to go along with her game and have her believe that I thought she'd passed out. It was a game that I hoped we'd play many times, a game which would bring us both immense sexual satisfaction. Nonchalantly wandering back into the room and smiling at her as she sat on the edge of the bed, I asked her why she hadn't joined me in the other room.

'I must have fallen asleep,' she murmured, looking around her.

'Fallen asleep?' I laughed. 'I thought you were coming to see the next room.'

'What happened, Alison?' she asked me. 'I ... I feel very wet.'

'Wet? Perhaps you had a dream about sex. Anyway, you couldn't have fallen asleep. I've only been in the other room for two minutes.'

'Something's not right,' she said, rising to her feet. 'I think I'll go and get dressed.'

'Too much bloody vodka last night,' I proffered.

I got the impression that Sally wasn't playing games. She'd seemed genuinely concerned, confused. And now *I* was becoming confused. Turning my thoughts to the old lady once more, I was sure that she couldn't exert some sort of power over Sally and influence her. It just wasn't possible – was it? My sexuality was also confusing me. I obviously harboured far more than mere lesbian tendencies. Having licked, fingered and sucked Sally to orgasm, I was now a fully-fledged lesbian. Was I bisexual? I wondered. I'd loved sucking Jim's cock and swallowing his sperm. And I'd loved drinking the warm sex milk from Sally's pussy. I was enjoying my new-found life so did it matter what I was?

I finally showed Sally around the house and grounds and, fortunately, she seemed to have forgotten about the episode in the spare room. Either forgotten, or didn't what to take her game too far. I knew that I'd soon discover whether or not she'd been feigning sleep or unconsciousness. She'd planned to spend a few days with me, so I was sure that I'd discover the truth at some stage.

We'd just had lunch when the doorbell rang. My clients weren't due and I hadn't arranged to see Jim until the evening. I couldn't think who it was, but I told Sally to wait in the lounge just in case one of my clients had decided to make an unexpected call. I opened the front door and knew instinctively what the good-looking young man wanted as he smiled and looked me up and down.

'Hi,' he said. 'I was wondering whether –'

'I'm sorry, but I'm busy,' I cut in.

'Oh, that's a shame,' he sighed. 'Any chance of fitting me in later today?'

'Who sent you?' I asked him. 'Who told you about me?'

'Word gets round.' He winked at me and chuckled. 'I was in the area, so I thought I'd look you up. Still, if you're busy . . .'

'Come in,' Sally said, joining me in the hall.

'Sally, what . . .' I began, noticing her glazed eyes, her blank expression.

'Are you busy or not?' the young man asked.

'We can fit you in,' Sally breathed.

'Come on in,' I invited him as intrigue gripped me. 'Come through to the lounge.'

Sally wasn't playing games now, I knew as we led the man into the lounge. Still unable to believe that she was being influenced by the old lady, I wondered what the hell she was going to do. She had no idea that I'd had male visitors, that I charged them for hand jobs. The situation was bizarre, and I could hardly wait to see what developed as Sally asked the man what it was he wanted.

'Two girls?' he chuckled.

'One,' I said. 'Sally is working today. I'm . . . I'm training her. What is it you want?'

'I'd like to strip her naked and fuck her,' he replied unashamedly.

'One hundred,' I said brazenly. 'Cash up front.'

'Yes, yes, of course.'

Taking the money from his wallet, he passed me the notes and stood in front of Sally. I sat on the sofa as he unbuttoned her blouse. Bizarre? This was crazy, I thought as he slipped her blouse off her shoulders and unhooked her bra. Sally just stood there, silent and motionless as he squeezed the naked mounds of her firm breasts. Like a zombie, she allowed the man to knead her breasts and tweak her ripening nipples. A dreadful thought occurred to me as he sucked on Sally's erect teats. If she was under the old lady's spell, then I could sell her to men for sex and she'd know nothing about it. What the hell was I thinking? It was a dreadful thought, and one that I had to push out of my mind.

Kneeling in front of Sally, the young man pulled her skirt down and pressed his face into the bulge of her tight panties. I could hear him breathing in, savouring the scent of her panties as Sally remained frozen to the spot. This was extremely arousing, but there was going to be a major problem, I knew as I imagined his hard cock shafting her tight vagina and filling her with spunk. When she returned to her normal state, she'd realise immediately that she was dripping with sperm. I was going to have to clean her up once our client had gone. But even then she'd be bound to realise that something had happened. Worse than that, she might wake up while the young man was there, while he was fucking her.

'She has a beautiful body,' he said, tugging her panties down and kissing her full sex lips. 'She doesn't say much, does she?'

'Sally is a girl of few words,' I replied. 'Besides, you didn't come here to have a chat with her.'

'That's true. How old is she?'

'She's eighteen.'

'I'll bet she's tight and hot and wet.'

Watching as the man ran his tongue up and down Sally's opening sex crack, I was looking forward to seeing him push his cock deep into her tight pussy. I'd never watched a couple fucking before and the notion gripped me, excited me. My panties soaking up my juices of desire, my clitoris stirring, I wondered whether Sally would attend my feminine needs once the man had left. Would she follow my instructions and lick and suck my clitoris to a massive orgasm?

In her strange state, Sally was like an obedient dog. Following the man's orders and bending forward over the back of the armchair, she parted her feet wide and jutted out her firm buttocks He stood behind her defenceless young body, admiring the curves of her naked bum as he tugged his zip down. She had a beautiful bottom. Firm, well rounded, smooth . . . As he lowered his trousers and displayed his erect cock, I turned my gaze to Sally's full sex lips bulging between her slender thighs. The pink wings of her inner lips protruded invitingly from her sweet crack and a globule of white liquid oozed from her teenage vagina – I knew that she was ready to receive the man's solid cock. My heart banging hard against my chest, my womb contracting, I waited in anticipation as the man retracted his fleshy foreskin and exposed the swollen globe of his knob.

The coupling was about to take place, I mused excitedly as he slipped his glans between Sally's well-juiced inner lips. Pushing into her teenage body, his knob sinking slowly into her vaginal duct, his shaft stretching her open, he impaled her completely on his huge organ. This was incredible, I thought as I gazed at her outer lips stretched tautly around the root of his huge cock. My best friend was naked, leaning over the back of an armchair with a stranger's prick embedded deep within her tight pussy. And she knew nothing about it. But, even more incredible, I'd been paid for this crude coupling.

As I watched the man withdraw his pussy-wet penis and slide his cock deep into her young vagina again, I became desperate to feel a huge prick deep inside my own yearning sex duct. It had been so long since

I'd been well and truly shafted, so long since my vagina had filled and overflowed with fresh sperm. Stuck in my flat with no money and no social life, I'd stagnated. My libido had gone into hibernation and I'd never given a thought to sex. Until now. I wanted a cock, the feel of a hard cock driving deep into my wet cunt and ... *Cunt*. I'd never used that word, never even thought it. It was vile, cold and hard. *Cunt*. It was also beautiful.

'God, she's a tight little whore,' the man breathed as he increased his shafting rhythm. 'I wouldn't mind giving *you* a length after I've finished with her.'

'You haven't paid to have me,' I returned, imagining that his solid cock was sliding in and out of my sperm-thirsty pussy.

'Will you do a deal?'

'What do you have in mind?'

'The two of you for one-fifty. I'll give you another fifty.'

'OK,' I agreed, my panties soaking up my plentiful juices of lust. 'If you can manage it, that is.'

He sniggered. 'No worries.'

Rising to my feet, I slipped my skirt and panties off. I'd never been so wet, so incredibly aroused as I stood beside the young man and watched him fuck Sally. Slipping his hand between my thighs as he repeatedly drove his cock deep into the girl's trembling body, he slipped a finger into the very hot and wet duct of my vagina. My clitoris swelling, my outer labia puffing up, I let out a sigh of pleasure as he massaged my inner flesh. One hundred and fifty pounds? I mused happily. The end of my financial worries was in sight.

Thinking again about Sally moving in permanently, I reckoned that we could earn a fortune. She'd never agree to become a prostitute – but then, she wouldn't know about it. The idea was good, but risky. As it was, I was going to have to clean her up once our client had gone. If she had several cocks shafting and spunking her several times each week, she was bound to realise that something was going on. But, in my soaring arousal, I didn't care. I'd sell my best friend's teenage body for sex, and make a fortune.

My clitoris swelled as the man continued to finger my tightening vagina and I watched his snatch-slick cock gliding in and out of Sally's sex hole. His purple knob appearing and disappearing, the squelching sound of Sally's copious juices resounding around the room, I grinned as he let out a gasp and announced that he was coming. Sally's naked body rocked back and forth over the armchair as he fucked her in his sexual frenzy, and I wondered when she'd last enjoyed a good shafting. Was she into oral sex? I asked myself as I watched the man's spunk oozing from the cock-bloated entrance to her young pussy and running down her inner thighs. Repeatedly ramming his fleshy rod into her sex duct, he breathed heavily and let out low moans of pleasure as he drained his swinging balls. He would become a regular client, I was sure. And Sally would be fucked regularly.

He finally withdrew his spent cock, leaving her vaginal entrance gaping wide open, sperm streaming from her inner sheath and gushing down her naked legs. Kneeling in front of him as he slipped his fingers out of my aching vagina, I sucked his dripping knob into my mouth and savoured the heady blend of sperm and girl-juice. He stiffened again quickly, his shaft swelling, his knob ballooning, and I knew that I'd soon have his magnificent cock embedded deep within my neglected pussy. Fondling his rolling balls, I sucked and gobbled fervently on the man's bulbous knob as he towered over me, gasping in his pleasure. I wanted him, needed him.

'Fuck me,' I ordered him in my rising crudity as I slipped his knob out of my mouth. Kneeling on all fours, I lapped up the sperm oozing from Sally's gaping vaginal hole as the man positioned himself behind me. I'd never behaved like this in my life, like an animal, and couldn't understand what had possessed me as I drank from Sally's sperm-laden pussy. Possessed? Had the old lady possessed me? There was no other explanation, I decided. Both Sally and I were possessed.

The man's knob slipped between the engorged inner lips of my vulva. I felt my womb contract and my pelvis inflate as he rammed the entire length of his cock deep into my sex-starved vaginal sheath. His shaft filling me, bloating me, I realised just how much I'd missed sex. As he began his shafting motions, fucking me hard, I continued to suck out the cocktail of spunk and female sex juice from Sally's hot pussy. This was so far removed from the way I'd been before moving into Juniper House. Behaving like a sex-crazed whore, allowing a stranger to fuck me as I tongued my best friend's pussy hole, I knew that this was only the beginning of my new way of life. My financial worries were over, I was enjoying the best sex ever . . . And I had the old lady to thank.

'You're a dirty little cow,' the man gasped as he pistoned my contracting vagina with his massive penis. 'You're a couple of dirty little sluts.'

'I take it you'll be coming again?' I asked him.

'Definitely,' he replied, pressing his thumb into my anal hole. 'How much to fuck your tight little arse?'

'How much to . . .' I began, picturing his cock stretching my anal hole wide open. 'No, I . . . I'm not into that,' I finally replied.

'Shame,' he breathed. 'I'd like to feel your tight arse hugging my cock.'

Slurping between Sally's vaginal lips, I moved up and ran my wet tongue over the brown ring of her anus. She tasted beautiful – bitter, tangy . . . Pushing the tip of my tongue into her tight little hole, I thought about allowing the man to fuck her there. Sally would never know, I mused while licking the hot walls of her rectum. Delighting in the taste of her most private duct, I imagined sucking the man's sperm out of her sweet bottom-hole. Was there no limit to my debauchery? I wondered, breathing in the heady scent of her anal gully. How much deeper would I sink into the pit of depravity?

My tightening vaginal sheath flooding with sperm, I locked my lips to the brown flesh of Sally's anal ring and sucked hard. I'd found my niche in life, I knew as my clitoris swelled against the man's thrusting cock-shaft. The perfume of Sally's anal groove, the taste of her rectal canal, the feel of a hard cock fucking my tight vagina, sperm streaming down my inner thighs . . . My clitoris erupted in orgasm as I shuddered and sucked fervently on Sally's anal hole. Again and again, shock waves of pure sexual bliss crashed through my young body as I drifted in the grip of the most powerful orgasm I'd ever experienced. In my unbridled debauchery, I wanted now to feel the man's huge cock up my tight arse, his spunk flooding my bowels. Two cocks shafting my sex holes, three cocks pumping sperm into my young body . . .

As well as deriving my own incredible pleasure from our clients, I had an overwhelming desire to watch men use and abuse Sally's teenage body. The very idea that she was in a zombie-like state, allowing strangers to commit crude sexual acts with her, sent my libido soaring. Two men, three men . . . Not only would I earn a fortune from the girl's naked body, but I'd satisfy my new-found lust for crude sex. But before I made any firm plans for Sally I had to be sure that she'd remain oblivious to my using her for illicit sex. And she had to move in with me, permanently.

My orgasm finally receded as the man's sperm flow stemmed. I slipped my tongue out of Sally's hot bottom-hole and panted for breath. Exhausted in the aftermath of my coming, I shuddered as the deflating cock slipped out of my spermed vaginal sheath. This was real sex, I concluded as I managed to drag myself to my feet. Hard, cold, crude sex for the sake of sex. And I loved it.

'There's the extra fifty,' the man said, zipping up his trousers and passing me the cash. 'Worth every penny, I might add.'

'Thank you,' I breathed, my body trembling uncontrollably. 'Same day next week?'

'You bet. Although it's a shame you're not into anal.'

'We might be able to do something for you,' I said, eyeing Sally's salivated anus. 'We'll talk about it next week.'

'Right. Well, thanks for everything.'

It was all over too soon for me. I could have gone on for another hour or more. Fucking, spunking, tonguing, fingering . . . After seeing the man to the front door I returned to the lounge and flopped onto the sofa. Sally was still draped over the back of the armchair with sperm streaming down her inner thighs. I was going to have to clean her up, I mused, eyeing her tight little bottom-hole. Ordering her to kneel between my feet, I thought I might as well take advantage of her and have *her* clean *me* up. Obediently following my instructions, she peeled my pussy lips apart with her slender fingers and lapped up the sperm oozing from my inflamed vaginal sheath.

'Good girl,' I praised her, lying back and closing my eyes as her wet tongue repeatedly swept over the tip of my sensitive clitoris. 'We're going to make a good team. And earn a lot of money.'

Sally's long black hair tickled my inner thighs as she licked and sucked between my puffy pussy lips, the sensations driving me wild. I decided to talk to her about her moving in permanently. Perhaps the old lady could influence her? I mused as I parted my thighs further. Her parents would never agree, especially her father. But, with the old lady's influence, I reckoned that anything was possible.

Watching her tongue running up and down my gaping sex valley, I felt a quiver run through my womb. This was heaven, I thought dreamily as my sex milk flowed in torrents from my open vaginal entrance. I'd been fucked and spunked, I'd sucked sperm from Sally's vagina, licked her bottom-hole, tongued her hot rectal duct . . . and now I was enjoying her wet tongue lapping between my own swollen sex lips. Revelling in my illicit pleasure, I ordered Sally to move deeper into my sex hole. This really was heaven, I thought as she complied. Pushing her tongue deep into my vaginal sheath, lapping up the blend of the man's spunk and my own sex cream, she was an excellent sex slave, and I knew that she'd move in with me no matter what.

Moving forward on the sofa until my buttocks were over the edge of the cushion, I raised my legs and placed my feet either side of my hips. The sexual centre of my body was now blatantly displayed, my sex holes gaping wide open, and I ordered Sally to move down to my bottom-hole. Again complying with my demand, she ran her tongue over the bridge of skin dividing my holes, and then licked the delicate brown tissue of my anus.

'God, yes,' I breathed, yanking my buttocks wide apart and opening my anal hole wide to allow her better access. Her wet tongue entered me, slipping deep into my rectal tube, as she licked and slurped like an obedient dog. Never had I known such wonderful sensations as when she pressed her lips hard against my sensitive brown ring and sucked. Her tongue darted in and out of my rectal duct, waking sleeping nerve endings there, and she took me to hitherto unknown heights of sexual ecstasy.

Splaying my fingers and opening both holes wide, I ordered Sally to run her tongue from my anus to my clitoris. I could feel her tongue travelling slowly over my anal hole, slipping into my yawning vaginal entrance and sweeping over the tip of my solid clitoris. Again, she moved her tongue slowly over my holes and up to my sensitive clitoris as I writhed and whimpered in my sexual euphoria. Listening to the slurping of her saliva, the squishing of my sex milk, I lost myself in my desire as she held me on the brink of my orgasm.

'Faster,' I finally ordered her. 'Lick me faster.' Lapping and panting like a dog, her pretty face glistening with my sex juices, she took me to an orgasm of such strength and duration that I thought I was going to pass out. Again and again, tremors of sex rolled throughout my trembling body as she repeatedly swivelled her head and licked the entire length of my anal and vaginal valleys. Shuddering uncontrollably, gasping for breath, I knew that she would become my live-in sex slave and attend my feminine needs on my command.

'No more,' I finally gasped as my climax began to wane. My orgasmic milk spurting from my gaping sex hole and splattering her flushed face as my vaginal muscles spasmed, I lay quivering on the sofa in the aftermath of my incredible lesbian-induced pleasure. Finally floating down from my sexual heaven, I gazed at Sally's juice-wet face. I had to get her cleaned up, I decided, leaping up from the sofa. If she returned to her normal state with sperm dripping from her inflamed vagina and girl-juice dribbling from her chin . . . How would I explain that? I asked myself.

'Get up to the bathroom,' I ordered her, slipping my panties on and grabbing her clothes. 'Look at the state of you. You've been a naughty little girl.'

After washing her curvaceous young body, wiping away the sperm and girl-milk, I dried and dressed her and led her into my bedroom. I brushed her long black hair and kissed her succulent lips before ordering her to lie on the bed. She'd believe that she'd been sleeping, I thought as I closed the door and went down to the lounge. Sleeping, and dreaming about getting fucked over the back of the armchair? Clearing the lounge, checking for evidence of recent sex, I finally sat on the sofa and relaxed. All I had to do was wait until Sally came down. Wait, and hope that she wouldn't suspect anything. If she did . . . well, I'd cross that bridge when I came to it.

Four

'You must have been tired,' I said to Sally as she wandered into the lounge.

'I don't remember going up to bed,' she said softly, her dark eyes frowning.

'You've been sleeping for over an hour. Are you feeling all right?'

'Yes, yes, I think so,' she sighed, flopping into the armchair.

Eyeing her naked thighs, I knew that the time had come to talk to her. 'I've had an idea, Sally,' I began. 'Why don't you move in with me?'

'What, permanently?'

'Yes, why not? We get on well together and I need some company.'

'What about my job?'

'Work here, work for me.'

'Doing what? Anyway, I thought you said that you were broke?'

'I was broke, Sally. But things are beginning to change. If you'd work here as my housekeeper, cooking and cleaning, it would give me time to get on with my plans. I don't want to say anything at this stage, but I have plans to start my own business.'

'Bed and breakfast?'

'Er . . . yes, among other things. So, what do you say?'

'I'd love to, Alison. But, the thing is ... What about my dad? There's no way he'd allow me to ...'

'You're eighteen years old,' I cut in. 'Ring home now and tell them about it.'

'All right,' she said, getting up from her chair. 'But I know what the answer will be.'

I couldn't be sure, but I thought that I felt the old lady's presence as Sally rang her parents. If there was a plan, if this was being orchestrated, then Sally would move in with me no matter what her parents said. Gazing at the backs of her legs as she talked to her mother, I recalled sucking the sperm out of her teenage pussy. My stomach somersaulting, my juices of desire wetting my panties, I wanted sex with her again. Was I a bisexual nymphomaniac? I mused, imagining my sex slave licking my bottom-hole.

Just Sally and me living together, I mused hopefully. Loving, lusting, satisfying clients, making money ... I wanted Sally to move in more than I wanted anything else. My life would be complete, I thought happily. We'd share the double bed and make love and make lust. We'd have plenty of cocks and torrents of fresh sperm to keep us happy. And we'd have each other's tight pussies and pulsating clitorises. What more could a girl want?

'There's no way,' she finally said, replacing the receiver and retaking her seat. 'My mum said –'

'They'll soon come round to your way of thinking,' I interrupted her.

'I doubt that very much. They want me to go home.'

'What, today?'

'Yes. My dad's going to pick me up later this afternoon. I wish I hadn't phoned them now.'

'Sally, you can't ... Look, I'll have a chat with him. When he gets here, I'll talk to him about it.'

'You know what he's like, Alison. If you talk to him, you'll only make things worse.'

'We'll see about that,' I said with a giggle. 'I have a plan.'

'Oh?'

'When he gets here, I'll bring him into the lounge and talk to him. You stay upstairs, out of the way.'

'If you say so,' she sighed despondently. 'But it won't work. There's nothing you can do to change his mind.'

'We'll see about that,' I said again.

I didn't have long to wait for Sally's father to arrive. Within an hour, his car pulled up outside the house and the doorbell rang. Sally scurried upstairs like a frightened rabbit as I hovered in the hall. She was an adult, I thought as I heard her shut the bedroom door. Old enough to get fucked senseless, and old enough to leave home. Opening the door and inviting her father in, I hoped that the old lady was nearby. There was no way I'd be able to change his mind about Sally, but with help from beyond the grave . . .

'Where is she?' he snapped as I led him into the lounge.

'She's gone out for a walk,' I lied. 'She wasn't expecting you until later.'

'I don't mean to be rude, Alison. But I don't want her living here with you. She's young and vulnerable. She needs her mother and –'

'What is it you're afraid of?' I cut in, eyeing the crotch of his trousers.

'I'm not afraid of anything. It's just that . . .'

'Just that she might enjoy herself for a change?'

'What do you mean by that? She's perfectly happy at home.'

'I know she is. But you're going to have to give her some breathing space. She's eighteen years old.'

'She's still a child at heart,' he sighed, sitting in the armchair. 'She's innocent, unlike you . . . What I mean is . . .'

'I know what you mean. But what I don't know is, what makes you think she's innocent?'

'Sally is . . . She's . . .'

'She's what?'

'She's a virgin, Alison.'

'How do you know that?'

'Instinct.'

Reclining on the sofa, I parted my thighs and exposed the bulging crotch of my panties to his wide eyes. I hadn't planned to seduce him but, seeing as the old lady obviously wasn't helping me, I couldn't think what else to do. As he stared at my tight panties, I realised that he'd think me a slut and be even more determined to keep his daughter away from me. Blackmail? I wondered. If I had sex with him, and then threatened to tell his wife . . . I knew that I was treading on dangerous ground, but I couldn't help myself.

'Why don't you come and sit next to me?' I suggested huskily.

'I hope she won't be too long,' he muttered, joining me on the sofa. 'I don't have a great deal of time. Having to drive all the way down here and . . .'

'You can spend a little time with me, can't you?'

'Yes, I suppose so. This house is . . . Sally told me all about the money and the house. It's a nice place.'

'It's a lonely place,' I said, placing my hand on his knee. 'I get very lonely here.'

'What do you intend to do with the house? It'll cost you a fortune to run this place. And as for the heating bills in the winter . . .'

'I have plans.'

'That's as maybe, but what would Sally do? There's no work around here.'

'I'm thinking of going into bed and breakfast. Sally could work for me.'

'What sort of future is that? I want my daughter to –'

'You could visit her every weekend,' I said, moving my hand up to his crotch. 'And visit *me*.'

'Alison, I . . .'

Unzipping his trousers, I hauled out his flaccid cock and squeezed gently. Sally's father looked down at his cock in my hand, and then locked his stare to mine. What was he thinking? I wondered as I pulled his foreskin back and massaged his purple knob with my thumb. His penis stiffening, he said nothing as I ran my hand up and down his warm shaft. He obviously thought that I was a slut, but I didn't care. The old lady wasn't helping me, and this was the only way I could get him on side.

'You could visit Sally every weekend,' I repeated. 'I'm sure that you and I would be able to have a little time alone together.'

'I . . . I don't know,' he murmured shakily.

'You and your wife could come down and see Sally every weekend, and we could sneak away for –'

'My wife would never agree to it,' he cut in.

'I'm sure you'll be able to convince her that Sally would be happy here with me.'

Leaning over, I sucked his purple glans into my hot mouth and savoured the taste of his salty globe. He gasped and breathed heavily as I ran my tongue over his sperm slit. Was I winning him over? I wondered, bobbing my head up and down and mouth-fucking myself on his magnificent cock. One thing was for sure. He'd be visiting me regularly whether Sally lived with me or not. Another client? Should I charge him? If he thought I was a prostitute, he'd never allow his daughter within a million miles of Juniper House.

'Is this what you do to all your visitors?' he asked me accusingly.

'Of course not,' I replied, slipping his knob out of my mouth. 'I've always fancied you. I thought you knew that?'

'No, no, I didn't. Why have you never said anything? We could have got together ages ago.'

He was weakening, I knew. 'I didn't know what to say. I mean, you're my best friend's dad, you're married and . . .'

'And you're a beautiful girl, Alison. Had I known that you wanted this . . . God, I wish you'd said something before.'

'Well, you know now,' I breathed, running my thumb over his silky-smooth knob.

Sucking his swollen knob into my mouth again, I reckoned that he'd agree to his daughter living with me. Sally, innocent? I thought it was funny that he believed her to be a virgin. She'd had a few boy-friends, and I knew that she'd had sex. Living with me, she was going to have sex on a regular basis. Lesbian sex, anal sex, oral, vaginal . . . and she was going to earn me a fortune. Her dad would enjoy his weekly visits, I was sure as his cock shaft twitched and his knob swelled within my sperm-thirsty mouth. We could slip upstairs or out into the garden for a quick blow job or a fuck. I was becoming naughtier by the day.

'I've always thought about you,' he gasped, clutching my head and rocking his hips. 'I've thought about your body for years. I've thought about fucking you and . . . God, I'm coming.'

His sperm flooding my mouth; I allowed my cheeks to fill before swallowing hard. He'd thought about my body, had he? I mused as I drank from his fountainhead. He'd thought about fucking me?

Sally's father wasn't the sort of man I'd believed him to be, I reflected as I wanked his cock faster and sucked harder on his throbbing glans. He must have thought about fucking me as he'd fucked his wife, thought about fucking me as he'd wanked and brought out his spunk. He was a normal man. A man weak in his powerful sexual desires. Sucking out the last of his spunk, I reckoned that the time had come to bring Sally in. I had her dad on side now, and I didn't think there'd be a problem.

'Was that nice?' I asked him, slipping his deflating cock out of my mouth and licking my sperm-glossed lips. 'Was that good?'

'God, yes,' he gasped, his eyes rolling. 'I've never . . .'

'Never had a young girl suck you off?'

'No, no, I . . . You're amazing, Alison. I just wish that I'd known how you felt about me.'

'We'll be able to enjoy each other every weekend,' I giggled.

'If only I'd known. Alison, I am the only one, aren't I?'

'Of course you are,' I lied. 'I don't have a boyfriend. In fact, I haven't had a relationship for two years or more. But now I have you.'

'I can't believe this,' he said, grinning as he zipped his trousers.

'I think I heard Sally come in. You wait there, and I'll send her in. Oh, and don't forget that we can only see each other if she lives here. You'll have the perfect excuse to come and visit me.'

'Yes, yes, I know.'

I sent Sally into the lounge and then made myself a cup of coffee while she chatted to her father. I hadn't needed the old lady's help, I mused. Sitting at the kitchen table, I thought about how I had used the power of sex to get my own way. As I sipped my coffee, I made my plans for Sally. She'd share my bed, I decided. But we'd need another bed to entertain our clients. Not every man would want sex in the lounge. There were bound to be some who'd want to take Sally to bed and give her the fucking of her young life. Grinning, I thought about preparing a special room, a sex room. A sex den? Recalling an old boyfriend talking about schoolgirls, I wondered whether to buy Sally a school uniform. If I was going to earn some real money, then I'd have to cater for all tastes and sexual preferences.

'Bye,' Sally's dad called from the hall.

'Oh, right,' I said, leaving the kitchen. 'Is everything all right?'

'I'll be staying,' Sally said.

'Oh, that *is* good news.'

'I'd better be going,' her dad said, winking at me. 'I'll see you at the weekend.'

'Yes, of course.'

Sally saw her father out and closed the front door behind him. She shook her head in disbelief. 'I don't know what you said to him,' she murmured. 'But he has no problem about my living here. How on earth did you change his mind?'

'I have my methods,' I replied. 'Right, we'd better make some plans. As you're now my employee, I think you'd better do some housework.'

'Yes, of course,' she trilled. 'I'm so pleased that my dad agreed. God only knows how you did it, but it worked. Right, I'll get to work and then make some lunch.'

'We'll have to get you a maid's uniform,' I said, looking her up and down. 'Once I start the bed-and-breakfast business, I'll want you to look the part.'

'I'm really looking forward to this, Alison. Living here with you, away from my parents and . . .'

'A short skirt,' I said pensively. 'And you'd better shave.'

'Shave?' she echoed, her dark eyes frowning at me.

'Er . . . what I mean is . . .' I stammered, wondering what the hell I'd said. 'I want you to wear a short skirt and I want you to shave.'

'OK, I'll do it now,' she said, bounding up the stairs.

I want you to wear a short skirt and I want you to shave. They were the old lady's words, I knew as I wandered into the lounge. Shave? Nothing could have been further from my mind. Had the old lady influenced me, or had she managed to speak through me? Sally hadn't seemed at all bothered about shaving. If anything, she'd been keen. I'd pondered on the idea of a school uniform, but hadn't dreamed about getting Sally to shave her pubic hair off. Just how much influence, how much power, did the old lady have?

A dead woman couldn't have influence over living people, I decided. It was the stuff of daft movies. And I was daft even to consider it. I'd always liked ghost stories and my mind was going off on a tangent. Ghosts were fiction, I knew. Then I recalled my arrangement to meet Jim in the pub that evening. What to do with Sally? I wondered. I didn't want her going to the pub or wandering around the village. I didn't want people asking awkward questions about her. She had to stay in the house, I decided. She was my housekeeper, my cook, my maid, my sex slave . . . There was no need for her to leave the house.

Hearing her banging about in the kitchen, I wondered whether she'd shaved her pussy. Would she do anything I asked, I mused, walking into the hall. Seeing her through the kitchen doorway, my eyes widened as I gazed at her very short skirt. She had beautifully long legs, slender thighs ... Had she shaved her pussy? I wondered again. My mind was once more riddled with thoughts of lesbian sex, but I had no idea why. As she bent over and opened the cupboard beneath the sink, I glimpsed the rounded cheeks of her naked buttocks. She wasn't wearing any panties.

'All right?' I asked her, wandering into the kitchen.

'I'm going to make some lunch,' she said. 'Are you hungry?'

'Er ... no, no, I'm not. I like your skirt.'

'It's rather short, but I think I look the part.'

'The part?' I echoed.

'A maid. They wear short black skirts.'

'Oh, yes, of course. Sally, did you –'

'I'm not wearing any panties,' she cut in. 'I did as you asked and took them off.'

I hadn't mentioned her panties, I reflected. Where on earth had she got the idea that I'd told her not to wear her panties? All I'd said was that she was to shave and wear a short skirt. Was this the old lady's influence? I had to stop thinking about bloody ghosts. Feeling a little guilty, I wondered what Sally was becoming, what I was turning her into. A tart, a slut ... A prostitute. Eyeing her naked buttocks again as she bent over, I spied the hairless lips of her vagina nestling between her shapely thighs. She was so young, so fresh ... and I wanted to lick her there, taste her there.

'I have things to do,' I said, dragging my eyes away from her teenage body as she stood up. 'I'll leave you to get on.'

'OK, just shout if you need me.'

God, how I needed her. Her young body, her firm little tits and puffy vaginal lips ... Returning to the lounge, I wondered again whether the old lady had power over us and, if so, how much? Was I in control of Sally and the house? Or had the previous owner taken complete charge? Could she make me do things against my will? Sitting at the bureau, I gazed at the key with the label marked *den*. Was there a sex den somewhere in the house? There were too many unanswered questions for my liking. Hearing the front doorbell, I decided not to answer it. I had no clients due that afternoon and had arranged to meet Jim in the pub that evening. Whoever it was could go away or come back later.

'There's a gentleman to see you, madam,' Sally said, appearing in the lounge doorway.

Madam? 'Sally, I . . . . Who is it? What does he want?'

'He didn't say, madam.'

'All right, show him in.'

Pondering on the word *madam*, I thought that Sally might be taking the role of maid a little too far. There again, I rather liked the idea of her being my slave in more ways than one. Maid, cook, house-keeper, sex kitten . . . Getting up from the bureau as she showed a middle-aged man into the lounge, I wished that she hadn't answered the doorbell. He wasn't bad-looking, and he was dressed well in a dark suit, white shirt and tie. But I hadn't wanted any visitors. Hoping that he wasn't a client, I decided to get rid of him as quickly as possible.

'I'm rather busy,' I said, flashing a frown at Sally. 'What is it that you want?'

'I'm sorry to trouble you,' he said. 'I wish to make an appointment.'

'An appointment?'

'For your services. I was wondering whether you could fit me in one evening each week? I was passing through the village, you see. I live about ten miles away and –'

'Er . . . yes, of course,' I interrupted him before he poured out his life story.

'Shall I deal with this, madam?' Sally asked, turning to the man. 'Which evening would suit you, sir?'

'Friday,' he replied, smiling at the girl. 'Every Friday at seven, if that's all right?'

'Yes, of course. And what's your preference?'

'Well, I . . . I don't know. I think I'd enjoy a massage.'

'A full body massage it is,' Sally said. 'Our terms are cash up front. Fifty pounds for a full massage.'

'That's fine. I'll see you on Friday, then?'

'Yes, sir,' Sally said, showing him out of the room. 'If there's anything else we can do for you, please don't hesitate to ask.'

I couldn't believe what I'd heard. I sat back down at the bureau. Sally seemed to know exactly what was going on. More than that, she was taking control. This was the old lady's doing, I knew as the front door closed as the man left. Initially, I felt angry to think that Sally had taken charge and had not only made an appointment but had named the price. But then I realised that this was exactly what I wanted. She'd make appointments, take the money, please the clients . . . and all I had to do was sit back and count the cash.

'Sally,' I called as she passed the lounge door on her way to the kitchen.

'Yes, madam?' she said, walking into the room and standing in front of me.

'You . . . you did very well.'

'Thank you, madam.'

'How did you know how much to charge?'

'We always charge fifty pounds for a massage,' she replied. 'That *is* right, isn't it?'

'Always charge . . . yes, yes, that's right.' Noticing her eyeing the key, I wondered whether she'd know what it was for. 'Perhaps you'd be good enough to clean the den?' I said, passing her the key.

'Certainly, madam.'

My head spinning as she walked into the hall, a thousand thoughts battering my confused mind, I couldn't understand the change in her. Had the old lady taken complete control over Sally? Had she possessed her? I followed the girl into the dining room and watched her walk across the floor towards the far wall. She obviously knew where the den was, and I thought it odd that I couldn't see the door. Was there a secret panel? I wondered as the doorbell rang again. This was bizarre, I thought as Sally returned to the hall and opened the front door. She was in charge, and I might as well have not been there. Wandering into the lounge as she spoke to a man on the doorstep, I thought it best to leave her to it.

'There's a gentleman, madam,' she said, peering round the lounge doorway. 'He wants hand relief. May I bring him in here?'

'Er . . . yes, of course,' I replied. There was no point in trying to keep clients away.

'It's just that I thought you might not want to be disturbed. It'll only take me a few minutes.'

'No, no. You just carry on, Sally.'

'Thank you, madam. Come in, sir,' she said, looking over her shoulder. 'This is Madam Alison,' she said, introducing me as he walked into the room.

'Oh, two girls?' he breathed.

'I'm training Sally,' I said, sitting in the armchair. 'Do you mind if I stay?'

'Not at all,' he replied. 'I rather like the idea of another girl watching.'

Where were these men coming from? I wondered as Sally took his money and sat on the sofa. Ordering him to stand in front of her, she unbuckled his trousers and tugged his zip down. After pulling his trousers down to his knees, she stroked his flaccid penis and tickled his rolling balls. It was as if she'd done this dozens of times before. This was more than bizarre, I thought as she grabbed his cock and began her wanking motions. Was I dreaming? What her father would say if he discovered the truth, I dreaded to think.

Watching the man's cock stiffen fully as Sally wanked his veined shaft, I wondered again where these males were coming from. Had they been clients when the old lady had run her brothel? If that was the case, didn't they wonder where she was? I needed answers, I told myself as the man began to gasp and tremble. The way Sally was behaving, the men arriving on the doorstep . . . I needed answers. There again, they were paying customers so did it matter where they'd come from? Ours is not to question why, as my mother always said.

Sally certainly knew what she was doing. Wanking the man's cock with one hand and fondling his heavy balls with the other, she was obviously well practised in the art of male masturbation. His solid organ was only inches from her fresh face, her pretty mouth, and I wondered why the man hadn't asked her for a blow job. Perhaps he couldn't afford it, I mused. His shirt was creased and his dark hair in need of cutting. He didn't look the well-off type. Perhaps he only had enough cash for hand relief.

'I'd like to give you a facial,' he said shakily, looking down expectantly at Sally.

'That'll be another twenty pounds, sir,' she said, her dark eyes flashing as she smiled. 'Will that be all right?'

'Yes, yes, that's fine. I'd like you to make it last. I don't want to come just yet.'

'You leave it to me, sir. I know exactly what you want.'

A facial? I thought excitedly. Sally didn't need any training, I concluded. She knew exactly what to do. Or the old lady knew exactly what to do. Was this Sally or was this the old lady? I was confused, and more than a little concerned. If Sally was possessed, was it permanent? Had her soul, her spirit, been cast from her body to make way for the old lady? I was going off on a tangent again. Wherever the men were coming from, whether Sally was possessed or not . . . It didn't matter. I was making money, *that* was all that mattered. Besides, Sally seemed happy enough so why should I worry? We were all happy. Watching expectantly, waiting for the man's sperm to shoot over Sally's pretty face, I stifled a chuckle as he asked her to talk dirty. He was certainly happy.

'I like wanking your beautiful cock,' she breathed huskily. 'Wanking your hard cock, feeling your full balls . . . I can't wait for your spunk to rain over my face. You have a lovely knob, swollen and a beautiful deep purple colour. Your shaft is so hard, your balls so heavy. I want you to come now. I want you to spurt your lovely spunk all over my face. Think about my wet cunt, your cock fucking my tight wet little cunt. Imagine your knob in my hot mouth, my tongue licking your slit, my teeth sinking into your cock as I suck out your spunk.'

Unable to hold back as he listened to Sally's crude words, the man let out a gasp as his white liquid jetted from his purple knob and splattered her face. My arousal was riding high, and I felt rather envious of the girl as his sperm rained over her face and dribbled down her chin. Massaging his purple knob

73

against her cheek, bringing out his orgasmic cream, she was obviously enjoying herself. I wouldn't have been able to control myself in her position. I'd have sucked his beautiful knob into my mouth and swallowed every drop of his fresh spunk. But Sally was obviously a professional. Or the old lady was a professional.

'That was amazing,' the man breathed as the last of his sperm dribbled from his knob-slit. 'God, you're perfect. I . . . I'll be visiting you again.'

'Thank you, sir,' Sally said, finally releasing his cock and wiping the sperm from her face with the back of her hand. 'I'm glad you liked it. Same time next week?'

'I won't be able to make regular appointments as I'm not sure when I'll be in the area,' he said, pulling his trousers up. 'If I could call in on the off chance . . .'

'Certainly, sir. You call whenever you can and I'm sure I'll be able to accommodate you.'

Sally took a twenty-pound note from the man and led him into the hall. One satisfied customer, I mused as he turned in the doorway and said goodbye. The time had come to have a talk with Sally, I decided as the front door closed. A talk with Sally – or with the old lady? As she returned to the lounge and passed me the money, I retook my seat at the bureau and grabbed an exercise book.

'I'll keep a record of the money we take,' I said. 'And I'd better make a note of the appointments. You did very well, Sally. I'm very pleased with you.'

'Thank you, madam,' she said, standing beside me as I wrote the amount in the book. 'Will that be all, madam? Only I have to go and wash my face.'

'No, I . . . I need to talk to you. It'll only take a minute or two. Sally, I need to know who you are.'

'Who I am?' she echoed, her dark eyes mirroring her puzzlement. 'I'm Sally, madam.'

'Yes, I know, but . . . Why did you shave?'

'Because you told me to, madam.'

'You didn't mind? I mean, did you *want* to shave?'

'What I want doesn't matter, madam.'

'Sally, you don't have to call me madam. We're friends, best friends, remember?'

'Yes, madam. May I go and wash now?'

'Yes, yes, of course. Oh, and then you can clean the den.'

As Sally went upstairs to wash, I wandered into the dining room and looked at the wood-panelled walls. If there was a door, then I couldn't see it. Was there a basement? I wondered. The situation was ridiculous. This was my house, this was my business . . . and yet Sally seemed to know far more about the house and the business than I did. Was I jealous of her? She looked even younger than eighteen, and she was very attractive. I felt a little jealous as she finally walked into the room in her short skirt. Her long black hair tossed over her shoulder, her pretty face smiling, she was a beautiful girl.

'I'll clean the den now,' she said. She was clutching a duster and a tin of polish as she moved to the far wall. Watching as she slipped the key into a hole, I stared wide-eyed as she pushed open an entire section of the panelling. 'Are you coming down?' she asked me, flicking a light switch.

'Yes, I'll join you,' I said, following her down several wooden steps to the basement.

Looking around the large room as she switched on more lights, I stared in disbelief at several vibrators and other sex toys displayed on a trolley next to a leather-topped table. Leather whips and handcuffs hung from the walls, vaginal speculums and rubber

gloves lined a shelf, bamboo canes, dog collars . . .
Sally commented on the dust as she began cleaning
the table, but I wasn't really listening. Gazing around
the sex den, I was too stunned to speak.

Noticing two chains hanging down from the low
ceiling, I thought the place looked like a sexual
torture chamber. Vaginal speculums and vibrators? I
mused. Did we cater for female clients? Again feeling
completely in the dark as Sally sprayed the leather-
topped table with polish, I wondered why our clients
hadn't mentioned the sex den. Perhaps it was only for
certain clients? Female clients? It was an amazing
place and must have taken a long time to construct.
The lighting and the table, the chains fixed to the
ceiling . . . It must have taken a lot of time and work.
The floor was carpeted and a couple of chairs stood in
one corner. There were paintings on the walls, erotic
paintings of naked young girls. The air was a little
musty but the place must have been shut up for ages.

'Do we have any female clients booked?' I asked
Sally, again eyeing the vibrators.

'Miss Saunders will be here this evening,' she
replied matter-of-factly.

'Miss Saunders?'

'The schoolteacher's daughter, madam. Surely you
know that she –'

'Yes, yes, of course,' I cut in. 'I was forgetting
which day it was.'

'That reminds me,' Sally breathed, opening a
cupboard door. 'I must clean my nurse's uniform.'

'Er . . . right,' I murmured as she took the uniform
from the cupboard. 'This Miss Saunders – what is it
that she likes, exactly?'

'You know what she likes, madam,' Sally replied
with a giggle. 'She's a young patient, and she comes
to see Doctor Graham, the gynaecologist.'

'Ah, yes. I must be losing my memory. So, Doctor Graham is . . .'

'An accountant, madam. You *have* lost your memory, haven't you?'

'Yes, I . . . I have a headache coming on. I can't think straight. Well, I'll leave you to it.'

Returning to the lounge, I sat at the bureau and held my hand to my head. Feeling dizzy in my confusion, I wondered again why the old lady had kept me in the dark. If she was around, if she was influencing us, then why keep things from me? Sally seemed to know everything about the house and the clients and I knew nothing. This is *my* house, I mused. So why hadn't I been told about the basement sex den? Eyeing the cash on the bureau, I realised how well I was doing financially. I dared not ask Sally any more questions, I thought as the phone rang. I didn't want her to believe that I was crazy and really had lost my memory. All I could do was play things by ear.

'Alison?' a man asked as I lifted the receiver. 'It's Jim.'

'Oh, Jim. How are you?'

'I'm fine. I hope you don't mind my ringing you? I was cheeky enough to make a note of your number when I was there.'

'No, no, that's fine. It's nice to hear from you.'

'I'm calling about this evening. I won't be able to make it until at least nine o'clock, I'm afraid.'

'Oh, right. Actually, I have one or two things to do. Shall we make it tomorrow instead?'

'Yes, that's a good idea. It's a shame because I was really looking forward to seeing you.'

'We'll spend the evening together tomorrow, Jim.'

'OK, that's great. Oh, by the way, I was talking to a customer this morning. We got chatting about

Juniper House and he reckons that the old lady had several girls working for her. Putting two and two together, I'd say that she was running a brothel.'

'Really? What else did he say?'

'Nothing much. I got the impression that he didn't want to say a great deal about it. Look, I'd better go. I have several people milling around the shop. I'll see you tomorrow.'

'OK, I'll look forward to it.'

I replaced the receiver. I was sure that the old lady had been behind everything from somehow putting the money into my bank account to my buying Juniper House. But what I didn't know was why. Why me? Was it because we shared the same Christian name? Why Sally? Because she was young and beautiful? And vulnerable? Did it matter why? I mused. I had a lovely home, a maid and housekeeper, a thriving business . . . And now I had money.

Five

Sally answered the door at seven o'clock dressed in her nurse's uniform. With her black hair tied up, she really did look the part. But it was Miss Saunders I was interested in. A schoolteacher's daughter? And who was Doctor Graham? Inviting a young girl into the hall, Sally introduced her to me and suggested that we go down to the den. I could hardly wait to see the girl's naked body and get my hands on her sweet little pussy. Would I be allowed to attend her most private place? I wondered excitedly. I was forgetting that I was in charge, I was the boss. Sally was my employee and would do as she was told.

The girl was very young, probably a sixth-form schoolgirl, and I wondered why she was into crude sex. She looked pretty with her long blonde hair framing her fresh face. She had big blue eyes and full red lips. She was wearing a red miniskirt and a white blouse, and I reckoned that she should have been out with her school friends having fun rather than visiting a sex den. But the choice was hers, I thought, again imagining her naked body. Slim and yet curvaceous, firm and unblemished in her youth . . . She was beautiful, and I was thirsty for her teenage love juices.

'Where's the doctor?' I asked Sally as we went down to the basement.

'He'll be along in a while, madam,' she replied. 'I have to prepare his patient before he arrives.'

Sitting on a chair in the corner of the den, I watched Sally unbutton the girl's blouse. Her skimpy bra coming into view, I lowered my eyes to the small indent of her navel adorning the smooth plateau of her stomach. She was so young, I thought again, eyeing the petite mounds of her teenage breasts as Sally removed her bra. Her nipples were long, ripe, standing proud from the dark discs of her areolae. Was she a virgin? I wondered, imagining sinking my teeth into her erect milk teats. Or did the so-called doctor push his cock into her tight little pussy and fuck her? My mind filling with crude thoughts, I felt my clitoris swell in anticipation. The evening was going to be most enjoyable, I knew as Sally slipped the girl's skirt off and pulled her red panties down.

Staring in awe at the hairless lips of the girl's vulva as she clambered onto the table, I left my chair and stood by her side. Rising alluringly either side of her tightly closed crack, her sex lips were full, puffy, and perfectly symmetrical. I wanted to touch her there, kiss her there, lick her there, but Sally moved me to one side. Pulling the girl's arms behind her head and cuffing her wrists to a steel ring set in the end of the table, Sally parted our female client's legs so that her feet hung down either side of the table. The girl's crack opening, the pinken wings of her inner lips unfurling, I was desperate to push my tongue into her sweet valley of desire and lick her.

'That'll be the doctor,' Sally said as the doorbell rang.

As she bounded up the stairs, I smiled at the young girl. 'What does the doctor do?' I asked her, moving my gaze to the beautifully smooth lips of her vulva.

'He examines me,' she replied softly.

'And? I mean, does he . . .'

'He's a gynaecologist. He examines me internally.'

'Yes, but does he –'

'This is Doctor Graham,' Sally announced, leading an ageing man down the steps.

'Hi,' I breathed as he dumped a leather bag on the floor. 'I'm Alison.'

'Good evening,' he murmured, his grey eyes widening as he gazed at the girl's naked body. 'This is our patient, I presume?'

'She has pains in her lower stomach, doctor,' Sally said.

'I see. Well, I'd better get started.'

Parting the fleshy lips of the girl's vulva, the doctor wasted no time in slipping a finger deep into her young vagina. Mumbling something as he parted the fleshy pads of her pussy lips with his free hand, he drove a second finger into her tight sex sheath. I could hear her juices of arousal squelching as he twisted and thrust his fingers in and out of her young vagina. The girl was obviously enjoying his crude attention, but she grimaced as he pressed on the pink flesh surrounding her clitoris. The doctor must have been in his late sixties, I reckoned as he pressed harder on the girl's flesh and forced the entire length of her erect clitoris out from beneath its pink bonnet. A sad old pervert, I reflected. But he was a paying client, and so was the girl.

'Do you masturbate?' he asked his young patient.

'No, doctor,' she replied softly.

'I think you do,' he breathed accusingly. 'You've been pushing things into your vagina, haven't you?'

'No, I . . . I haven't.'

'What is it you use? A candle or . . .'

'Nothing, doctor.'

'Nurse, the speculum, please.'

Slipping his fingers out of the girl's juice-dripping pussy, the doctor took the speculum from Sally and pushed the steel wings deep into his vulnerable patient's vagina. The girl grimaced and let out a rush of breath as he squeezed the levers and opened her tight duct. When her hairless outer lips were parted wide and stretched around the speculum, he squeezed on the levers again, forcing her teenage vagina open to fullest capacity. Her clitoris forced out from its pinken hide, her urethral outlet fully exposed, he peered into her gaping hole and again mumbled something.

The sight of the young girl's gaping sex hole sent my arousal soaring and I felt my juices of desire seeping between the swelling lips of my pussy. My clitoris stiffening, my mouth watering, I could almost taste her sex cream as I gazed into her open sheath. The walls of her vagina were pink and very creamy, and invited my tongue. But as the doctor examined her inner flesh with his probing finger I didn't think he'd allow me to taste her there.

'There's no doubt about it,' he said sternly. 'I can see that you've been masturbating. Why did you lie to me?'

'I . . . I don't know,' she whimpered.

'Have you been with boys?'

'No, doctor. I've never been with a boy.'

'I don't believe you,' he said, withdrawing the vaginal speculum. 'Nurse, I want her feet up and the table down.'

'Yes, doctor,' Sally said as he moved back.

Fixing leather straps to the ends of the chains hanging down from the ceiling, Sally lifted the young girl's feet and secured the straps to her ankles. Moving to the wall as I watched in amazement, she pulled on the chains and raised the girl's legs high into the air. Her feet wide apart above her head, her vulval crack gaping, the girl again grimaced as the doctor stared at her crudely exposed sex holes. This was weird, I thought as Sally secured the chains to a hook on the wall. Folding the end of the table down, leaving the girl's buttocks hanging over the edge, she moved aside to make way for the doctor. Weird, degrading, humiliating . . .

'Now, let's take a proper look at you,' the doctor said, pulling up a chair and parting the girl's firm buttocks to the extreme. Examining her tight anal hole, he massaged her delicate brown tissue with his fingertip. 'She's had anal sex,' he said, looking up at Sally.

'No, no, I haven't,' the girl whimpered. 'I haven't done anything, I've never been with a boy or –'

'She's lying again, doctor,' Sally breathed.

'You're a slut, Miss Saunders. A lying slut.'

'What are you going to do to me?'

'Punish you. Nurse, pass me the anal speculum, please.'

This was a bizarre game, I thought, watching Sally take the instrument from the trolley beside the table. Realising that I didn't know how much they'd paid, I thought again that Sally was in charge of the business. She was running the show, I mused, standing by her side and whispering in her ear as the doctor fiddled with the anal speculum. I asked her how much they'd paid, and she took a wad of notes from her pocket. The doctor was busy with the speculum and didn't notice as I discreetly counted the cash. One hundred pounds? Clutching the money, I smiled at Sally and indicated for her to follow me to the corner of the room.

'Why don't they meet each other somewhere else?' I whispered. 'Why pay to meet here and play their games?'

83

'This is realistic, madam,' she said softly. 'I'm a nurse, we have the examination table and all the necessary instruments ... Basically, they pay to use the facilities.'

'Yes, yes, I see. Does he end up having sex with her?'

'Nurse,' the doctor called. 'I need the Vaseline, please.'

Passing the man a jar of Vaseline, Sally held the girl's buttocks wide apart as he smeared a good helping of grease into her tight anal ring. I was going to be rich, I thought happily, squeezing the notes in my hand. One hundred pounds just for using the basement? How many other clients did we have? How much money were we going to take each week? Hardly able to believe that I was the owner of such a lucrative business, I knew that I had the old lady to thank. How she was doing this – and why – didn't matter. After years of poverty I was now in the money.

'No, please,' the girl cried as the doctor forced the steel speculum deep into her anal canal. 'God, no, it won't fit.'

'You've not only lied to me,' the doctor snapped, 'but you're a dirty little slut. You've had boys' cocks up your bottom, haven't you?'

'No, no, I haven't.'

'Nurse, would you be good enough to silence our patient? I cannot tolerate lying little sluts. Silence her with your vagina, please.'

'Certainly, doctor.'

Gazing in awe as Sally clambered onto the table and placed her knees either side of the girl's head, I focused on the hairless lips of her pussy as she lifted her short skirt up over her stomach. Lowering her body, settling her gaping vaginal valley over the girl's mouth, she threw her head back and breathed a sigh of satisfaction. I could see Sally's clitoris emerging between her gaping sex lips, the pink protrusion becoming solid in arousal as she rocked her hips and slid her open valley back and forth over the girl's gasping mouth. Her pussy milk flowing from her open hole and flooding the girl's face, she was obviously already close to her lesbian-induced climax.

Moving my attention to the doctor, I watched him sink the speculum deep into the girl's tight rectal duct as she squirmed and writhed on the table. Squeezing the levers, opening her anal sheath to capacity, he chuckled as she cried out and protested through a mouthful of Sally's cream-dripping vaginal flesh. This *was* a game, wasn't it? I wondered as the girl pulled against her bonds and struggled to free herself from what appeared to be enforced anal abuse. Locking the speculum in place, the doctor stood up and lowered his trousers. I stared in awe at his huge cock standing to attention above his heaving balls as he gazed at his victim's tight sex crack. Leaving the speculum in place, he was going to fuck her. Was that what she wanted? This was amazing, I thought as he looked at me.

'Perhaps you'd like to guide me in?' he asked, smiling at me.

'Yes, of course,' I breathed, standing by his side and grabbing his cock by the root. 'You're big,' I added, barely able to wrap my fingers around his solid organ. 'I hope the girl can accommodate you.'

'She'll have to,' he replied. 'She's a lying slut, and she deserves to be fucked hard. After that, I'll thrash her with a leather whip.'

'What about the speculum? You'll never push your cock into her with that in her bum.'

'I'll force my cock into her,' he replied, chuckling wickedly. 'I'll fuck her, even if I have to tear her open.'

Wondering again whether this was a game or whether the girl was an unwilling participant, I slipped the man's purple knob between the splayed lips of her vulva and eased his swollen globe into her very tight sex sheath. Her mouth full of Sally's vaginal flesh, she coughed and spluttered on my colleague's juices of lust as I eased the entire length of the doctor's solid penis deep into her young pussy. With both her holes bloated, stretched wide open, she arched her back and writhed on the table.

Watching the doctor's massive penis sliding in and out of the trembling girl's pussy, I finally moved my attention to Sally. The sight of her hairless pussy lips forced over the girl's mouth sending quivers through my womb, I felt rather neglected. I'd have Sally attend my feminine needs later, I decided. She'd suck and lick my clitoris to orgasm, and then lick my bottom-hole. I'd run my tongue over the smooth flesh of her vulva, take her to her climax, and then have her bring me to another massive orgasm.

Deciding to have at least some pleasure, I leaned over the young girl's naked body and sucked hard on her erect nipple. With her legs in the air and Sally over her face, I had just enough room to mouth and nibble on her beautifully ripe teats. She squirmed on the table as the doctor's cock repeatedly rammed into her tight little pussy. Her gasps stifled by Sally's dripping sex slit as I bit on each nipple in turn, she shook and writhed again and I knew she was close to her coming. Biting her nipples hard to add to her pleasure, I hoped that she'd come and visit me without her gynaecologist in attendance. To get the little cutie alone in the sex den would be sheer heaven. I'd have to make plans for the girl, I mused.

The doctor came quickly. Pumping his sperm into the young girl, gasping as his swinging balls drained, he fucked the girl with force as Sally reached her lesbian-induced climax and cried out in the grip of her lesbian ecstasy. Feeling neglected, I again found myself wondering whether the young girl would visit me without her doctor friend. To pull her tight panties down and lick the smooth flesh of her hairless outer lips would be . . . More uncharacteristic thoughts, I mused. But *were* they uncharacteristic now? I'd changed, and was still going through a change.

Hearing a dull thud upstairs, I left the threesome to their orgasms and climbed the steps to the dining room. Someone was moving around in the kitchen, opening drawers and cupboards. Wondering how they'd got into the house, I wasn't sure what to do. I could hardly call Sally or the doctor for help. Tentatively walking to the hall, I peered into the kitchen just in time to see someone slip out of the back door. I dashed to the door but they'd already disappeared into the bushes. From the glimpse I'd had I thought that it might be Jim. What he'd be doing poking around in my kitchen, I had no idea. Was it Jim? I wondered. It could have been a girl, I wasn't sure. There was just a shadow . . . Who the hell was it?

Nothing appeared to be missing, so I closed and locked the back door. As Sally's orgasmic cries sounded from the basement, I wondered whether the intruder had realised what was going on. Had he or she crossed the dining room and looked down the basement steps? Whoever it was must have heard something, I decided. Filling the kettle for coffee, I was no longer in the mood for sex. Watching the three-way coupling in the basement had sent my arousal soaring to amazing heights, but now? Now I was worried. The last thing I wanted was word about the sex den getting around the village.

I should never have left the back door unlocked, I reflected as Sally cried out in the grip of what must have been a powerful multiple orgasm. If I wasn't careful, half the village would hear about my brothel and there was no way I wanted that. Pondering on the villagers as I poured myself a cup of coffee, I wondered again where the clients were coming from, who had sent them to Juniper House. I shouldn't underestimate the old lady's power and influence, I mused as a knock sounded on the back door.

'Jim,' I breathed, stepping out onto the patio and closing the door behind me. 'I thought it was you. What were you doing in my kitchen?'

'In your kitchen?' he echoed, looking somewhat bewildered.

'Just now, about ten minutes ago.'

'I've come straight from my shop.'

'So why not go to the front door?'

'I saw a fox and followed it ... Why all these questions?'

'I'm sorry,' I sighed. 'Someone was in the kitchen earlier. I thought it was you.'

'I wouldn't just walk into your house, Alison. So someone broke in? Is anything missing?'

'They didn't break in. The door wasn't locked.'

'You're cut off here, away from the village. You should be more careful.'

'Yes, yes, I know.'

'Anyway, you mentioned that you were trying to let a room.'

'A room? You want to rent a room?'

'No, no. My niece wants to move down from Yorkshire and my cottage is pretty small. She's a lovely girl, quiet, reserved, no trouble. She's nineteen.'

'Er ... as it happens, a girlfriend of mine has just moved in. I suppose I have enough rooms but ...'

'I'll be paying the rent, if that's what you're worried about?'

'No, no. Does she work?'

'She's going to work for me, in the shop. It's a long story, but her parents have split up. My brother has gone off with some woman or other and . . . well, I suppose it's down to me to help out.'

'All right, she can come here,' I finally conceded. 'When will she be down?'

'Er . . . tomorrow morning. I know that it's short notice and if you can't . . .'

'No, no problem. I'll have to get the room ready.'

'Thanks, Alison. You don't know what a relief it is.'

'It's no problem. I'll go and sort the room out. What's the girl's name?'

'Caroline. OK, I'll see you in the morning and we'll talk about the rent.'

Caroline, I mused as Jim left. Nineteen years old, young, firm, fresh, tight and very wet . . . Could I trust myself with a teenage beauty? More to the point, could I trust Sally? But it wasn't Sally that I had to worry about, it was the old lady. I dared not involve Jim's niece in my illicit business. I dared not allow the girl to become a prostitute. Turning my thoughts to the intruder I left the kitchen and wandered around the huge back garden, looking for clues. Dusk was falling rapidly. Was someone still there, lurking in the bushes? What the hell had they wanted? Perhaps it was a common thief, I mused. Someone trying their luck by snooping around country houses.

The doctor and the girl had left by the time I'd returned to the house and got to the basement. Sally was in the sex den, tidying, cleaning, placing the instruments back on the shelves and wiping away the cocktail of sperm and girl juice from the table. Would Caroline visit the sex den? I wondered. Nineteen years old, firm small tits, tight little pussy . . . Would her naked body be tethered to the table, her teenage vagina used and abused by my clients? Definitely not, I decided.

'We're ready for the next client, madam,' Sally said, standing in front of me.

'Sally, why do you insist on calling me madam?' I asked her. 'We're friends, remember?'

'You're my employer,' she replied.

'Yes, but . . . Calling me madam when clients are here is fine. When we're alone, just call me Alison.'

'I can't break the rules, madam.'

'Rules?'

'I've finished down here, so shall I prepare Caroline's room?' she asked, shocking me to the core.

'How . . . Sally, how do you know . . .' I stammered. 'How do you know about Caroline?'

'She'll be here tomorrow morning, madam. I'll prepare the back room,' she said, heading for the steps. 'She'll like the back room.'

My hands trembling, my heart banging hard against my chest, I said nothing as she left the basement. She hadn't overheard Jim and me talking in the garden. She'd been in the den with the doctor and the girl . . . There was only one way she could have known about Caroline. Somehow, the old lady had told her. The time had come for some answers, I decided, bounding up the steps to the dining room. This was my house, my business, and yet Sally had taken charge. Marching into the back bedroom, I grabbed her arm and spun her round to face me.

'Right,' I said sternly. 'I want some answers.'

'Answers, madam?'

'How did you know about the basement? How did

you know about the doctor and Miss Saunders? How did you know about Caroline?'

'You told me,' she replied, obviously confused.

'I told you nothing, Sally. I didn't know about the basement until you went down there. I knew nothing about the doctor and the girl. And I've only just found out about Caroline. I've only just agreed to her moving in. Who are you?'

'I'm Sally. Are you feeling all right, madam?'

'No, I'm not. What else do you know? For example, who is our next client and when are they due?'

'Mr Brookes will be here at five o'clock tomorrow afternoon, madam.'

'And where did he come from? What is he into?'

'I knew nothing about him until you told me this morning, madam.'

'Until *I* told you?'

'This morning, in the lounge . . . You said that we have a Mr Brookes arriving at five tomorrow. Don't you remember?'

'No, I . . . We didn't have a conversation about a client, Sally.'

'We did, madam. You said that Mr Brookes wanted hand relief and he'd be Caroline's first client. You said that Caroline–.'

'What was I wearing when we had this conversation?'

'Your pink dress, madam. The one you always wear when we talk about the clients.'

Leaving the room, I held my hand to my head. I didn't own a pink dress. I'd never owned a pink dress. Sally believed that she'd been talking to me but . . . She wasn't mad, I reflected, heading for my bedroom. She'd obviously been talking to someone who looked like me, sounded like me . . . Flopping onto my bed,

I looked up at the ceiling, the very ceiling that the old lady would have looked up at when she'd been in her bed. Was she there, in the room with me? I wondered. Would she show herself? Had Sally not only seen her but spoken to her?

If that was the case, then the old lady must have appeared as me. But why a pink dress? Sally obviously believed that it was me so . . . Deciding not to try to work it out, I thought about Caroline. So the old lady had plans for the girl. Mr Brookes was to be Caroline's first client. As I closed my eyes and began to drift off to sleep, I knew that there was nothing I could do to change things. The old lady was in charge. There was nothing I could do to save Caroline from her fate.

Sally was up and about by the time I woke in the morning. To my surprise, I was naked beneath the quilt. She must have undressed me, I mused dreamily. What else had she done to me? Had she licked me, licked my pussy and tasted my hot milk? Thoughts of Caroline filtering into my mind as sleep left me, I climbed out of bed and took a shower. The day was going to be interesting. What did Caroline look like? Was she slim, curvaceous? What colour was her hair? I had to stop thinking about girls like that, I thought as I wandered into the bathroom.

Finally trotting down the stairs, dressed in a miniskirt and a T-shirt, I found Sally in the kitchen. 'Hi, Sally,' I said, pouring myself a cup of coffee.

'Good morning, madam,' she trilled. 'It's a lovely day. It's going to be hotter than ever.'

'In more ways than one,' I murmured, sitting down at the table with my coffee. 'Is Caroline's room ready?'

'Yes, madam, all done. I'll take charge of her when

she arrives. She'll need to be shaved and dressed properly before –'

'What if she doesn't want to be shaved? Will she be given a choice?'

'Yes, and she'll choose to be shaved. I've taken a school uniform from the sex den. I'll dress her in a gymslip and white blouse and . . .'

'You seem to have everything organised.'

'That's what I'm here for, madam. Now, what would you like for breakfast?'

'Er . . . nothing at the moment. I'll sort something out later.'

'In that case, I'll put a few finishing touches to Caroline's room.'

I toyed with my coffee cup. Not only did I feel that Sally had taken complete control, but I felt that I was becoming more or less redundant. Was that part of the plan? I wondered. If so, why? Was I supposed to sit back and rake in the cash without really doing anything? Perhaps that was what the old lady did, I reflected. Girls worked for her, one was in charge, and she counted the money. Glancing at my watch as the front doorbell rang, I wondered whether Jim had arrived with his niece. Eight-thirty. It was rather early. Gulping down my coffee, I dashed through the hall before Sally had a chance to come downstairs.

Answering the door, I was amazed to see an extremely pretty and angelic-looking girl standing on the step. It was Caroline, I knew as her succulent lips furled into a smile. Tall, slim, with a beautifully curvaceous body, she was stunning. Long blonde hair framed her fresh face and cascaded down over her white blouse, veiling the mounds of her young breasts. She was wearing jeans, and I knew that Sally would soon have her in a microskirt. And shaved?

'I'm Caroline,' she announced sheepishly. 'My uncle couldn't leave the shop. He got me a taxi and I've come alone.'

'I'm Alison,' I said, returning her smile and taking her suitcase. 'Please, come in.'

'I hope I'm not too early,' she said as I led her into the lounge.

'No, not at all. We'll take your case up to your room in a minute. Sally, that's my . . . my maid, is just finishing your room. Er . . . would you like some tea or coffee?'

'No, I'm fine, thanks. This is a lovely house.'

'I've not been here long. Ah, this is Sally,' I said as my friend walked into the room. 'Sally, this is Caroline.'

'Pleased to meet you, Caroline,' Sally breathed. 'Your room is ready. If you'd follow me?'

'Yes, of course. I'll see you later, Alison.'

'I hope you like the room.'

'I'm sure I will.'

As the girls climbed the stairs, I wondered whether Caroline moving in was a good idea. Her first client due at five o'clock? She was to be shaved, dressed as a young schoolgirl . . . What Jim would say if he discovered that his niece was going to work for me as a prostitute, I dreaded to think. Hearing movements upstairs, I half expected Caroline to scream and run out of the house. The bathroom door closed, followed by silence. Had the old lady taken a grip on Caroline?

I paced the lounge floor for half an hour, thinking, worrying. If Jim turned up and found his niece dressed as a schoolgirl . . . She was going to work for him in his shop. Would he notice the change in her? Would he question me? I had to stop worrying, I decided. Unlike Sally's father who had originally been against his daughter moving in, Jim had actually asked me whether his niece could move in. It had been his idea. The old lady was in charge. She'd make sure that nothing went wrong. Wouldn't she?

Caroline finally walked into the lounge dressed in a white blouse, a gymslip and white knee-length socks. She really did look the part, I thought, scrutinising her school uniform. She looked younger than her age, and was bound to be a big hit with the clients. Wondering whether Sally had shaved the girl, I imagined the soft, smooth flesh of her teenage pussy lips. Her gymslip was short, revealing her naked thighs. Was she wearing panties? Or was her hairless crack naked beneath the pleats of her gymslip?

'I'll do the lounge now, madam,' she said, standing in front of me.

'Do the lounge?' I breathed.

'You asked me to do the housework, starting with the lounge.'

'Er . . . when was that?'

'Just now, madam. You came into my room and asked me to –'

'Yes, yes, of course,' I cut in. 'Yes, you carry on.'

Sitting in the armchair, I watched as she took a duster and a can of polish from the understairs cupboard, regarding her closely as she cleaned the coffee table. What the hell was going on? I wondered. I'd asked her to do the housework? I hadn't even seen her since she'd gone upstairs with Sally. This was uncanny. Was she aware that she was dressed as a schoolgirl? I wondered. Did she know what she was doing? Or was she under some kind of spell? As Caroline leaned over, I followed with my gaze the smooth flesh of her slender thighs up to the rounded cheeks of her naked buttocks. Seeing the puffy lips of her hairless pussy nestling between her thighs, her pink crack displayed, I felt my stomach somersault.

Trying not to imagine pressing my mouth against the sweet lips of her vulva and pushing my tongue into her little sex hole, I wondered again why the old lady hadn't shown herself to me. Sally had seen her, spoken to her. And Caroline had seen her. Perhaps the girls had been dreaming, I thought. Perhaps they'd seen the old lady, appearing as a young woman, in their minds. Or had they seen, and conversed with, a ghost?

'Did you like my pink dress?' I asked Caroline as she leaned over further and exposed the full length of her vaginal slit. 'Do you think it suits me?'

'I thought it was rather old-fashioned, madam,' she replied, moving to the bureau.

'Yes, I . . . I've had it for years.'

'It's very nice,' she said, turning and smiling at me. 'Do you like the way you're dressed?'

'Oh, yes, madam. Sally said that it suits me.'

'Yes, yes, it does. And you've . . . you've shaved?'

'Sally did that for me, madam. She's very helpful. I think we're going to get on well together.'

'Yes, I'm sure you will,' I returned with a giggle. Extremely helpful, I thought.

As the phone rang, I decided to take the call in the kitchen. I had a feeling that it was Jim, and I didn't want Caroline listening to my conversation. I was right: Jim was checking up on his young niece, his sweet little girl. Had she arrived? Was she all right? What was she doing? I didn't know what to say. Walking around with her shaved pussy on display? Clutching the receiver with both hands, I bit my lip and said that she was fine and very happy.

'She's a very shy girl,' he said. 'I'm pleased that she's with you, Alison. You're kind and understanding. I know that you'll keep an eye on her for me.'

'Yes, of course I will,' I replied. Did I feel guilty? 'She . . . she seems to be fitting in well.'

'That's good. I'll be over later and we'll talk about the rent. As I said yesterday, I'll be paying the rent. I'll pay her for working in the shop, of course. She'll need money for clothes and make-up and stuff like that.'

'I might be able to give her a little money for doing the odd job around the house,' I said, imagining the girl taking a man's cock into her mouth.

'That would help me out no end. I don't want you to feel obliged to look after her, Alison. After all, she's a paying tenant. I don't want you giving her money for nothing.'

'Don't worry, Jim. She'll be earning money.'

'Great. OK, I'll see you later. In an hour or so, if that's all right?'

'Oh . . . er . . . OK, that's fine. Bye for now.'

An hour or so? I couldn't hide the girl. Jim was bound to want to see her and . . . She'd have to get out of her school uniform, I decided, returning to the lounge. To have her walking around in a short gymslip with her hairless pussy on show would be disastrous. This whole thing was too risky, I thought, eyeing the girl's pert buttocks as she bent over to pick up her duster. Her vulval lips bulging invitingly between her beautiful thighs, her tight crack seemingly smiling at me, beckoning my tongue . . .

'Sally,' I called as the girl walked through the hall into the kitchen. 'Sally, I have to talk to you,' I said, chasing after her.

'Yes, madam?'

'Caroline's uncle will be here soon. I don't want him to see her dressed like that.'

'Like what, madam?' she asked me, filling the kettle.

'In that bloody school uniform with her shaved pussy hanging out. If he sees her like that . . .'

'It's the rules, madam. I can't break the rules.'

'Look ... Fuck the rules. Dress her in her jeans and –'

'I'm sorry, madam. I won't break the rules. Besides, her uncle might be willing to pay for –'

'Don't even think about it,' I cut in. 'She's his niece, for God's sake.'

'When I was shaving her, you came into the bathroom and suggested that her uncle might become one of her clients.'

'Sally, I ... I didn't say ...'

'She's a teenage girl, madam. And he's a normal man. As you said, she's here for one reason and one reason only. To earn money.'

This was getting totally out of hand, I realised as Sally switched the kettle on and left the kitchen. To charge Jim for having sex with his niece ... God, there *were* limits. But how could I enforce those limits? The rules that Sally kept on about were obviously the old lady's. I had no say in the matter. The very thought of Jim and his niece was ... I had to do something. But what?

Six

Fortunately, Caroline had changed into her jeans and T-shirt by the time Jim arrived. Had the old lady influenced her? Or had Sally seen sense and got her to change out of her school uniform? Caroline grinned as her uncle hugged her and said how good it was to see her. Then he asked her about her journey and whether she'd settled into her room. Thanking God that the girl was dressed properly, I made my excuses and left them to have a chat as they sat on the sofa. Hovering in the hall, I could hear what they were saying. I don't normally eavesdrop, but I wanted to make sure that Caroline said nothing incriminating.

'I like it here,' she said. 'Alison is nice and I get on really well with Sally.'

'I'm pleased,' Jim said. 'I haven't met Sally yet.'

'She's the maid. Well, she's sort of everything rolled into one. She does the cooking and . . . I really like her.'

'That's good. Now, how about starting at the shop tomorrow?'

'OK. I'm really looking forward to it.'

'At your age, you'll probably find antiques some-what boring, but at least you'll be earning some money. As I said, I'll pay the rent. Oh, and Alison said that she'd pay you for doing a few jobs around the house.'

'I'm going to be happy here,' Caroline breathed. 'Away from ... well, mum and dad and all their problems, I'll be happy.'

As Sally came down the stairs, I beckoned for her to follow me into the kitchen. I didn't want Jim to see her ridiculously short skirt or glimpse her hairless pussy lips. What the hell would he think of her dressing like a slut? Ordering Sally to make some coffee, I told her to keep out of sight while Jim was there. I doubted that he'd be calling round very often as he'd be seeing Caroline at the shop every day. And when he came to see me ... That might be a problem, I mused. Wondering whether it would be best to go to his cottage, I knew that I had to keep friends and clients well apart.

'I see that Caroline is wearing jeans,' I said as Sally poured the coffee.

'She'll be punished later, madam,' the girl returned. 'I specifically told her not to –'

'No, Sally,' I cut in. 'She won't be punished. I don't want her uncle seeing her dressed as a schoolgirl. I don't want him to discover what's going on here, do you understand?'

'She's broken the rules, madam.'

'*I* make the rules, Sally.'

'That's what I don't understand, madam. One minute you're telling me the way things are to be and the next minute you change your mind. When I saw you upstairs earlier, you said that I was to punish the girl if she misbehaved.'

'I didn't say ... She hasn't misbehaved, Sally. I *wanted* her to wear her jeans.'

'Then why did you tell me to punish her in the usual way?'

'The usual way?'

'The frame, madam. You said that she's to be taken down to the frame and given the bamboo cane if she's insubordinate.'

'I'm going now,' Jim called from the hall.

'Oh, right,' I said, leaving the kitchen. 'Caroline seems happy enough here, doesn't she?'

'Very much so. I can't thank you enough, Alison. About the rent . . .'

'Make it fifty pounds a week. I was going to charge more but, seeing as Caroline is your niece, fifty will be fine.'

'Thanks.' He passed me the money and opened the front door. He was a nice man – I liked him. And I felt as guilty as hell. 'I'll be in touch,' I said, smiling at him. 'I'll have to come and see your cottage.'

'I'd love to see you,' he whispered. 'I really enjoyed our evening together. Make it soon.'

'I will. I'll call you, OK?'

'OK. And thanks again.'

Closing the door, I breathed a sigh of relief. What with Caroline's school uniform and Sally's short skirt, I was going to have to keep Jim away from the house. Perhaps it wasn't such a good idea to have Caroline living with me. I walked into the lounge, intending to talk to her and find out what she'd said to her uncle, but she'd gone. Sally wasn't in the kitchen, and I wondered whether she'd taken Caroline upstairs to change her clothes. No, they couldn't have gone upstairs. I'd been with Jim at the front door and I would have spotted them if they'd climbed the stairs. Reckoning that they'd gone down to the basement, I crossed the dining room and was hovering by the basement door when I heard Sally's voice.

'You are not to disobey me, Caroline,' she said sternly. 'You are not to break the rules. Bend over the frame.'

'I didn't know,' the girl whimpered. 'I thought I had to wear my jeans.'

'You know very well . . .' Sally's words tailed off and I wondered what was going on. 'Yes, madam,' she finally said. 'I'll use the leather strap instead of the cane.'

As I crept down the steps, I knew that she'd been talking to the mysterious girl in the pink dress. But I could see only Sally and Caroline. Watching as Caroline bent over a wooden frame, I felt uneasy, fearful. Was Sally talking to a ghost? I wondered as she turned away from Caroline and spoke to someone I couldn't see from where I stood. Taking a leather strap from a hook on the wall, she said that she'd punish the girl severely for breaking the rules. Hovering on the steps, I gazed at Caroline's curvaceous young body, her rounded buttocks, the swell of her pussy lips nestling between her slender thighs. I wanted to halt the imminent lashing of her naked bottom, but I didn't dare to intervene. If the old lady was there, wearing a pink dress and appearing as me . . . Was that possible?

Sally reckoned that she'd spoken several times to someone who looked like me, someone in a pink dress. Had she been dreaming or . . . She wasn't mad. Was it really some kind of apparition? It was no wonder that she was confused. What with me telling her one thing and my lookalike contradicting me, she probably thought that *I* was mad. Gazing again at Caroline's naked buttocks, the beautifully firm and rounded orbs of her teenage bottom, I wondered where this would all end. How many more girls would I employ as prostitutes?

The first crack of the leather belt echoed around the basement. I grimaced as Caroline let out a yelp. Again, the leather strap landed squarely across the tensed flesh of her naked buttocks with a deafening crack. She was squealing, pleading. But there was nothing I could do to save her from her fate. I was no longer in charge, I reflected. Had I *ever* been in charge? Had I ever been in control? What was I there for? What was my role? As Caroline let out another yelp and begged for mercy, I knew that she didn't deserve this. She'd been told to wear jeans, Sally and the old lady had told her to wear her school uniform ... The poor girl must have been totally confused. And she must have wondered why I appeared to change my mind every five minutes.

I couldn't allow confusion to reign like this. Either the old lady was in charge, or I was. One of us had to back down. But it wouldn't be her, I knew. But why should I stand back and allow her to use my house as a brothel? I was taking the money, but she was running the business. Was that what I wanted? I wondered. I'd wanted money, a decent income, a nice home, and I'd got it. But had I wanted this? What the hell was I thinking? I asked myself. The old lady was dead and there were no such things as ghosts.

Gazing at the red weals fanning out across Caroline's naked buttocks, I lowered my eyes and focused on the swollen cushions of her hairless vulval lips. She was a beautiful young girl, I thought, watching a globule of sex milk drip from her gaping sex crack. Young, fresh, nubile ... I now had two little beauties in my house. Two young girls with shaved pussy lips and ... and no ghosts. As Caroline cried out again, I bit my lip. If her uncle knew what was going on, if he knew how his young niece was being treated ... But he didn't know. And I'd make sure that he never discovered the shocking truth.

'Let that be a lesson to you,' Sally said, lowering the leather strap to her side. 'In future, you'll do as you're told. Do you understand?'

'Yes, mistress,' the girl replied with a whimper.

'I will *not* tolerate disobedience,' Sally said. Turning away from the girl, she smiled. 'Of course, madam,' she breathed, moving to a cupboard. 'I'll make sure that she wears them for the rest of the day.'

I couldn't see what Sally was holding until she knelt on the floor in front of Caroline. As she fixed metal clamps to Caroline's outer sex lips, I held my hand to my mouth to stifle a gasp. My eyes widened as I gazed at two weights attached to chains hanging from the clips and I winced. The weights swinging between the girl's slender thighs, her outer lips stretched, pulled away from her hairless vulva – I couldn't imagine her walking around like that all day. But the old lady had given her instructions, and there was nothing I could do.

'Now, get upstairs and put your school uniform on,' Sally snapped. 'And then get on with the housework.'

'Yes, mistress,' Caroline breathed.

'And remember: if you defy me again, you'll be severely punished.'

I stole back up the steps, dashed across the dining room, slipped into the lounge and sat down at the bureau. As I heard the girls go upstairs I felt that I was having to hide. Cowering at the bureau, I thought it best to pretend that I knew nothing of the episode in the basement. The situation was ridiculous, I reflected. This was *my* house, *my* home. Why should I have to bow down to Sally? Perhaps I should never have allowed her to move in, I thought again as I sifted through a pile of bills. There again, at least I was making money.

Dressed in her school uniform, Caroline finally wandered into the room with the weights swinging between her slender thighs. She'd be starting work at her uncle's shop the following day, so I'd only have to worry about her during the evenings. And the weekends, of course. But I didn't want to have to worry about her at all, I mused as she reached up with a cloth and started to clean the windows. Eyeing the crimsoned flesh of her naked buttocks, the weights hanging from her distended outer lips, I wondered what she was thinking. Was she aware that she was a slave to Sally? What had she thought about the sex den? Did she know that she was about to be plunged into prostitution?

'Are you all right?' I asked her.

'Yes, madam,' she replied, turning and smiling at me.

'The weights . . . are you in pain?'

'Only a little, madam. I'm getting used to it now.'

'Sally thrashed you with a leather belt, didn't she?'

'Yes, madam. I misbehaved, defied her. I deserved to be punished.'

'Caroline, are you a virgin?'

'Yes, madam.'

'Do you know why you're here? I mean, do you know what you're going to have to do?'

Sally walked into the room. Caroline spun round and carried on cleaning the windows. After the gruelling thrashing she'd received, she had good reason to be wary of Sally. I'd hoped that the atmosphere would be warm and friendly with the three of us getting on well and chatting together. But that obviously wasn't to be. I didn't know what to say as Sally checked the weights hanging between Caroline's thighs. Stupid though it was, I felt a little afraid of my friend. It was as if she was the boss and I had to sit quietly and keep out of the way.

'I've made a shopping list, madam,' Sally said, standing by my side and placing the list on the bureau.

'Er ... I don't think Caroline should go into the village,' I replied.

'I agree. And I have to stay here to look after things – so if you'd be good enough to go?'

'*Me*? No, *I*'ll stay here and look after things, Sally. You go into the village. Oh, and you'd better change into something more suitable.'

'I'm sorry, madam, but I can't leave the house. I have the business to run and –'

'Sally, you seem to be forgetting that this is *my* house and *my* business.'

'With all due respect, madam ... I think you'd better come down to the den with me.'

'The den? Why?'

'We have a client arriving shortly.'

'When was this arranged? And why wasn't I told about it?'

'Just follow me, madam,' Sally said, marching out of the room. 'We'll sort out the shopping later.'

As I followed the girl I knew that I was going to have to put her straight. She'd been trying to push me aside and take charge, and now the time had come to lay down a few rules. I didn't want to feel somehow beholden to her. She was my tenant, for God's sake. But I didn't want arguments. I'd wanted us to be friends, all three of us. But now? As she stood by the leather-topped table and ordered me to strip off, I couldn't believe the situation. She ordered me again to remove my clothes and to lie on the table on my back.

'Sally,' I began, looking down as my fingers unbuttoned my blouse. This wasn't my doing, I didn't want to take my clothes off ... Tossing my blouse onto the floor, I slipped my skirt off and tugged my panties down. I had no control over my actions as I lay on the table and gazed up at the low ceiling. I tried to speak, tried to protest, as Sally slipped my ankles into the leather straps hanging from the chains. But the words wouldn't come. I couldn't move, I couldn't. My feet lifted into the air as she pulled on the chains, my sex holes gaped – I was completely defenceless.

'Hierarchy,' she said, cuffing my wrists behind my head before taking something from the cupboard. 'The chain of command, from the top to the bottom. This is your house – on paper. But *I* run the business. I'm the boss: you are beneath me and Caroline is beneath you. It's known as the pecking order, madam. As it is, I've had to punish Caroline most severely. And now I have to put *you* in your place.'

Put me in my place? I thought as she massaged shaving foam into my vulval flesh. *This is your house – on paper.* Recalling her words, I was fuming. But I couldn't speak, I couldn't move. Had she somehow drugged me? Who the hell did the bitch think she was? I mused angrily as she began shaving off my pubic fleece. Once I was released, I'd throw her out of the house, I decided as she dragged the razor over my outer lips. I'd send her packing and ... But I couldn't speak – I had no control. Whether I liked it or not, with the old lady's help Sally was in charge.

After cleaning me between my legs with a towel, she stood back and admired her handiwork. Why had she shaved me? I wondered as she moved to the cupboard. What the hell did she plan to do? As the doorbell rang out, I imagined Jim trotting down the steps and discovering me in my embarrassing predicament. If Caroline answered the door with the weights hanging between her young thighs ... This was a nightmare, I thought fearfully as Caroline bounded down the steps. This was worse than a nightmare.

'Our client is here, mistress,' Caroline said.

'Then bring him down, girl,' Sally snapped.

'He's here,' she said as a boy of seventeen or so came down the steps. 'This is Ian.'

'Hello, Ian,' Sally said cheerily. 'I expect you're looking forward to this?'

'Very much,' he breathed, gazing in awe at my shaved vulva, my exposed sex holes.

'I was going to allow you to practise on Caroline, but there's been a change of plan. This is Alison, and she's going to accommodate you.'

'I'm stiff already,' he murmured, scrutinising my gaping sex crack again.

'You're a virgin, Ian. Virgin boys have a tendency to hurry things. Anyway, you're here to lose your virginity. That's what you've paid for, and that's what you're going to get. I suggest that you strip naked. Caroline and I will watch you – all right?'

'Yes, great.'

Slipping out of his clothes with an eager urgency, Ian stood by the table with his youthful cock pointing at the ceiling. His pubic curls shone in the light and his heavy balls rolled. He had a good body, taut and muscled. But I'd known nothing about a client, I reflected as he pressed his knob between the inner lips of my vulval slit. When had this been arranged? Why hadn't I been told? Sally was in charge, I thought again angrily as the boy drove the entire length of his solid cock deep into my wetting vaginal sheath and let out a gasp. Hierarchy, the chain of command . . .

'Don't come too soon,' Sally instructed the boy as she stood next to him. 'Take your time and fuck her slowly.'

'God, it feels good,' Ian gasped, watching his pussy-wet cock withdrawing before gliding back deep into my vagina. 'She's hot and very wet.'

'Better than wanking?'

'You bet.'

'How many times can you come, Ian?'

'I've managed five times in a row,' he replied proudly.

'Then you'll be able to fuck her five times, won't you?'

'Six, I reckon,' he boasted. 'Yes, six.'

Caroline stood beside the young man, gazing in awe as his rock-hard cock glided in and out of my tightening pussy. My feet high above my head, my tethered body rocking with the gentle fucking, I tried to plan what I'd do once I was released. Would I regain control over my body? I couldn't allow Sally to become the madam. I wasn't prepared to become one of her girls. There again, would I have a choice? Caroline had had no choice, I reflected as the boy began gasping. I could feel the hardness of his knob battering my cervix as he increased his fucking rhythm. My inner lips rolling back and forth along his solid shaft, I knew that the gushing of his spunk was imminent. Caroline had to do as Sally ordered her.

'What do you think, Caroline?' Sally asked the girl. 'Are you enjoying the show?'

'Yes, mistress,' Caroline breathed, her eyes locked to the illicit coupling.

'Is the sight of his hard cock making you wet?'

'Very wet, mistress.'

'And your clitoris is swollen?'

'Yes, mistress.'

'I think we'll have to bring you some relief later, Caroline. You'll find that the weights pulling on your outer lips will heighten your arousal. Later, when you're positively craving for sexual relief, I might allow you to lose your virginity. You'd like the feel of a hard cock fucking your tight little cunt, wouldn't you?'

'God, yes,' the girl breathed.

'If you behave, I might allow you the pleasure of a client's solid cock.'

'Thank you, mistress.'

Sally had said that she – as the old lady – had planned to have Caroline give a hand job to Mr Brookes as her first act of prostitution. And now she was planning to have some other client actually fuck her. The girl was a virgin, I thought anxiously. I should never have agreed to her moving in. Deciding to take her to her uncle's cottage before she was used and abused by a client, I hoped that I could get her out of the house without Sally realising what was going on. I'd talk to Jim, make up some story or other and . . . My thoughts turning to sex as the boy increased his shafting rhythm and began to gasp, I imagined Caroline in my position on the table. The lad's solid penis shafting her tight little virgin pussy, her inner lips stretched by the sheer girth of his teenage cock, his spunk flooding her . . . I'd love to watch her get fucked hard. Why had my thinking changed? I wondered. Was the old lady influencing me?

'Slow down,' Sally instructed her young client. 'You don't want it to be over within a few minutes, do you?'

'It's too late,' he breathed, repeatedly ramming his cock into me. 'I'm . . . I'm coming.'

'OK, fill her with your spunk,' Sally trilled excitedly. 'That's it, fuck her hard and pump her full of spunk.'

I could feel Ian's creamy sperm pumping into my cunt, filling my bloated vagina, lubricating his pistoning cock as he fucked me with a vengeance. My clitoris swelled as its sensitive tip was massaged by his pussy-wet shaft and I felt the birth of my orgasm stirring deep within my contracting womb. I needed to come, desperately needed the relief of orgasm. My thoughts turning again to Caroline as she watched the crude fucking, I pictured her naked body tethered to the table. Her feet high in the air, her teenage crack gaping wide open, her tight sex holes crudely exposed ... I'd have loved to watch the lad fuck her and strip her of her virginity.

'See her clitoris?' Sally trilled. 'See how it's swelled? She's going to come.'

'Yes, mistress,' Caroline breathed, her stare locked on my shaved vulva. 'It's amazing.'

'You'd like to come, wouldn't you, Caroline?'

'Yes, yes, I would.'

My body shook uncontrollably and I gasped as my clitoris exploded in massive orgasm. Waves of pure sexual ecstasy rolled through my glowing body as I threw my head back and breathed heavily while the young guy sustained my incredible climax with his thrusting cock. His sperm ran down to the tight ring of my anus and I imagined him fucking me there, pumping his spunk deep into my arse. Recalling a client shafting Sally's bottom-hole, I remembered sucking the sperm out of her rectal duct. The beautiful taste, creamy, bitter, heady ... What had I become? I wondered as my orgasm peaked and shook me to the core. Did I *really* want a cock thrusting deep into my anal canal?

As Ian's sperm flow ceased and his cock began to deflate within my inflamed vagina, my orgasm began to recede. I was left quivering, gasping, as he slid his spent cock out of my sex-drenched pussy. He'd lost his virginity, fucked and spunked me, used me to practise on, as Sally had put it. Would he manage another erection? I mused dreamily. Four, five, six times. He was young, his hormones were running wild ... I'd never been fucked several times in succession. In the wake of my coming, I hoped that he'd manage to shaft and spunk me again.

'Good boy,' Sally praised him. 'You're now a man.'

'That was amazing,' Ian breathed. 'This place is amazing – you're all amazing.'

'I take it that you'll become a regular visitor?'

'Definitely. I can't believe that I've fucked a girl, a girl with a shaved pussy.'

'So do you still reckon that you can do her six times?'

'Yes, I think so,' he replied, looking down at his flaccid penis.

'Caroline, kneel down and suck his cock,' Sally ordered the girl. 'Make him stiff and then we'll watch him fuck Alison again.'

Lifting my head, I watched Caroline kneel down and open her pretty mouth. Taking Ian's sperm-dripping penis inside, closing her full lips around his wet shaft, she breathed heavily through her nose as she sucked on his sex-sticky cock. The sight sent my arousal soaring and I knew that I'd plunged into the depths of depravity as my clitoris swelled and my vaginal muscles tightened. The lad had a firm body, muscular and youthful, and I wanted his beautiful cock in my mouth. Caroline was obviously enjoying her first taste of sex, I mused jealously. Would she enjoy having his young penis driving deep into her virgin pussy? I had to get her away from Juniper House, I had to save her from ...

'That's enough,' Sally said, pulling the girl away.

'Please, mistress, just a little more,' Caroline begged as she stood up.

'You'll have plenty of opportunities to suck cocks and drink sperm. The way things are going, you'll probably be sucking several cocks every day. As

112

you've been a good girl, you can suck the spunk out of Alison's pussy. Clean her up with your tongue and then Ian will fuck her again.'

A den of debauchery, I thought as Caroline knelt at the foot of the table and began lapping at my gaping vaginal entrance. A teenage virgin plunged into a den of iniquity and introduced to the crudest sexual acts imaginable. Although I wanted to save the girl from her inevitable fate, I knew that I was weakening. I wanted to rescue her, but I also wanted to watch her get fucked senseless. She was so young, firm, curvaceous, beautiful . . . and her pussy would be very tight. Were these the old lady's thoughts filtering into my mind? I wondered as Caroline's tongue slipped into my sperm-flooded vagina. Was she influencing me?

'What are the chains for between her legs?' Ian asked.

'She misbehaved,' Sally replied. 'The chains are hanging from her pussy lips as a punishment.'

'Wow,' the boy breathed. 'It must hurt her.'

'That's the idea,' Sally said with a giggle. 'But she'll also find it arousing.'

I could feel Caroline's hot breath against my hairless vulva as she tongued my contracting pussy. Did she like the taste? I wondered as Sally and the boy discussed Caroline's distended vulval lips. Lapping up the cocktail of sperm and girl-juice from my sex hole, she sucked and nibbled on my engorged inner lips. The sensations were heavenly, and my clitoris responded by sending ripples of sex throughout my naked body. My pussy milk flowing in torrents from my vaginal sheath, my womb rhythmically contracting, I was desperate for another massive orgasm. Shuddering, gasping as Caroline's tongue swept over the sensitive tip of my clitoris, I wanted to come and spurt my orgasmic cream into her pretty mouth. Again and again her wet tongue snaked over my solid clitoris and drove deep into my contracting vagina, taking me ever closer to my goal.

Following Sally's instructions, Caroline moved down to the tight ring of my bottom-hole. My clitoris neglected, leaving me teetering on the verge of orgasm, I knew, as she lapped at the delicate brown tissue surrounding my anus, that I was to be teased and left craving for relief. Shaking violently, I gasped and whimpered as she slipped the tip of her tongue into the hot duct of my rectum. Licking me, tasting me there, she pressed her full lips hard against my brown ring and sucked rhythmically. The sensations drove me crazy and I wanted to beg her to suck on my clitoris and allow me my orgasm. But my thoughts wouldn't turn into words.

'Enough,' Sally said, pulling Caroline away. 'It's time for Ian to enjoy his second fuck.'

'Great,' the lad breathed eagerly, standing at the foot of the table with his solid cock waving from side to side.

'Wait,' Sally said. 'I want you to do her bottom.'

'What?' he murmured. 'Do her bottom?'

'Caroline has wet her there, so you'll have no problem. Push your cock deep into her bottom – and fuck her hard.'

The boy needed no further encouragement. Pressing his purple plum hard against my tight private ring, he pushed his swollen glans past my defeated anal sphincter muscles. I could feel my nether entrance stretched tautly around the rim of his cock helmet, his thumbs pressing into the orbs of my firm buttocks, easing my bum cheeks wide apart and opening my rectal inlet. His knob driving into me slowly, journeying along my anal sheath to the hot depths of my bowels, he finally impaled me completely on his teenage cock. The sensations were amazing. My pelvic cavity was inflated, bloated, and I could feel his bulbous knob deep inside my rectum.

'Very good,' Sally praised him. 'By the look of her clitoris, I'd say that she's ready to come again. Caroline, use your pretty little mouth and suck her clitty to orgasm.'

The feel of a girl's tongue sweeping over the sensitive tip of my clitoris as a huge cock shafted my tight rectum sent me into a sexual frenzy. My womb contracting, my nostrils flaring, my eyes rolling . . . Never had I known such beautiful sensations, never had I experienced such an incredibly crude sexual act. My heart banging hard against my chest, my naked body shaking wildly, I teetered again on the brink of orgasm as the boy fucked my inflamed bottom-hole and the young girl sucked and mouthed on the solid protrusion of my aching clitoris.

As the boy gasped and announced his second coming, my clitoris exploded in a massive orgasm within the girl's hot mouth. I thought that I was going to pass out as wave after wave of pure sexual bliss rocked my tethered body. The sperm squelching within my anal duct as the boy arse-fucked me, the sound of Caroline's mouth slurping and sucking as she sustained my incredible pleasure . . . I knew that I'd found my sexual heaven as my body shook fiercely in the grip of a powerful orgasm. In my thoughts of crudity, my thoughts of debased sexual acts, I imagined a swollen knob bloating my mouth, pumping sperm over my darting tongue. Three cocks? I mused dreamily as my orgasm peaked and rocked my body to the core. Two massive flesh rods shafting my tight sex holes, another fucking my sperm-thirsty mouth . . . What had I become?

My rectal sheath burning like fire as the boy continued his crude shafting, my clitoris aching as it pumped out wave after wave of orgasm, I knew that I couldn't take much more. My feet hanging from chains above my head, my sex holes crudely exposed, my arse fucked with a vengeance, my clitoris pulsating wildly within a teenage girl's wet mouth . . . I was exhausted and prayed for my beautiful ordeal to come to an end. Finally, my orgasm began to wane. The boy's balls drained and his sperm flow ceased. He withdrew his cock slowly as Caroline sucked out the last ripples of sex from my deflating clitoris. Quivering uncontrollably, I imagined the boy fucking me again, and again. Six times?

'Would you like to use the leather strap on her?' Sally asked him as he swayed on his trembling legs.

'The strap?' Ian murmured. 'What do you mean?'

'Lash her bum with this,' she said, taking a leather belt from a hook on the wall. 'Give her a good thrashing before you fuck her again.'

'Won't she mind?'

'She loves it, believe me. Go on, give her a good thrashing.'

'If you say so.'

Powerless to defend myself, I couldn't believe what the cow was ordering the boy to do as she passed him the strap. Thrash my naked buttocks? She was a bitch, I thought, gazing at the strap. My feet high in the air, the cheeks of my bottom were jutting out, perfectly positioned for a thrashing. I could feel my buttocks tensing as the boy raised the strap above his head. What the hell had happened to Sally? I wondered fearfully. How the hell had I got myself into this situation?

The strap swished through the air, landing across the orbs of my bottom cheeks with a loud crack, and

I let out a scream. Again the strap lashed me, jolting my tethered body as Sally and Caroline grinned and whispered to each other. I couldn't take this, I knew as the boy repeatedly lashed my burning buttocks. The leather strap caught the swollen lips of my vulva and I screamed again as the pain permeated my burning flesh. Was the boy deliberately lashing me there? I wondered, lifting my head and gazing in horror at the glowing cushions of my outer lips.

'Keep going,' Sally ordered the boy. 'Make sure you thrash her cunt lips. I want them glowing a fire-red before you finish.'

Caroline sniggered as the strap landed squarely across my puffy lips. She was a bitch, I thought, focusing again on my reddening vulval flesh. My inner lips emerged from my sex valley and I shrieked once more as the strap swiped my delicate petals. Gasping, shaking, I watched my inner lips engorge and swell as they protruded fully from my milk-drenched crack. Squeezing my eyes shut as the strap again stung my inner labia, I let out another scream.

'Is that enough?' Ian asked Sally as he lowered the belt to his side.

'It's nowhere near enough,' she replied. 'I told you that I want her cunt lips glowing red, so you'd better carry on.'

Tensing my buttocks as the lad raised the strap above his head, I held my breath as the strap swished through the air and flailed my bloated outer lips. My crimsoned inner lips unfurled beneath the leather and I let out a gasp as my pussy milk spewed from my vaginal entrance. Again and again the strap lashed my vulval flesh until I screamed out yet again and Sally finally ordered the boy to halt the gruelling thrashing. Quivering, gasping, I gazed at my burning vulva and prayed for my release. I couldn't take another thrashing – and I wouldn't survive another anal shafting.

Sally finally ordered the two other teenagers to stand back as she moved to the wall and released the chains. As my legs lowered and my feet finally hung over the end of the table, I hoped that my ordeal was over. Sperm was oozing from my gaping vaginal entrance, draining from my inflamed anus, and I quivered as I drifted down from my amazing orgasms. I needed to rest, I thought. My body aching, my inner thighs sticky with a blend of sperm and girl-juice, I needed to wash and rest. Six times? Would the boy really manage to fuck and spunk me six times?

I wondered what was going on as Sally ordered Ian to dress and told Caroline to go up to the lounge. Was it over? I wondered as the girl bounded up the steps. Once I was free I'd order Caroline out of the house. I'd tell her to go to her uncle's shop and never return to Juniper House. She was still a virgin, and I wanted her to stay that way. The lad finished dressing and Sally ushered him up the steps. Was I to remain tethered to the table? I needed to wash and rest. Surely Sally didn't intend to leave me there?

Alone in the basement, the sex den, I wondered whether I was to be kept prisoner in my own home. *This is your house – on paper.* Why had I been given the money, why had I been drawn to Juniper House, why . . . What was I there for? I asked myself. Was I now one of the working girls to be used and abused by the clients? Was I to be sold for sex? I'd be better off getting Sally out of the house rather than Caroline. But Sally was under the powerful influence of the old lady. Sally was in charge, I was a prisoner . . . And there was nothing I could do.

Seven

I'd been imprisoned in the sex den for what seemed like hours when Sally finally came down and released me. She said that our client had arrived, the one Caroline was to deal with, and she wanted me to watch. Helping me off the table, she told me as she walked me up the steps that I was to remain naked. My legs sagging beneath me, my vulval flesh burning and stinging, I managed to make it to the lounge and sit in the armchair. Caroline was standing in the centre of the room. She too was naked, the metal clamps still attached to the distended lips of her vulva, the weights hanging from the chains between her slender thighs.

I had no power to help the girl, to save her from her inevitable fate. Unable to speak, I was sure that I was under the old lady's control. As Sally left the room to answer the doorbell, I gazed at Caroline's hairless vulva, her puffy outer lips pulled away from her young body by the heavy weights. Her breasts were firm and hard, the cone-shaped swell of her areolae topped with long, erect nipples. Sally had said that this client was the original one, the one who wanted hand relief. And Caroline was to oblige. Hopefully, that was all the man wanted.

'This is Caroline,' Sally said, leading a middle-aged man into the room. 'Caroline, this is Mr Brookes.'

'Well,' the man breathed, looking the naked girl up and down. 'There's a real little beauty if ever there was one. God, I love the clamps and the weights.'

'And that's Alison,' Sally said, flashing a glance in my direction.

'Another naked beauty? I can see that I'm going to enjoy my visit.'

'It *was* hand relief you wanted? Nothing more?'

'That's right. I'm a little short of cash at the moment. But once I get back on track I'll be able to afford to screw the little beauty senseless.'

'I'm sure you will, sir. Now, if you'd like to get ready and sit on the sofa –'

'I'd rather stand,' he cut in. 'I have this thing about a young girl kneeling before me.'

'As you wish. Caroline, get on your knees.'

Brookes dropped his trousers, his erect penis standing to attention above his rolling balls as Caroline knelt in front of him. The heavy weights swung between her thighs as she gazed in awe at the man's solid cock, the purple globe of his knob as he retracted his foreskin. She grabbed his shaft and began her wanking motions, watching his balls bounce in time with the motion of her hand. Brookes looked down at her young breasts and mumbled something about her teenage body. I knew what he had in mind as the girl looked up at his grinning face. He wanted to spunk over her, give her a facial.

This was going to be over within minutes, I knew as Brookes began gasping and trembling. He'd probably been thinking about it all day, thinking about a young girl wanking him and bringing out his sperm. Was he married? I wondered. Did he have a wife waiting at home? One thing was for certain: there was a fortune to be made from sex. Simply spending a few minutes wanking a man to orgasm paid well. Employing a couple of young girls and selling them for sex was extremely profitable. But I was no longer in charge. Had I *ever* been in charge?

Sally was a bitch, I thought for the umpteenth time. My vaginal lips were burning like hell, my inner petals stinging, and I swore to turn the tables and give her a damned good pussy-thrashing. If I could somehow lure her to the den, get her on the table, handcuffed and naked, her pussy wide open ... She needed disciplining, I concluded. A bloody good cunt-thrashing until she begged and pleaded for me to stop. Should I lash her firm little tits? I mused in my rising wickedness. Half a dozen lashes across each nipple with the leather strap would be interesting. I'd have to make my plans, plans for revenge.

Watching Mr Brookes's balls bouncing as Caroline ran her hand up and down the length of his solid shaft, I wondered whether it would be possible to take charge. There was only one way, I reckoned. Banish the old lady from Juniper House. Was that possible? I should never have allowed Sally to move in, I reflected. But had I had a choice? Was it the old lady's doing? And Caroline moving in ... had that been my decision? No, probably not. Deciding to escape from the house once I had the opportunity, I wondered whether the old lady would be able to use her influence outside the building. If I could lure Sally and Caroline out of the house ...

'Not so fast,' Sally snapped at Caroline. 'For goodness' sake, girl. Give Mr Brookes time to enjoy himself.'

'Yes, mistress,' Caroline breathed, slowing her wanking rhythm. 'I'm sorry.'

'I'm nearly there,' the man gasped.

'Let go of his cock,' Sally said. 'We want to make sure that Mr Brookes gets his money's worth. Play with his balls – run your fingernails over them and make him wait for his orgasm.'

Complying, Caroline fondled and tickled the man's hairy scrotum. His penis swelled and twitched, and I knew that he was on the verge of pumping his spunk all over Caroline's pretty face. Would Sally charge him more for that? I wondered. He'd paid for hand relief. If he gave the girl a facial, he'd have to pay more. Sally was a conniving little bitch and had probably told Caroline to make sure that his spunk rained over her face so that she could charge him more. She was a scheming little bitch, hard and uncaring, and that was why she was doing so well with the business.

As a globule of clear liquid emerged from the man's knob-slit and dripped onto Caroline's head, Sally ordered the girl to wank him for all she was worth. Grabbing his cock, Caroline ran her hand up and down his shaft, wanking him with a vengeance as he shook and let out a low moan of pleasure. His white liquid shot from his purple knob and rained over the girl's hair as he mumbled crude words of sex. *Dirty schoolgirl slut, spunk-loving whore, tight-arsed little bitch* ... I watched his orgasmic cream running over Caroline's hand as she continued to wank his swollen cock. Her eyes sparkling as his sperm splattered her face, I knew that she was well and truly under the old lady's spell. Sadly, it was all over too quickly.

'Enough,' Sally snapped, grabbing Caroline's arm and pulling her upright. 'You've done it, he's finished. Go and clean yourself up, girl.'

'Yes, mistress,' Caroline said, scurrying out of the room.

'That'll be another twenty pounds,' Sally said as she looked down at Brookes's sperm-dripping cock.

'But you said –'

'You gave her a facial, Mr Brookes. That wasn't part of the deal.'

'She was in the way. It's not my fault if the little cow was in the line of fire.'

'The rules are the rules, Mr Brookes. Now hand over the money.'

'You've had all you're getting from me,' he retorted.

'In that case, you haven't had all that you'll be getting from *me*. I don't like being ripped off, Mr Brookes. I'll give you one last chance to pay up. If you don't . . . You have a daughter, don't you?'

'Yes, I . . . How do you know that?'

'A sixteen-year-old daughter. Recently developed, fresh, tight and hot . . .'

'Now wait a minute. What are you implying?'

'The money, Mr Brookes.'

Passing Sally the money, Brookes adjusted his clothing and left the house. Sally had powers beyond belief, I mused as she placed the cash in the bureau. Or the old lady had powers. This was all becoming too much. I was unable to speak, unable to take control of the situation . . . After watching Sally walk across the room and disappear into the hall, I left the armchair and went up to my bedroom. At least I had the power to dress myself, I thought as I reached into the wardrobe and grabbed the first thing that came to hand. Gazing wide-eyed at the pink dress, I felt a shiver run up my spine. I didn't own a pink dress – I'd *never* owned a pink dress.

I slipped into the garment and stood in front of the full-length mirror, gazing at my reflection. The dress fitted perfectly – but where the hell had it come from? It had belonged to the old lady, I knew. But I'd taken all her clothes out of the wardrobe, hadn't I? Caroline appeared in the doorway and looked me up and down. She'd washed the sperm from her hair, her fresh face, and was wearing her school uniform. The weights swung between her thighs as she said that Sally wanted me to go down to the basement.

'No,' I breathed. 'I'm busy at the moment. Tell her that it will have to wait.'

'Yes, madam,' she said, turning to leave.

'Caroline, wait. I want you to come into the village with me. Put a long coat on to cover yourself and –'

'It's against the rules, madam,' she cut in. 'I'm not allowed to leave the house without Mistress Sally.'

'Fuck Mistress Sally,' I replied angrily. 'I'm in charge, and you'll do as I say.'

'Yes, madam,' she finally conceded, leaving the room.

I was sure that if I could get the girl away from Juniper House I'd be able to set her free. Sally was in the basement, the old lady ... Where was the old lady? Was she lurking? I wondered fearfully. All I could do was try to get the girl away from the house, I decided. Better to have tried and failed. Aware of the swollen lips of my naked pussy – my hairless pussy – I was about to grab a pair of panties from the drawer but then I had a change of mind. There was no time to dress properly, I thought as I crossed the landing to Caroline's room. My priority was to get the girl, and myself, out of the house.

Caroline was standing by her bed, folding clothes. 'What the hell are you doing?' I asked her. 'I told you to –'

'You told me to fold my clothes and put them away, madam,' she broke in.

'What?'

'Not one minute ago, you came in here and –'

'All right, all right,' I snapped, leaving the room.

I bounded down the stairs, slipped into the kitchen and opened the back door. Running out into the garden, the warm summer air wafting up my dress and playing around the burning lips of my pussy, I headed for the woods. At least I'd escaped, I thought happily. I was away from the house, away from the old lady . . . I should never have left Caroline in the house, I reflected guiltily. But I'd had no choice. Under cover of the trees, at least I was safe. Wondering what to do, I decided to go into the village and get help. If I explained everything to Jim he'd come to the house with me and . . . Hearing twigs cracking underfoot, I dived into the bushes and hid like a frightened rabbit. Was Sally after me?

'You might as well come out, Alison,' a female voice said. 'You can't hide from me.'

Emerging from the bushes, I stared open-mouthed at a girl in a pink dress. 'Who are you?' I asked shakily, dreading the answer.

'Go back to the house,' she said, smiling at me.

'No, I . . . I don't want to go anywhere near that house. If you're who I think you are, then you shouldn't be here. You should be in some other world, not here in mine.'

'The house was my home. Don't you want to be rich? Don't you want a lovely house with more than enough money?'

'No, not if it means imprisoning young teenage girls and . . .'

'No one is imprisoned, Alison,' she said, chuckling. 'People only imprison themselves, as you did when you were in that rented flat with no future and no money. You have an opportunity now. You have a chance to make something of yourself. And so does Caroline.'

'Caroline is being sold for sex.'

125

'Caroline is happy. For the first time in her life she is away from her parents and their problems. She has a future.'

'You shouldn't be here,' I repeated. '*I* bought the house, and *I* should be running things. You shouldn't be here.'

'You *are* running things. Or you would be if you settled down and accepted your role in life. Go back to the house, Alison.'

As she wandered off I held my hand to my head. I'd been talking to a bloody ghost, I thought fearfully. A dead woman, a ghost . . . Chasing after her, I shouted that I wanted answers, answers to a thousand questions. But she'd gone, disappeared into the woods. Ambling back to the house, I convinced myself that I'd been imagining things. Ghosts didn't exist. I'd either been imagining the old lady or dreaming. Perhaps I'd been daydreaming and it was instinct telling me that I had an opportunity to make something of myself. A nice house with plenty of money? That's what I had, and to throw it all away would be . . . But I'd have to accept that I'd be running a brothel. Was Caroline happy? She hadn't once complained, I reflected. There again, she was under the influence of . . . Or was she? Perhaps she had more than willingly slipped into the role of sex slave. My mind was beginning to ache with too much thinking.

Reaching the house, I made myself a cup of coffee and sat at the kitchen table. I needed to clear my mind and relax, calm down after seeing a . . . a ghost? Recalling my poky flat, I knew that I was doing well. I had a beautiful house, and money. And two girls working for me. Feeling more at ease with the situation, I was sure that I hadn't seen a ghost. I'd been thinking so hard all day that my head had gone into a spin and I'd momentarily gone crazy. I needed to relax, I mused again as I sipped my coffee. Calm down, forget about old ladies and ghosts, and relax.

I decided to say nothing to Sally or Caroline. Although Sally had been talking to someone in the basement, someone I couldn't see, I wanted to stick to my conclusion. There were no ghosts. Maybe Juniper House did have some kind of influence over us. Over time, thoughts and memories might have been soaked up by the walls of the building and were now seeping into our minds. Dark and distant memories, experiences . . .

'Excuse me, madam,' Caroline said as she entered the room.

'Yes, Caroline,' I said, smiling at her. 'What is it?'

'Mistress Sally has gone into the village. She couldn't find you so she asked me to tell you that she's doing some shopping.'

'I'm pleased to hear it. Er . . . I think you'd better remove those weights. We don't want you permanently stretched, do we?'

'No, madam,' she replied, lifting her skirt and removing the clamps from her swollen and very red outer labia.

'That's better. So, do we have any clients booked for this evening?'

'Not as far as I know, madam,' she said, rubbing her puffy vulval lips.

'Place one foot on the table and let me take a look at you,' I instructed her. 'You might need some cream rubbed into you.'

Lifting her skirt and placing her left foot on the table, Caroline looked down at the reddened flesh of her distended outer lips as I moved closer and examined her. She was so young and beautifully fresh, so vulnerable. Stroking the swollen cushions of her puffy labia, I couldn't help myself as I eased a finger between her inner lips and pushed it deep into the virgin sheath of her pussy. She was so tight, hot and extremely wet. And I wanted her. Slipping off the chair and dropping to my knees, I drove a second finger into her teenage vagina and kissed and licked the hairless flesh of her outer love lips.

'Is that nice?' I asked her, massaging her creamy-wet inner flesh.

'Yes, madam,' she replied softly, shakily. 'It's very nice.'

'Caroline, are you happy here? I mean, Sally made you wear those weights and . . .'

'I'm very happy here, madam. I wouldn't want to be anywhere else. Mistress Sally said that she's arranged for a boy to come and see me.'

'A boy?'

'One of Ian's sixth-form friends. He's going to come here and we're going to lose our virginity together. He'll be paying, of course.'

'Of course,' I breathed, managing to force a third finger deep into her tight vagina. 'Had you had any sexual experience before you came here? You said that you're a virgin, but have you, er, *done* anything?'

'Nothing, madam. Nothing at all.'

'Have you not thought about falling in love and enjoying sex for the first time in a loving relationship?'

'Mistress Sally said . . .'

'It's what *you* have to say that I'm interested in, Caroline. Not Mistress Sally.'

'Love brings problems, madam. Mistress . . . I mean, I think that I'll be better off without love. My parents fell in love, and look what happened to them.'

'Point taken, but . . .'

'I don't want the pain that love brings. Pain, suspicion, doubt, insecurity – I don't want that. Have you ever been in love, madam?'

Slipping my pussy-wet fingers out of Caroline's hot vagina and massaging her erect clitoris, I smiled at her. 'I've thought that I've been in love,' I replied. 'You're right, there was pain and . . . But it's not always that way.'

'Isn't it?' she asked wryly.

'You endured the physical pain of the weights and . . .'

'Yes, but mental pain never goes away.'

'Lie on the table with your legs either side of me,' I ordered her, slipping my fingers out of her juice-drenched sex valley and sitting on the chair. 'I want to bring you physical pleasure, Caroline.'

Her feet hung down to either side of me and her rounded buttocks jutted over the edge of the kitchen table. I pulled the chair closer and gazed longingly at the open crack of her teenage vulva. She was wet, her sex milk oozing from her vaginal entrance and trickling down to her bottom-hole. Her clitoris was fully erect, protruding from beneath its pinken bonnet as if inviting my hot mouth. I'd been waiting for this, I thought, leaning forward and running my tongue up and down her gaping valley of desire. Her lubricious sex juices tasted beautiful, and I began lapping fervently at her open sex hole. I'd been longing for this.

Hoping that Sally wouldn't return too soon and interrupt my lesbian loving, I eased my tongue deep into the girl's hot love-sheath and licked the creamed walls of her tight vagina. She writhed on the table, her breathing fast and shallow as I probed her urethral opening with the tip of my tongue. Did I need Sally? I mused. I had Caroline, so why bother with Sally? But Sally was good with the clients, and she ran the business well. If I could get her to obey me, to allow me to be in charge, things might work out.

Reckoning that Sally would go mad because I'd told Caroline to remove the metal clamps, I decided to take no nonsense from her. Whatever had happened to me in the woods had changed my thinking. I must have been listening to my subconscious, I reflected as I sucked out Caroline's juices of lust. I'd probably heard my inner voice, and thought that I'd seen an apparition. No, I must have been daydreaming. Whatever had happened, I was determined to bring about changes at Juniper House.

Moving up Caroline's vulval slit, I parted her swollen pussy lips and sucked her ripe clitoris into my hot mouth. She gasped, writhing again on the table and trembling uncontrollably as I took her closer to her climax. Slipping two fingers into the tightening sheath of her vagina, I imagined a cock there, fucking her, spunking her. It would be a shame to allow her to lose her virginity, I mused, sweeping my tongue over the sensitive tip of her solid clitoris. She was young and fresh, untouched, unsoiled. To have some teenage lad driving his cock deep into her pussy and defiling her with his spunk would be such a shame. There again, she was one of my girls and had to earn her keep. Although Jim was paying her rent, she had to bring in real money if I was going to survive. Pondering on her virginity, I decided that a teenage boy fucking her would be far preferable to having some middle-aged man using and abusing her young body. I'd save her for young, fresh males, I decided as she whimpered in the beginning of her orgasm.

Caroline came with a deluge of vaginal milk. I'd read somewhere about female ejaculation, but this was amazing. Her vaginal muscles rhythmically tightening around my thrusting fingers, she pumped out her orgasmic cream in torrents. Again and again, fountains of white liquid spurted from her finger-bloated sex sheath, splattering my chin as I sucked her orgasm from her pulsating clitoris. The fleshy cushions of her outer sex lips had swollen to an incredible size, bulging either side of my thrusting fingers like balloons. Caroline was all girl, all sex, and I swore to attend her young pussy daily. I'd finger her, lick her and suck her and bring out her pleasure several times every day.

Finally beginning to drift down from her shuddering climax, she lay writhing and whimpering on the table as I teased the last ripples of orgasm from her pink clitoris. Her sex milk had flooded my face, streamed down my fingers and drenched my hand. This was real lesbian sex, I mused as I slipped my fingers out of her inflamed vagina and pressed my lips to the pink cone of flesh surrounding her love hole. Sucking out her pussy milk, drinking from her young body, I wondered whether this was lesbian *love*. Had I fallen in love?

I'd felt responsible for the girl ever since she'd arrived. I hadn't wanted men touching her, fucking and defiling her. Did I want her all to myself? I wondered, repeatedly sucking out her milk and swallowing her creamy offering. Was this cold sex, or was it lesbian love? Dreading Sally's return, I cleaned Caroline's vulva, lapped up the spilt milk from her bloated lips, her crimsoned crack. Helping her to sit up, I could see that she was dazed, dizzy in the aftermath of her massive orgasm. My clitoris swelling, yearning for the girl's wet tongue, I thought about swapping places with her. To have her reciprocate, to tongue-fuck my vagina and . . .

'Anyone around?' Sally called from the hall.

'In here,' I replied, helping Caroline off the table and adjusting her short skirt. Suggesting that she go out into the garden, I grabbed a tissue and wiped up the pool of girl-juice from the table.

'I've been shopping,' Sally called as Caroline closed the back door. Joining me in the kitchen, Sally dumped several carrier bags on the table. 'One of us had to do it,' she sighed. 'Anything happen while I was out?'

I'd met the girl in the woods, tongued and fingered Caroline to orgasm . . . 'No, nothing,' I muttered as I helped her to put the shopping away. I was pleased to see that she was wearing a long coat over her revealing skirt.

'Where's Caroline?'

'In the back garden. I thought she could do with some fresh air.'

'What are the weights doing there?' Sally murmured, gazing at the chains on the table.

'I told her to remove them,' I replied, hoping that she wasn't going to complain. 'Sally, when I was in the basement . . . I couldn't speak.'

'What do you mean?'

'I was powerless to speak. Also, when I did as you asked and stripped naked . . . It was as if I was under a spell.'

'A sex spell,' she replied, giggling as she slipped her coat off. 'Did you enjoy the thrashing? You like a nice cunt-thrashing, don't you?'

'No, I don't. I didn't want that.'

'Then why didn't you protest.'

'I couldn't speak. Hang on a minute – why aren't you calling me madam?'

'You told me not to.'

'Yes, so I did. Sally, I need some answers.'

'Answers to what? You're the boss, Alison. You should have all the answers.'

'Yes, I *am* the boss. You've changed your tune. I thought . . . It doesn't matter what I thought.'

'By the way, there's a man calling round later. I met him in the village and –'

'You've been talking to people in the village about our business?'

'I wasn't blabbing about us. He approached me. He asked me whether Juniper House was open for business.'

'How did he know about the house?'

'He said that he used to visit the lady years ago.'

'The lady?' I echoed.

'The lady of the house, as he put it. Anyway, he's in his late sixties now and he reckons that he's forgotten what naked young girls look like. I said that we'd soon refresh his memory. That is all right, isn't it?'

'Yes, yes, of course. Sally, I ... I don't want Caroline to get fucked, to put it crudely.'

'Why ever not? That's what she's here for.'

'I've made my decision, and that's the end of the matter. I don't mind her attending men, wanking them. But I don't want them fucking her. Besides, it's getting late. I think she should get to bed before too long.'

'As you wish. In that case, I suppose *I*'ll have to look after our client. I'll go and get ready.'

I finished putting the shopping away and then called Caroline in from the back garden. Eyeing the swell of her pussy lips just visible below the hem of her very short skirt, I told her to make herself something to eat and then get to bed. If our client glimpsed the little beauty's hairless crack, her puffy vaginal lips, he'd go into a sexual frenzy. In her bed, she'd be out of the way. I wanted to protect her, I thought as she made herself a sandwich. Keep her under wraps? Keep her for myself. She'd be safe in her bed, playing with herself, fingering her little pussy, masturbating her beautiful clitoris to orgasm.

The front doorbell finally rang and Sally invited the man in. She was right: he was in his late sixties. He

133

had thinning grey hair and a lined face, and I wondered when he'd last feasted his eyes on a naked teenage girl. Decades, I concluded as I followed Sally and her client into the lounge. Passing her some money, he looked her up and down approvingly and then asked why there were two of us.

'Don't mind me,' I said, hoping that this wasn't going to take too long as I made myself comfortable in the armchair. After a busy day, all I needed was a good night's sleep. 'I'll just sit here out of the way.'

'Right,' Sally said, smiling at the man. 'So, you want to see a naked teenage girl?'

'Very much,' he murmured, rubbing his chin as he eyed her long legs. 'It's been a long time.'

'Firm young breasts, a hairless pussy . . . Sit on the sofa and, after the show, I'll bring you your much-needed relief.'

I felt that I was in control again as Sally unbuttoned her blouse and exposed the cups of her white bra. I didn't like being called madam, and I certainly didn't like being told what to do. I'd get my own back for the pussy-thrashing. She wasn't going to get away with that. At least things were beginning to change. Sally had been shopping, which pleased me. The day she'd moved in she'd agreed to do the household chores. And that was the way I wanted it. Caroline would help out, of course. But she'd be working in her uncle's shop during the day and wouldn't have a great deal of time left over.

I watched the old man's eyes widen as he waited patiently for Sally to remove her bra and expose her teenage breasts. Then I turned my head and gazed into the hall as I heard Caroline trotting down the stairs. Before I'd had a chance to dash into the hall and order her back to her room, she appeared in the doorway. Fortunately she was wearing white panties beneath her short skirt. If the old man had seen her shaved pussy lips, her tightly closed sex crack . . .

'Come and stand over here,' Sally ordered the girl.

'Yes, mistress,' Caroline said, standing in front of the grinning man.

'This is Caroline,' Sally said, turning to the man. 'She's a young schoolgirl, and she's eager to show you her naked body.'

'And I'm eager to take a look,' he breathed excitedly.

'Sally,' I began. 'I thought –'

'It's all right, madam,' she cut in. 'I'll deal with this.'

I was fuming, but I didn't want to say too much in front of our client. I didn't mind him gawping at Caroline's young body, but I wasn't going to allow him to push his cock into her virgin pussy. As he eyed the swell of her tight panties and licked his lips, I thought it was sad that elderly men were denied the beauty of the naked teenage form. All they could do was try to remember and dream and fantasise. At least we'd make *one* old man happy, I mused as he moved forward on the sofa and gazed longingly at the triangular patch of material straining to contain her full sex lips. Beginning to calm down, I relaxed and lay back in the armchair. I was going to enjoy the show as much as our client.

'Tight little panties,' Sally said. 'She has beautifully smooth, hairless pussy lips beneath the thin material of her panties. Caroline, lift your skirt up and show the man your smooth stomach. There,' she breathed as the girl complied. 'See the indent of her little navel?'

'God, yes,' the man breathed, his eyes bulging.

'She's young and virginal. A young schoolgirl. And she's going to show you everything she has. But

135

you're not going to see her little pussy just yet. We'll save that for later. Now, Caroline, slip your skirt and blouse off, but keep your bra and panties on.'

Caroline obeyed her mistress like an obedient dog. Stepping out of her skirt as it crumpled around her feet, she slipped her blouse off and tossed it onto the sofa. The man looked up at her skimpy bra and grinned. His cock would be as hard as rock, I was sure as he lowered his head and focused again on the swell of her panties. Caroline was slim but had curves in the right places. She was a real beauty, I mused, recalling sucking on her ripe clitoris and taking her to orgasm. Sensual, sexy, young and fresh . . . And her cunt milk tasted beautiful.

'Turn round, Caroline,' Sally said. 'I'm sure that our client would like to see how your tight panties cling to your firm little bottom cheeks.' Turning, the girl stood with her feet slightly parted. The bulge of her succulent vaginal lips was clearly outlined by her panties between the tops of her slender thighs and I knew that the man was now becoming desperate to see the girl in all her naked glory. Her panties faithfully following the contours of her rounded buttocks, I too was desperate to see her naked. I couldn't stop thinking about her sweet girl-crack, couldn't get the image of her inner folds, her open hole, out of my mind. Was I in love?

Following Sally's instructions, Caroline lowered the back of her panties just enough to reveal the top of her bottom crack. The man reached out to touch her, but Sally grabbed his hand and ordered him to be patient. I could see the bulge of his penis straining the crotch of his trousers, and I reckoned that he'd spurt his spunk the minute a teenage girl's hand touched his solid cock. He might even come in his trousers, I mused excitedly. My clitoris swelling, my vaginal milk oozing between the hairless lips of my pussy, I thought that *I* might come in my own panties.

Again following Sally's orders, Caroline spun round on her heels and lowered the front of her panties just enough to expose the top of her sex slit. Sally certainly knew how to tease a man, I thought as she pulled down the cups of Caroline's bra and revealed the brown teats of her ripe nipples. Suggesting that the man pull his trousers down, she said that he'd soon enjoy the feel of a young girl's warm hand around his solid shaft. He was visibly trembling, his eyes wide as he gazed at the ripe teats of Caroline's firm little breasts. Eagerly yanking his trousers down to his ankles, he lay back on the sofa with his erect cock standing to attention above his heaving balls.

'God, you're big,' Sally gasped, staring in awe at his magnificent organ.

He looked down at his cock and grinned. 'Big, and desperate to come,' he breathed.

'All in good time. Since you've been a good boy, you may pull Caroline's panties down to her knees. But don't touch her.'

Wasting no time, he yanked the girl's panties down and let out a rush of breath as he locked his wide-eyed stare on her closed pussy crack. Her swollen outer lips rose on either side of her valley of desire – she was a real beauty, I thought. She'd be wet, I knew as I imagined driving my tongue into her teenage pussy. Wet and hot. I thought that our client would be unable to control himself and would thrust his fingers deep into her tight vagina, but he sat back on the sofa and gazed admiringly at the most private part of her curvaceous body. His cock twitching, his balls rolling within their hairy sac, he was still trembling. I'd have liked to take his cock into my mouth and suck out his sperm, but thought I'd better leave it to the other girls.

'Would you like to taste her?' Sally asked him. 'Would you like to taste her girlie milk?'

'Yes, yes,' he breathed, leaning forward and running his tongue up and down the tightly closed crack of her vulva.

'All right, you may push your tongue into her groove. But keep your hands away.'

Lapping at her sex slit, the old man pushed his tongue between her fleshy hillocks. Caroline gasped and threw her head back as he licked her there. She'd be very wet, I thought, recalling her milky orgasmic gush. I felt a little jealous as the man slurped at her vaginal crack. I'd loved taking her to orgasm, fingering her tight pussy and sucking hard on her pulsating clitoris. And now *he* was there, savouring the taste of her teenage milk. A little jealous? I was *extremely* jealous.

'OK,' Sally said. 'Lie back and we'll sort out your cock. You've paid for hand relief. Are you sure that you don't want to feel the heat of her mouth around your knob?'

'Yes, yes, I do,' he said, taking the money from his trouser pocket. 'There you are. Now, I want her to suck it hard and swallow my sperm.'

'You heard the man, Caroline. Get down on your knees and suck his knob.'

Dropping to her knees, the girl parted her full lips and sucked his purple plum into her wet mouth. She'd sucked Ian's cock, but she hadn't had the pleasure of giving a full blow job. Would she enjoy swallowing sperm? I wondered as she bobbed her head up and down, repeatedly taking his swollen knob to the back of her throat. The old man gasped and shuddered as he watched Caroline mouth-fuck herself on his ageing cock. This was what he'd wanted, I mused. He'd never forget this. Whenever he wanked, he'd picture the teenage girl taking his knob into her mouth.

His orgasm came quickly, too quickly. Writhing and moaning softly, he thrust his hips forward and pumped Caroline's pretty mouth full of sperm. Watching the girl as she swallowed hard, he grabbed her head and rocked his hips faster, forcing her to take his orgasming knob down her throat as he drained his heavy balls. I could hear her gulping, breathing heavily through her nose as she swallowed his creamy liquid. She was doing well, I thought, feeling a little envious of her. The man might have been old but his cock was huge, bloating her pretty mouth and filling her cheeks. She was a lucky girl. But I still didn't want a cock shafting her sweet pussy.

Finally slipping his spent penis out of her mouth, she coughed and spluttered and wiped her sperm-glossed lips on the back of her hand. Sally helped her to her feet and praised her repeatedly as the man lay on the sofa trembling and panting for breath. The girl was learning fast. And I'd have liked to watch her restiffen the man's cock and suck him to orgasm again. But she had to work in her uncle's shop the following morning. She needed to rest, and so did I.

The old man finally recovered and booked an appointment before leaving. I knew that my business would soon be booming. The more clients, the better, I reflected as I climbed the stairs, wondering whether to employ another girl. Sally and Caroline were doing well, but with a third girl I could entertain three clients at once.

Sally wanted to sleep with Caroline, but I wouldn't allow it. Caroline was to get a good night's sleep, not spend the night entwined in lesbian lust with Sally.

Naked beneath the quilt with Sally, I was going to suck on my friend's hairless pussy lips, run my tongue up and down her sex crack and suck her clitoris to orgasm. But sleep engulfed us and dreams of lesbian sex comforted me.

Eight

Actually, I didn't sleep at all well. Gazing into the darkness for hours on end, thinking about the girl in the woods, I'd imagined ghosts roaming the house in the dark of the night. I must have had a few hours' sleep, but it didn't feel like it. Glancing at the clock, I couldn't believe that it was gone nine. There was no sign of Sally, apart from an indent left in her pillow, and I wondered whether Caroline was up and about.

I left my bed and gazed out of the window. It was lashing with rain, but that didn't matter. I had no plans to go anywhere. Catching my reflection in the mirror, I gazed at the hairless lips of my vulva. I looked so young, I thought, running my fingertips over the smooth hillocks of flesh rising either side of my sex valley. Young, fresh, virginal . . . My clitoris responded as I slipped my finger between my smooth outer lips and massaged its sensitive tip. I needed to come, I knew as my vaginal muscles tightened. I needed Caroline's wet tongue there, licking, teasing, taking me to a multiple orgasm.

Leaving my swollen clitoris and slipping into my pink dress, I decided to find Caroline and have her attend my feminine needs. If I could get Sally out of the way for a while, I'd kneel over Caroline's face and have her tongue me to a much-needed climax. The very notion sending ripples of sex through my womb as I made my way downstairs, I remembered that Caroline was working at her uncle's shop. Perhaps Sally would lick me to orgasm, I mused. Hearing a male voice coming from the lounge, I wondered whether it was Jim. Had Caroline not gone to work?

'I know what's going on,' a man said. 'And unless you accept me as a non-paying customer –'

'You're blackmailing me?' Sally cut in.

'All I'm saying is, if you allow me to enjoy myself here I won't mention your illegal business to the police.'

'What's going on?' I asked, entering the lounge and staring at another middle-aged man.

'This gentleman is blackmailing us, madam,' Sally said.

'I know what's going on here,' he said, staring at me accusingly. 'All I'm asking is that you allow me to visit and enjoy your girls in return for my keeping quiet.'

'I think we can sort something out,' I replied, smiling at him.

'I'm pleased to hear it,' he murmured. 'You're obviously a sensible woman.'

'Anything for a quiet life,' I said.

'I'm into young schoolgirls. Are you able to offer –'

'Indeed we are, sir,' I interrupted him, winking at Sally. 'In fact, your timing is spot on. We have a new girl starting today. She's young, and she's a virgin.'

'Perfect,' he breathed, grinning at me.

'The girl will be here any minute now. Sally, show the gentleman down to the den.'

'Certainly, madam. If you'll come this way, sir?'

I followed them down to the basement, determined to nip this in the bud. There was no way I was going to be blackmailed by some sad pervert. He was in his late forties with dark hair swept back from his forehead. A businessman, I reckoned, eyeing his shirt and tie. Ordering him to strip naked and lie on the table, I winked again at Sally. She obviously knew what I had in mind as she helped our non-paying client to slip out of his clothes and take his position on the table. He protested as she pulled his hands behind his head and cuffed his wrists to the steel ring set in the top of the table. But she explained that our young girl was into male domination.

'She'll be here soon,' I said as Sally parted his legs and hung his feet down either side of the table. Cuffing his ankles to the table legs, Sally stood back as I stroked the man's flaccid cock.

'Are you married?' I asked him.

'Yes,' he replied. 'But my wife isn't into anything kinky. My fetish is young girls. Young virgin girls in school uniforms.'

'Sally,' I said, grinning at the girl. 'Would you shave our client, please?'

'Shave?' he breathed, lifting his head and staring at me. 'No, you can't . . . My wife will –'

'Your wife will wonder what on earth you've been up to,' I cut in.

'Don't you dare,' he hissed, glaring at Sally as she massaged foam into his dark pubic curls.

'Sally does as I tell her,' I said. 'Once you've been shaved . . .'

'If you shave me, I'll ruin you.'

'What's this?' I murmured, taking his wallet from his jacket pocket. 'Ah, your name and address. I might have to call in and have a chat with your wife.'

'For God's sake,' the man gasped as Sally began the job of shaving his pubes. 'Look, I'll pay for your services.'

'I know you will,' I returned, taking fifty pounds from his wallet. 'This will do nicely.'

Feeling wicked, and vengeful, I decided that this man was going to pay dearly for attempting to blackmail me. I hadn't had a good night, I'd wanted Caroline to attend my intimate needs and she'd gone to work . . . and I'd come downstairs to find that my business was being threatened by a sad pervert. Pacing the floor as Sally finished shaving our victim, I finally grabbed a vibrator from the shelf and stood at the foot of the table. Parting his buttocks, I pressed the rounded end of the pink shaft hard against his anus. He protested: he didn't want the vibrator there, he didn't want to be shaved.

'Too late,' I said, giggling and forcing the plastic shaft deep into his rectal duct. 'You have to be punished for trying to blackmail me. I have to teach you a lesson – and one that you'll never forget. I'm sure your wife will be delighted when she sees that you've been shaved. She'll question you, of course. Why did you do it? Have you got another woman? I can feel divorce in the air. Sally, pass me the leather strap.'

Taking the strap, I ran it over the man's semi-erect penis. I'd never lashed a cock before, and the notion gripped me as he lifted his head and gazed at his defenceless manhood. His anxiety was mirrored in his dark eyes – he was probably wondering how to explain things to his wife. How long before his pubic hair grew back? I wondered. Four weeks? Longer, maybe? He asked me what I intended to do with the leather strap. His voice was shaky, he was fearful. Rather than tell him, I decided to show him.

Bringing the strap down across the shaft of his cock with a loud crack, I grinned as he yelped and begged for mercy. Blackmailers would receive no mercy from me. And adulterous men would receive no mercy from their betrayed wives. Again, the strap lashed his twitching cock. His cries resounding around the sex den, the torture chamber, he struggled and pulled futilely against his bonds. The vibrator bloating his rectum, the shaft of his penis reddening beneath the blows of the leather belt, I was surprised to see his cock stiffening. Lashed to orgasm? I mused, repeatedly bringing the strap down across his convulsing penile shaft. Sally watched in amazement as his cock became solid. Little did she know that her own sweet cunt lips were to be thrashed before long. Suggesting that I lash his balls, she asked me whether I'd allow her to use the bamboo cane on our victim.

'There are limits,' I said, lowering the strap to my side.

'Please . . .' the man gasped. 'Please . . .'

'You want the cane?' I asked him.

'No, no, I don't. I can't take any more. For God's sake, stop now.'

'I've barely started. And I won't stop until your spunk shoots out.'

Lashing his solid penis again, I was sure that he'd soon achieve his orgasm as Sally rammed the vibrator fully home into his rectal duct and switched it on. The man gasped and writhed on the table as the belt landed squarely across his rock-hard cock. His purple knob emerged as his foreskin retracted and I kept an eye on his sperm-slit. Would he come? I wondered again as the belt caught the purple flesh of his sex globe. Would he shoot his spunk all over his stomach? He cried out as the belt again landed on his twitching cock, his naked body convulsing as the loudest crack of the strap yet echoed around the den. He was almost there.

'Yes,' I breathed, increasing my lashing rhythm as his white liquid jetted from his knob-slit and splattered his stomach. His cream ran down to the shaved

145

flesh surrounding the base of his crimsoned cock, and he moaned and squirmed as the strap caught the purple globe of his penis. I brought the belt down again and again across his glowing sex shaft as his sperm gushed from his swollen knob. What his wife would say when she saw his inflamed cock, his hairless balls, I dreaded to think. But it served him right. How dare he try to blackmail me? One thing was for sure: he wouldn't be back. I had his name and address, and he knew that I wouldn't hesitate to have a chat with his wife about his adultery.

His sperm flow finally ceased. I lowered the strap and admired my handiwork. The vibrator was still buzzing deep within his rectal sheath, his spunk still streaming over his shaved flesh. I wondered whether he'd be able to achieve another orgasm. I was in a strange mood, torn between wanting to torture the bastard and using him to satisfy my lust for debased sex. I ordered Sally to lap up the spilled spunk and cleanse the man as I moved to the top of the table and lifted my dress up over my stomach.

'Like it?' I asked him as he gazed wide-eyed at my hairless vulva.

'Yes,' he breathed softly as Sally sucked up the sperm from his shaved flesh. 'You're beautiful. You're both very beautiful girls.'

'It's a shame you had to threaten me. You could have become a regular client.'

'I was only joking,' he sighed.

'How did you hear about me, about this house?'

'I used to come here years ago, when I was in my teens.'

'Really?' I murmured, lowering my dress. 'Who was here? Who was running things?'

'Alison was the lady in charge. And there was a young girl called Caroline.'

'Are you sure?' I asked him, unable to believe what I was hearing.

'Of course I'm sure. Have you taken over the business?'

'Yes, yes, I have. What about Sally? Was there a girl called Sally?'

'I don't know. I didn't meet all the girls. Apart from Alison, there was Caroline, Tracey . . .'

'Tracey?' I breathed 'Why didn't you say that you used to be a client? Why try to blackmail me?'

'I'm very short of money at the moment. I'm going through a bad patch and –'

'I'm not interested in your problems,' I cut in coldly. 'But I *am* interested in the past. Tell me about Alison.'

'I think that's enough, madam,' Sally said sternly.

'What do you mean?'

'The past has gone, let's leave it that way.'

'Sally, I want to know . . .'

'I said, that's enough,' she shot back. 'Go and sit on that chair, and leave this to me.'

I was about to have a go at Sally, but then I decided to see what she was going to do. Nothing had changed, I mused angrily as she began wanking the man and restiffening his cock. I wasn't in charge. Was the old lady influencing Sally? She didn't want me to hear about the past, and had somehow influenced Sally to intervene and stop my questioning. Confused, I couldn't begin to work out what was going on. The man had been to the house during his teens, he'd met Alison and Caroline . . . Who the hell was Tracey? I was certain of one thing: Juniper House was haunted. And I didn't like it.

The man's cock was soon fully erect again and Sally leaned over and sucked his purple plum into her mouth. As she gobbled and slurped, I gazed at the rounded cheeks of her naked buttocks clearly visible below her short skirt. I wasn't sure whether the old lady had possessed her completely, or was just influencing her. If she was possessed, then where was Sally? Where was her soul? I didn't like the situation at all, and was pleased that Caroline wasn't around. Ghosts, I mused fearfully. Did they exist? Whoever I'd met in the woods ... The time had come to put an end to the haunting or whatever it was.

I left the basement as Sally lost herself in her knob-sucking, went to the lounge and sat at the bureau. Although I'd sifted through the papers several times, I felt sure that I'd missed something. I didn't know what I was looking for. A note scribbled on the back of an envelope, an old bill ... There had to be something. Opening the top drawer, I began to rummage through the papers. I examined every envelope, every scrap of paper, and finally discovered something very interesting.

'Tracey arriving on evening train,' I read aloud. Tracey? The man hadn't been lying, I reflected. There again, why would he lie? I felt a chill run up my spine as I stuffed the papers back into the drawer. There was more to this haunted house than I'd realised. A spirit, an entity was trying to return to the physical world and ... Was the old lady trying to return through Sally? Was she in the process of moving into Sally's body? Or was I overreacting? Perhaps I'd watched too many films about ghosts and possessions, I mused. But, in my heart, I knew that the old lady was trying to return to the physical world.

Leaving the house by the back door, I walked down the garden to the woods. The rain had stopped and the sun was shining. I should have been enjoying the summer, I thought, finding the very spot where

I'd talked to the girl in the pink dress. I should have been enjoying my life, not worrying about ghosts. I wanted to meet her again, to speak to her and ask her a thousand questions. I should never have allowed her to walk away, I reflected. I should have grabbed her arm and held on to her. Sitting on the wet ground with my back against a pine tree, I closed my eyes. Would she come to me? I wondered. As an apparition, or in my thoughts, would she come to me?

In the darkness behind my eyelids, I saw a swirling mist. Bright pinpoints of silver light penetrated the dark as I mentally urged the old lady to come to me. I saw a face in the mist. Was it my imagination? A young girl, naked, attractive ... 'Alison,' a girl's voice called. I opened my eyes but saw no one. Again, I heard my name. Closing my eyes, I tried to blank out the sound of the singing birds. 'Alison,' I heard again. Urging the girl to speak, I sensed someone approaching and opened my eyes.

'You?' I said, leaping to my feet as the girl in the pink dress smiled at me. 'Who are you?'

'I live in the village,' she replied. 'We met before, remember?'

'In the village, but ...'

'I like your dress. It's the same as mine.'

'You're not real,' I breathed shakily.

'Not real? What do you mean?'

'You shouldn't be in this world. If you're real, then how do you know things about me? You mentioned my flat and said that I could be rich and ... How do you know so much about me?'

'Word soon gets round in a small village. Besides, I'd been talking to Sally. She told me about your flat and the money and –'

'Have you been to the house?'

'I met Sally in the village.'

'How come we have the same clothes? And how come you look like me and . . .'

'The lady who lived in the house . . . She was my mother.'

'Your mother?'

'She had me late in her life. Sadly, we never got on. To make matters worse, my brother and I never spoke. I finally left the house and moved into the village with a friend. It's a long and sad story. My mother was a prostitute, and I have no idea who my father is. I know what you're doing with the house, I know that you're running the business as my mother used to. When we met before, I said that you could be rich. I said that you were in charge.'

'But I'm not in charge. Wait a minute, I don't understand. What's your name?'

'Tracey.'

'Tracey, the evening train.'

'I'm sorry?'

'Nothing. I thought you were a ghost.'

'No, no, I'm not a ghost. Mind you, it wouldn't surprise me if Juniper House had a few ghosts roaming around. I liked living there but . . . The main reason I left the house was because my mother wanted me to work for her.'

'Work for her? You mean, as a –'

'Prostitute. I moved in with my friend, and her parents looked upon me as their daughter.'

'But the pink dress . . . Sally reckons that she's seen a girl in the house wearing a pink dress. And she's spoken to her.'

'This was my mother's dress. I always wear it when I come up to the house. I usually stay in the woods or wander into the back garden in the hope of . . . You see, my brother sold the house without my knowledge. Half the money should have been mine, but it's too late now. May I come up to the house this evening?'

'Yes, of course.'

'I'd like to have a look round. Are you sure you don't mind?'

'You're more than welcome,' I said softly. 'I really did think that you were a ghost. You knew so much about me, and you were wearing that dress . . . Come to the house this evening and you can have a look round.'

'I will, thank you. I have to go now.'

'Yes, I'd better get back. Until this evening, then.'

As she followed the path into the woods, I breathed a sigh of relief. There were no such things as ghosts, I thought happily. But if Tracey hadn't been to the house, who had Sally been talking to? I'd seen no one in the basement when she'd been talking, I reflected. Perhaps the very walls of the building were oozing with memories. And some of the distant memories had seeped into our minds? Sally had been talking to someone. Or she had appeared to be. There were no ghosts, I decided as I walked through the back garden to the kitchen door. Only distant memories. Memories haunt people, don't they?

There were still many unanswered questions, I thought as I closed the back door behind me. Caroline had said that I'd been into her room and ordered her to do this and that, she'd said that I'd changed my mind and . . . She must have been talking to someone, some girl or other who'd been wearing a pink dress. Tracey had probably sneaked into the house and met Caroline. I decided to stop trying to work things out and get on with running the house, the business. Perhaps the place was haunted, after all. If that was the case, then I wasn't going to allow it to affect me.

'Sally,' I called, making my way down the basement steps. She'd gone, and so had the man. I hadn't liked him at all, and I hoped that I'd never see him again. Since I'd threatened to talk to his wife, I doubted very much that he'd return. He'd have a hell of a lot of explaining to do when his wife confronted him, I mused happily. His pubic hair shaved off, his cock red and raw ... Divorce, I reflected, thanking God that I'd never married.

Searching the house, I could only imagine that Sally had gone out. She shouldn't have left the back door unlocked, I thought. After the intruder ... There again, it was just as well, otherwise I'd have been locked out. This was the first time I'd had the house to myself for a while, and the peace and quiet made a pleasant change. It wasn't that the girls were noisy, but they were always around. I didn't even have my bedroom to myself, and decided that I'd have to make a few changes. If I needed lesbian sex, I could always slip into Caroline's bed and enjoy her beautiful young body.

'So, there are no ghosts here,' I said, standing in the middle of the lounge and looking around the room. There were many things that I didn't understand, but I was determined not to waste time thinking about them. What I wanted to do was move on, build the business and enjoy the profits. Start afresh, I thought. I had to make Sally understand that I was in charge. Make sure that Caroline was under my control. And as for Tracey ...

Tracey was an unknown entity, I mused. She was real enough, but she belonged to the past. The old lady was her mother, she'd grown up in the house ... And she'd mentioned that she should have had half the money from the sale of the house. I didn't want her becoming a regular visitor. If we became too friendly, she might want to move into the house. I'd show her around and offer tea or coffee, but that was as far as it would go. I'd make it clear that she wasn't to call round every day.

I wondered again where Sally had got to. Then I felt an overwhelming urge to masturbate. I was alone in the house, I'd be undisturbed, have time to enjoy an orgasm . . . Sitting in the armchair, I pulled up my dress and parted my thighs. I had no idea why my arousal had suddenly heightened. I hadn't been thinking about sex, but I knew that I desperately needed to come. My pussy lips were still red from the thrashing, red and swollen. In a way I'd enjoyed the abuse. The leather strap lashing my vulval flesh . . . Did I want the strap again? I wondered. Perhaps I'd slip into the world of bondage and whipping and enjoy even bigger and better orgasms.

Peeling the fleshy lips of my pussy wide apart, I focused on the tip of my ballooning clitoris. Solid, pink, ready to be sucked. I needed Caroline. My inner lips unfurled as I stroked the tip of my sensitive clitoris and I smiled as my cunt milk trickled from my gaping love hole. I could feel my nipples inflating beneath my pink dress, becoming acutely sensitive, waiting for a hot mouth. Caroline was beautiful, I thought for the umpteenth time. If only she was home, if only her pink tongue was lapping around the solid nub of my clitoris.

Perhaps Caroline and Sally would attend my feminine needs, I thought, slipping two fingers deep into my contracting vagina. Two tongues licking my vulval crack, two hot mouths sucking my pussy lips. Imagining several fingers delving deep into my vagina, I massaged my creamy inner flesh. Dragging my sex juices up my yawning valley and lubricating the swollen bulb of my clitoris, I felt my womb contract, my nipples harden. I would have slipped down to the basement and enjoyed a vibrator, but I didn't like the idea of being in the den alone. Ghosts might get me, I mused dreamily, again thrusting two fingers into my tight vagina. Ghosts might fuck me.

Massaging the erect nub of my clitoris with my free hand, I closed my eyes and relaxed. The house was quiet, calm. There were no ghosts, I mused again as my juices of lust seeped between the engorged petals of my inner lips. There were only memories of orgasms, spurting spunk and flowing girl-juice. Managing to force three fingers into my yearning vaginal duct, I pictured a swollen knob, my tongue licking the slit. The knob in my mouth, I sucked it, brought out the creamy sperm and swallowed hard. Did I need a man or a woman? Both, I mused.

I'd never had such a powerful urge to masturbate. Perhaps it was because I was surrounded by sex, the sounds and smell of sex. I was running a brothel, witnessing crude sexual acts every day, so my libido was bound to heighten. I recalled the young boy's cock driving in and out of my tight pussy, his shaft opening my rectal duct and spunking my bowels. I'd enjoyed the experience, I reflected as I began to tremble and my breathing became heavy. His fresh young cock fucking my sex holes ... It was a shame that he hadn't managed to fuck and spunk me six times after all. Maybe next time.

My arousal reached frightening heights. I pulled my dress over my head and tossed it onto the floor. Naked in the armchair, my legs wide apart, my hairless vulval crack gaping, I massaged again the swollen bulb of my sensitive clitoris. Things had changed dramatically since I'd left my flat, I thought dreamily as I dragged my creamy juices up my valley of desire and lubricated my clitoris. I'd come into money, bought a beautiful house, experienced incredible sex . . . and was now running my own successful business. As my climax neared, I was thinking how well I'd done. Then I heard a noise in the kitchen.

'Shit,' I breathed, leaping out of the armchair. Wishing that I'd locked the back door, I was about to grab my dress when a man wandered into the room. 'Oh,' I gasped, folding my arms to conceal the mounds of my firm breasts. 'Who the hell are you?'

'Sorry,' he said, his dark-eyed stare fixed on the hairless lips of my sex-dripping pussy. 'The door was open.'

'You don't just walk into someone's house because the door . . .' Grabbing my dress, I held it up against my naked body. 'Who are you?' I asked him again. 'What do you want?'

'I was looking for Alison,' he replied.

'I'm Alison.'

He chuckled and then frowned at me. 'You're not the Alison I remember,' he said. 'I've not been here for a few years. If anything, you should look older, not younger.'

'Ah, you're talking about the old lady.' Turning my back on him, I slipped the dress over my head. 'The old lady . . . This is my house, now.'

'Oh, I see.'

Facing him again, I straightened the dress. 'I'm afraid the old lady died,' I told him.

'Oh, I'm sorry to hear that. Mind you, she was getting on a bit.'

'What was your connection with her?'

'Er . . . business.'

'You were a client? It's all right, I know what her business was.'

'Yes, yes, I was a client. I moved abroad a few years ago and I'm back in England for a couple of weeks, looking up old friends.'

155

'Do you remember Tracey?' I asked him. 'She was the old lady's daughter.'

'Yes, I do. She didn't like her mother's business, which was understandable. Eventually, she moved out and . . . Look, I've interrupted you. I'm sorry for the intrusion. I'd better be going.'

'No, not yet. Tell me about the old lady.'

'I'm David, by the way. The old lady, Alison, knew what men wanted. She provided a service which was second to none. She never married. I suppose she didn't have the time or the inclination to settle down. She was too busy making money to bother about things like that.'

'And the girls? What were they like?'

'There was Caroline – she was a lovely young thing. She saw most of the clients. As I said, Tracey didn't like her mother's business. But she did see a few clients.'

'Oh, I thought that she kept out of it?'

'Her mother . . . I wouldn't say that she forced the girl to work, but she did encourage her. You must have had one or two old clients call at the house? I suppose not all of them know that the business has closed.'

'It hasn't closed,' I said, hoping that David would become a regular client.

'You mean . . .'

'I run the business now. You're right, when I moved in, one or two old clients called at the house. I saw the potential and . . . and here I am.'

'I see. What a coincidence. Your name being Alison, I mean.'

'There are too many coincidences for my liking,' I murmured. 'So, would you like my services?'

'Very much so. But may I come back later? I have a few things to do, a few people to see. Would six o'clock suit you?'

'Yes, that's fine. The more clients, the better. I'll look forward to seeing you.'

Showing David to the front door I decided that he'd be my client, not Sally's. I didn't want Sally taking charge of this one. He was good-looking, in his late thirties, well dressed . . . I'd keep him for myself. After all, it was my business so I should get the best. Closing the door, I thought about Tracey. So, she had worked as a prostitute for her mother. Everyone has their price, I mused, returning to the lounge. Although I hadn't wanted her to move into the house, I was beginning to have second thoughts. If that was what she was after, if she had it in her mind to move in, then she could become one of my working girls.

At least I could forget about ghosts, I decided as I sat in the armchair. Things were becoming clearer in my mind now. My first client, the man who'd enjoyed being spanked, had known where the leather belt was because he was an old customer. He'd been to the house before and obviously knew where the belt was kept. But why had he called me Alison? He couldn't have known my name. Perhaps it was a slip of the tongue, I reflected. He'd met the other Alison on numerous occasions and had simply made a mistake. Deciding again to move on rather than dwell on the past, I was about to lift my dress and resume masturbating when I heard the front door open.

'Hello, madam,' Sally said as she entered the lounge.

'Where have you been?' I asked her.

'Into the village, madam.'

'Sally, you can cut out the *madam* crap. If you have to call me madam, then only do it when we have a client here. What did you do in the village?'

'There's a boys' school, a private school. I'd arranged to meet Ian, the young lad who came here.'

'You'd arranged to meet him? You didn't tell me.'

'I'm sorry, madam. It must have slipped my mind. He has a few friends – older boys from the sixth form – who'd like to visit the house. They have money and –'

'I wish you'd told me about this, Sally. For God's sake, we can't have a load of sex-crazy schoolboys trooping up the lane to Juniper House. Word is bound to get back to the teachers.'

'No, madam. They understand the importance of discretion. After all, they face expulsion if they're caught coming here.'

'Have you booked them in, made appointments?'

'Yes, madam. There are four lads arriving this evening, at eight o'clock.'

'I do wish you'd spoken to me about this, Sally. I have a visitor, a friend, calling this evening.'

'Caroline and I will entertain the boys in the den, madam. You'll be free to spend time with your friend in the lounge.'

'I don't want Caroline to ... She'll probably be tired by the time she gets home. The last thing she'll want is four lads fucking the juice out of her.'

'Fucking the juice out of her?' Holding her hand to her mouth, Sally laughed. 'I like the way you put it, madam.'

'I don't know why I said that,' I mumbled. 'I suppose it *is* rather funny. All right, we'll have to work something out. But in future come and see me before you go arranging things. We'll have half the bloody school up here if we're not careful.'

'We'd make a lot of money, madam.'

'Yes, but that's not the point. Look, I didn't sleep very well last night. I'm going upstairs to have a rest. Don't disturb me, OK?'

'I won't, madam.'

Climbing the stairs to my room, I knew that Sally was only trying to help build up the business. But to arrange for four boys to come to the house . . . David was due at six, and then Tracey was coming to see the house. Flopping onto my bed, I pondered again on having Tracey move in and work for me. We were booking more clients every day, and I needed another girl to share the workload. Another two girls, if I was to keep Caroline to myself. *The last thing she'll want is four lads fucking the juice out of her.* Recalling my own words, I smiled as I drifted off to sleep.

Nine

My client David arrived on time at six o'clock.
Fortunately, the girls were out of the way. Caroline
had gone to her uncle's cottage for dinner after a hard
day's work at his shop. Sally was having a bath and,
as usual, was bound to take an hour or so. I had
peace and quiet – and privacy – for a change. And I
was feeling as horny as hell. To have David's solid
cock shafting my hungry vagina, his spunk bathing
my cervix as I orgasmed, was just what I needed.

I led David into the lounge and asked him what he
wanted. A hand job? Full sex? Full sex, I hoped.
Stripping naked, he said that he wanted me to milk
him. His cock was stiff, standing to attention in front
of his stomach. His foreskin was retracted slightly, his
purple knob beckoning the wet heat of my sperm-
thirsty mouth, the hugging sheath of my pussy. I
assumed that he was talking about a hand job, but he
then got down on all fours. He had a lovely bum with
beautifully heavy balls hanging below his firm cheeks.
Did he want me on the floor beneath him?

'You're a farm girl,' he said. 'Milk me like you
would a cow.'

'OK,' I breathed, settling on the floor beside him.
'You'll want full sex with me I assume?'

'No, no,' he replied, much to my disappointment.

'Oh, well . . . I'll charge you twenty for this, OK?'

'That's fine. I want you to feel my udder to make sure that I'm full of milk.'

'Like this?' Cupping his heavy balls as if weighing them, I began wanking him with my free hand.

'Perfect,' he breathed. 'This is what my sister used to make me do. She liked playing farms, as she called it.'

'Your sister?'

'We used to play doctors and nurses. But she liked playing farms best.'

Stifling a laugh, I didn't dare ask him what else he did with his sister. I was an only child and had missed out on having a brother. Not that I'd have wanked him, I reflected. There again, it might have been fun playing at farms and milking him. This was all rather odd, I thought as David parted his knees further and rested his head on the floor. But in my line of business I was bound to come across the oddest of characters. Moving behind him, I pulled his cock back and watched his balls bulge on either side of his shaft. This was going to be over too soon, I mused as he gasped and trembled. I'd been hoping to give him a blow job or feel the sheer girth of his organ stretching my tight pussy open wide. But he wanted to be milked, and it was my job to obey him.

I thought about Tracey as I rolled David's foreskin back and forth over the purple globe of his cock. She'd entertained clients when her mother had run the business, so she might be willing to work for me. The more girls I employed, the more clients I could satisfy. And the more money I'd earn. Pleasing David would only take five minutes. Not bad going for twenty pounds. If Sally was in the den earning fifty pounds and Tracey was in a room upstairs earning fifty . . . Caroline? I mused. I didn't want her to get fucked. Maybe I was falling in love with her? God, no. That was the last thing I needed.

Ideally, I'd also need regular staff, someone to do the gardens and general maintenance on the property. The girls could do the cooking and housework, but the grounds, the upkeep of the property ... I was going to have to make plans, I mused as David's cock swelled in my hand. If the number of clients increased significantly, I'd need half a dozen girls working for me. If they all lived in, they'd have to share rooms. The house was large, but not large enough to accommodate six or more girls, each with their own room. If I worked things out properly, I could be raking in a thousand or more every week.

Breaking into my reverie, David announced the coming of his milk. Wanking his granite-hard cock faster, I realised that I should have put something on the floor to cover the carpet. But it was too late. His sperm jetting from his throbbing knob and splattering the carpet, he shook and gasped as I milked him. His balls bouncing and jerking as I ran my hand up and down his shaft, he told me to use both hands on his cock. Complying, I wanked him with two hands until his sperm flow ceased and his penis began to deflate.

That was that, I thought, finally releasing his cock. Gazing at the pool of white liquid on the carpet, I wondered how old his sister had been when she'd milked him. Did she still milk him? Was he married? Where did he live? It wasn't my place to question my clients. They came to me in confidence and I had to respect that. But I was still intrigued. Wondering why David was still on all fours, I noticed that his cock was stiffening again. Did he want more? He asked me to stroke his balls, and I knew that he'd want me to wank him again. Milk him.

Running the fingernails of one hand over his ball bag – his udder – I gazed at his swelling cock. He was soon fully erect, his shaft twitching, and I grinned as he asked me to milk him again. Grabbing his solid cock with my free hand, I wanked him and continued to stroke and tickle his scrotum. He breathed heavily, his naked body trembling, and I wondered how long it would be before he shot his second load of cream. Tracey was due to arrive at some point but I had plenty of time. Maybe I ought to buy a real milking machine? I stifled a giggle as I imagined David's cock in a plastic tube, the machine rhythmically sucking him.

I wanked him slowly, running my hand up and down the length of his shaft gently. I was enjoying myself, I thought happily. The girls were out of the way, and I had a beautiful cock to milk. There was no rush, no panic to bring out David's second load of cream. Kneading his heavy balls, feeling his sperm eggs through the thin skin of his scrotum, I thought it strange when he asked me to scoop up his milk from the carpet and massage it into his cock. But, like an obedient farm girl, I did as he'd asked. Rubbing the creamy liquid into his cock shaft, into the flesh of his scrotum, I continued to wank his sticky pole. Lathering his balls, his sperm almost like soap, I worked on him with both hands. I was good, I thought. I knew how to please a man. But what about my own feminine needs?

'Lie on the floor and drink my milk,' David ordered me. 'Squeeze my balls and wank me and suck out my milk.'

'I should charge you more for this,' I said, lying on my back with my head between his knees. But I was so desperate to drink sperm that I'd have paid *him*. 'You should have said that you wanted more than a milking.'

'Charge whatever you want. Just make it good.'

Taking his purple knob into my wet mouth, I rolled my tongue over its silky-smooth surface. Tasting his salt, sucking hard on his bulbous globe, I wanked his solid shaft and squeezed his balls gently as he breathed heavily. I loved sucking his cock, but my arousal had soared out of control. I wanted him to fuck me, to shaft my tight cunt with his beautiful organ and spunk my cervix. Caroline would attend my feminine needs, I decided. But she wouldn't be home until late. Sally had arranged for a bunch of sixth-formers to come to the house at eight o'clock. Perhaps I should have the lads take turns to fuck me? The notion of four fresh young cocks shafting my neglected pussy sent my arousal soaring higher. I needed to come before long, I thought as David announced that his milk was about to flow again.

Concentrating on my client's needs, I took his swollen knob to the back of my throat and sank my teeth gently into the root of his sperm-sticky shaft. Fondling and squeezing his full balls, his udder, sucking and biting his shaft, I felt a gush of sperm shoot down my throat. With my head right back, I managed to take his knob deep into my throat. His sperm jetting straight down my throat, there was no need for me to swallow. I'd heard about deep-throat fucking but had never believed that it was possible. Until now.

His swinging balls battered my neck as he rocked his hips and throat-fucked me, pumping out his spunk and letting out a long moan of pleasure. He was obviously pleased with me, I mused, deciding to charge him thirty pounds. I'd make deep-throat intercourse my speciality, I thought happily, imagining the randy sixth-formers ramming their cocks so far down my throat that I managed to take their balls into my mouth. Life was good, sex was good. But my pussy yearned for a cock.

David finally withdrew his deflating prick, rolled to one side and lay on his back, gasping in the aftermath of his second coming. He had a good body, I observed. Firm, muscular, suntanned . . . The taste of his sperm lingered on my tongue and I'd have given anything to kneel astride his body and drive his beautiful cock deep into my hungry pussy. But I'd fulfilled my duty and milked him as I would a cow. I'd allowed him to throat-fuck me. I'd satisfied him. He had no concern for my needs.

'You were great,' he said, finally clambering to his feet and swaying on his sagging legs.

'Will you want milking on a regular basis?' I asked him, standing in front of him as he dressed.

'Twice a week, if that's all right?'

'Certainly. That'll be thirty pounds.'

'Thanks.' Passing me the money, he finished dressing. 'You really were good,' he praised me again. 'How about every Wednesday and Sunday?'

'I'll put it in my diary. Milking time, six o'clock. Is six OK?'

'Yes, and . . . With all due respect, do you have a younger girl?'

'Er . . . Caroline is young,' I breathed. 'But she doesn't go any further than milking. You might be interested in another girl. I don't know whether she'll be working for me yet, but I hope so. Her name's Tracey.'

'Tracey?' he echoed, frowning at me.

'Does the name ring any bells? She's coming here this evening to look around the house.'

'God, for a minute I thought you meant Alison's daughter. That was tragic.'

'Tragic?' I breathed. 'What do you mean?'

'The way she went. She was so young and –'

'Wait a minute. Are you talking about the Tracey who lived here? Tracey, the old lady's daughter?'

'Yes, that's right.'

'She's dead?'

'Sadly, yes. Right, I'd better be going. Thanks for a great time. I'll see myself out.'

Dizzy with shock as David left the room, I was unable to question him further. Tracey? Dead? No, there must have been some mistake, some mix-up. I'd met the girl twice in the woods – she wasn't a ghost. I'd initially thought her to be a ghost but . . . David had been talking about the old lady's daughter, the same girl, but he'd obviously mixed her up with someone else.

Composing myself, I straightened my dress and went into the kitchen. I could hear Sally in the bathroom upstairs and reckoned that she was preparing herself for the young lads. Was she shaving the stubble from her pussy? I wasn't sure when Caroline would be home. As long as it was before the boys arrived . . . What the hell was I going to do with Tracey? I pondered, pouring myself a glass of wine. I didn't want her meeting the lads. If she was going to move in and work for me . . . I was worrying about nothing, I decided. She hadn't mentioned moving into the house. She was probably happy where she was, in the village with her friend.

Pacing the kitchen floor, I wished again that Sally hadn't gone and made arrangements behind my back. I wanted four paying lads in the house, but not when Tracey was due and Caroline . . . Well, what was done was done. Sally would have to take the boys to the den and if Caroline came back early she'd have to stay in her room. Things were out of hand, I mused dolefully. I shouldn't have invited Tracey to the house.

Pondering again on David's words, I wondered who he'd been talking about. Were there two girls called Tracey? He'd definitely been talking about the old lady's daughter. He wouldn't have made a mistake about her. Perhaps the girl I'd met in the woods had been lying, making out that she'd lived in the house and . . . But why would she do that? I had to clear my mind of crazy thoughts. Pouring another glass of wine, I almost jumped out of my skin as Tracey wandered in from the garden. Had she been lurking, spying?

'I didn't mean to make you jump,' she said, smiling at me. 'Am I too early?'

'Not at all,' I replied, holding her arm. She felt warm, physical – she was alive. 'Would you like some wine?' I asked her.

'No, thanks. The kitchen hasn't changed. It's the same as it was when . . . when I lived here.'

'I haven't changed anything in the house,' I said. 'I've moved a few things around, but changed nothing.'

'The business is doing well?'

'Yes, very well.' Deciding to ask Tracey a few searching questions, I led her into the lounge. 'So, tell me about yourself,' I said, standing with my back to the window as she sat on the sofa. 'You're living in the village?'

'Yes, with my friend and her parents.'

'Where do you work?'

'I . . . I'm not working at the moment,' she muttered hesitantly.

'It's funny to think that you grew up in this house. Which bedroom was yours?'

'The one at the back, the one with the hole in the ceiling. Mother never did get round to having it fixed. She was too busy to bother about my room. All she was interested in was making money.'

As Tracey rambled on, I grew more sure that she was the old lady's daughter. She certainly wasn't a ghost. I firmly believed that David had been talking about someone else as she mentioned the basement den. Wishing that I'd questioned him about it, found out exactly who he'd been talking about, I wondered again whether Tracey would like to move into the house. She was young and attractive, with a beautifully curvaceous body. And, having worked for her mother, she had experience.

'Tracey,' I interrupted her as she talked about her childhood. 'You said that you weren't working at the moment.'

'That's right.'

'It may be a little premature to ask you this. Would you consider moving into the house and working for me?'

'I was hoping that you'd ask me to move in,' she trilled. 'I'm not happy . . . Where I am doesn't suit me. As for working for you, that's fine. The reason I didn't like working for my mother was because she kept the money I earned.'

'OK, that's settled. You'll get your fair share of the money, so you've no need to worry about that. When would you like to move in? You'll have to tell your friend that you're leaving, of course.'

'Now – if that's all right?'

'Now? But . . . what about your things?'

'Oh, yes. I'll . . . I'll get them tomorrow. May I have my old room?'

'Yes, of course. Er . . . I have four virile young men arriving later. Four sixth-formers out to celebrate the end of their schooldays by having sex with an uninhibited slut. Are you ready to begin work?'

'Four? Well, yes, I suppose so.'

'You don't *have* to start this evening. If you'd rather settle in first, that's OK by me.'

'No, no. I'll start this evening.'

'Right, you go up to your room and take a look. Caroline's room is next to yours. She's out at the moment. Oh, you'd better make the bed. There are sheets and a quilt in the cupboard on the landing.'

'OK. I'll be down in a while.'

As Tracey left the room I felt a lot easier. I heard her talking to Sally on the landing and, as they'd met previously, there was no need for an introduction. This was going to work out well, I was sure as I heard them giggling. Three girls, I thought, imagining the cash pouring in. As the front doorbell rang, my heart leaped. Surely the lads hadn't turned up already? To my relief, it was Caroline. I'd have to get some keys cut, I decided, leading her into the lounge. She was wearing her jeans and a T-shirt, but she still looked beautiful, sensuous.

'So, how was the shop?' I asked her.

'I enjoyed it, madam,' she breathed.

'Caroline, you don't have to call me madam,' I said with a giggle. 'How is your uncle?'

'He's fine. We had a nice meal at his cottage.'

'That's good. By the way, there's a new girl who's moved in. She's got the room next to yours. Her name's Tracey – you might like to go and introduce yourself.'

'Yes, madam,' she murmured, leaving the room.

Hoping that Caroline would get on with Tracey, I wondered whether to allow Tracey to deal with the sixth-formers on her own. Four eager lads, four solid cocks? It might not be a good idea to throw her in at the deep end, I reflected. Sally had been getting more than her fair share of sex, and I decided that I'd help Tracey with the boys. Besides, I wanted to take a look at Tracey's young body. Sally could keep Caroline out of the way while Tracey and I enjoyed four youthful cocks.

In the kitchen I refilled my wine glass. I was looking forward to the evening. I was looking forward to enjoying the young men's solid cocks, but also to enjoying Tracey's young body. She was slim, and I wondered how firm her breasts were. Was her pussy tight and wet? What colour were her pubes? How big was her clitoris? My mind riddled with thoughts of crude sex, I thought about going up to her room. What was she wearing beneath her pink dress? She'd probably be talking to Caroline, I thought. It would be best to leave them alone for a while.

Tracey finally came downstairs dressed in a nurse's uniform. As she joined me in the kitchen she grinned. The hem of her uniform was only an inch or so below her pussy and I glimpsed her shaved vulval lips as she turned this way and that. Had Sally shaved her? I wondered. What else had she done to the girl? Tracey looked beautiful, and I was sure that the boys would appreciate her young body. But I wanted to take a closer look at her before they got their hands on her.

'Very nice,' I said, smiling at her. 'Let's take a closer look at your sweet pussy.'

'Yes, madam,' she breathed, pulling her uniform up and displaying the hairless flesh of her young vulva.

'Did Sally shave you?'

'Yes, madam.'

'You don't have to call me madam, Tracey. Right, as the time's moving on you'd better get yourself down to the den. I'll bring the lads down when they arrive.'

'Yes, madam,' she said, leaving the kitchen.

Arriving early, the young bucks were obviously eager to experience hardcore sex. Sally came downstairs as I invited the lads into the hall, so I ordered her to go and keep Caroline company. She didn't seem at all pleased but she did as she was told for a change. Perhaps, at long last, she'd accepted that I was in charge, I thought as each lad passed me his money. Leading my charges through the dining room and down the basement steps, I thought it was amazing how young and innocent they still looked at the ages of seventeen and eighteen. One was blond with a fresh face, another dark-haired and suntanned. They were good looking fellows, and I could hardly wait to see what they had between their legs. They wouldn't remain innocent for long, that was certain.

'This is the school nurse,' I said, deciding to play a game as the lads gazed in awe at Tracey. 'She needs to examine you before we start. All strip naked and form a queue, please.'

'Who are you?' one lad asked.

'Me? I'm the school governess. I punish naughty boys, so I hope you're all going to behave yourselves.'

I watched with bated breath as the lads stripped with a pleasing urgency. They had good bodies, I observed as they almost tore their shirts off. Then came the dropping of the trousers, the lowering of the shorts ... Their cocks were solid, standing to attention above their tight ball sacs. My mouth watered as they obediently formed a queue and I ordered the first lad to lie on the examination table. Taking his position on his back with his rock-hard penis pointing at the low ceiling, he looked up at Tracey as she cast her wide-eyed gaze over his naked body.

'I'll begin by examining your genitalia,' Tracey said, running her fingertips over the full sac of his tight scrotum. 'Do you masturbate?' she asked him.

171

'Er . . . no,' he breathed.

'Don't lie to the nurse, boy,' I said sternly as his friends sniggered. 'Remember, I'm the school governess. I wouldn't want to have to punish you for lying.'

'Do you masturbate?' Tracey asked him again.

'Well, I . . . yes, nurse,' he replied sheepishly.

Tracey had slipped into the role of nurse with ease, and she was doing very well. She'd be a great asset, I thought as she ran her fingertips up and down the lad's erect penis. A valued member of the team. And I didn't think she'd get any ideas about taking charge and running the business, unlike Sally. Again eyeing the young buck's solid cocks as they waited patiently for their turn to see the nurse, I didn't think that they should be kept waiting for too long. Standing in front of them I stroked each solid cock in turn. Weighing their balls in the palm of my hand I told them how pleased I was to see that their udders were full. They sniggered again, and I admonished them.

'No laughing,' I said, moving back to the table. 'Is everything all right, nurse?'

'Yes, governess,' Tracey replied.

'I think you'd better bring out each student's sperm quickly. One after the other – bring out their spunk and then we'll start with the first lad again.'

'Of course, governess,' she breathed, grabbing the lad's cock and wanking him.

'Use your mouth, nurse,' I ordered her. 'Drink the sperm from each young man in turn. By the time you've done the last lad, the first will be ready for your vagina.'

Obediently retracting the teenage male's fleshy foreskin, Tracey leaned over his naked body and sucked his purple plum into her pretty mouth. The lad gasped, his eyes rolling as the wet heat of Tracey's mouth engulfed his swollen cock-head. This was a good test for Tracey, I decided as she slurped and gobbled on the lad's rock-hard penis. With another three patiently awaiting her oral services, this was her initiation. And I knew that she'd pass with flying colours.

Thinking about the sixth-formers, I wondered whether they'd tell a few selected friends about the delights of Juniper House. Obviously, I didn't want word spreading like wildfire through the school. But a couple of dozen monied older teenagers visiting the house on a regular basis for crude sex would certainly boost my income. Turning to my previous thoughts, I knew that I'd need more girls to deal with the clients. Six, seven . . . They'd have to share rooms, of course. But that wouldn't be a problem. Turning my attention back to Tracey as the youth let out a long moan of pleasure, I watched her bob her head up and down as her mouth flooded with his fresh sperm.

The young guy's naked buttocks repeatedly left the table as he thrust his hips up to meet Tracey's bobbing head and I knew that he wouldn't take long to recover and enjoy the tight sheath of her hot pussy. His balls bouncing, his sperm trickling down his solid shaft as Tracey's mouth overflowed, he was obviously enjoying his pioneering mouth-fuck. The other lads watched open-mouthed and wide-eyed, no doubt eager to drive their own youthful cocks into the girl's sperm-thirsty mouth and give her an oral fucking.

'And the next one, please,' I said as Tracey slipped the youth's spent cock out of her mouth and stood upright.

'Me,' a lad said after some heated discussion with the others. 'I'm next.'

'There's no need to argue,' I said. 'There's more than enough time for you to enjoy yourselves. You'll all get to see the nurse, so don't panic.'

'Now *there*'s a nice specimen,' Tracey breathed as her next patient lay on the table with his erect penis standing to attention. 'You're a big fellow. Do you wank?'

'Er . . . yes, I do.'

'Have you ever fucked and spermed a girl's mouth?'

'No.'

'In that case, it's about time you did.'

Tracey was extremely good, I thought again as she leaned over the lad's naked body and sucked his swollen globe into her hot mouth. The sixth-formers would be talking non-stop about this once they were back at school, and I was sure that we'd be seeing quite a few of their friends. Attended by a teenage nurse, what more could a virgin lad ask for? Of course, they had yet to experience the expertise of the school governess, I mused happily, watching Tracey bob her head up and down as she squeezed her patient's full balls. The students weren't leaving the basement sex den until the governess herself had got her hands on their beautiful cocks.

The lad came quickly, pumping Tracey's gobbling mouth full of spunk within a few seconds. I could hear Tracey swallowing, gulping hard, as she wanked his cock shaft and fondled his youthful balls. I was getting very wet – my sex milk was streaming from my vulval crack and running down my inner thighs – and I knew that the time had come to join in. Kneeling in front of the first lad who'd filled Tracey's mouth with sperm, I took his flaccid cock in my hand and retracted his foreskin.

Cupping his balls in my hand and sucking his sperm-glistening knob into my mouth, I ran my wet tongue over its velveteen surface. He stiffened quickly, his balls rolling, his knob swelling against my pink tongue. I'd a good mind to suck him to orgasm and drink his fresh milk, but I knew that he'd want to feel the wet heat of Tracey's tight vagina hugging his knob. I finally stood up and took his hand and slipped it up my skirt. I wasn't wearing panties, and my hot milk flowed down my thighs. He explored my hairless pussy lips, running his fingers up and down my wet sex crack, and I felt my womb contract and my stomach somersault as he drove a finger deep into my contracting vagina.

The third youth took his place on the table and Tracey began fondling his rock-hard cock. Watching as she sucked his purple globe into her sperm-flooded mouth, I ordered my lad to kneel down and lick my crack. He dropped to his knees obediently as I lifted my skirt. Licking my crack, lapping up my cream, he finally drove his wet tongue between the puffy lips of my vulva. Shuddering as he worked his tongue over the sensitive tip of my clitoris and thrust at least three fingers into my hungry pussy, I knew that I was on the brink of orgasming. He sucked my clitoris into his hot mouth, massaged my inner vaginal flesh with his fingers, and I came with a gush of pussy milk. Whimpering in the grip of my climax, clinging to his head as my legs sagged, I ground my open cunt flesh hard against his mouth as my pleasure peaked and rocked my young body to its core.

I could hear Tracey's slurping mouth as she knob-sucked the third youngster, I could hear my fellow's sucking and licking as he sustained my orgasm. The smell of sex hung heavy in the air: the basement was a den of iniquity, a brothel. As my orgasm finally began to recede, I watched the naked lad on the table shuddering as he reached his goal and pumped his teenage sperm into Tracey's gobbling mouth. I was making real money, I thought happily as the boy at my feet slipped his fingers out of my sex-dripping vagina and sucked the last ripples of pleasure from my deflating clitoris. My sex den, my den of crude and illicit sex.

The fourth and final sixth-former took his place on the table and I gazed at his erect cock rising above his heaving balls. Standing opposite Tracey, I ordered her to kiss me. She frowned and cocked her head to one side. Pulling the lad's foreskin back, exposing the swollen globe of his glans, I suggested that she kiss me with his knob between our lips. She understood perfectly. Grinning, she bent down and grabbed his cock by the root as I leaned over. Our mouths open, we pressed our full lips together, sandwiching the lad's purple plum as we kissed.

The other young guys moved in, gazing in awe as Tracey and I sucked on the lad's ballooning knob and fondled his heavy balls. The heady blend of the boy's salt and Tracey's saliva driving me wild, I was desperate to taste his sperm, share his orgasmic liquid. We both slurped and gobbled on his cock-head, our tongues snaking over its silky-smooth surface as he gasped and writhed in the grip of the illicit act. He came with a gush of milk, and we both sucked and swallowed, drinking from his fountain-head, sharing his spunk. His cream splattered my face, dribbling down my chin as we frantically mouthed on his orgasming knob, and I was in my sexual heaven. His sperm flow finally ceased, but my libido had soared to awesome heights and I wanted more.

'You two,' I said, nodding at a couple of lads as I knelt on the floor. 'I want a double mouth-fucking. Stand either side of me.'

Grabbing the fellows' solid cocks, I rolled back their fleshy foreskins and exposed their bulbous knobs. This was a new experience, I mused dreamily, sucking the two purple plums into my sperm-thirsty mouth. Each lad had spunked once, but I knew that they'd be able to manage at least two or three comings before the evening was over. Young and fresh, with their hormones running wild, they'd have no erection or sperming problems.

Gripping the lads' hard shafts, one in each hand, I took their knobs as far as I could into my mouth and sucked and tongued in my sexual frenzy. The very thought of sucking on two cocks drove me crazy with lust, and I hoped that the young men would shoot out their cream together and give me a double mouth-spunking. Three cocks? I mused in my debauchery. Could I manage to gobble three knobs to orgasm? I'd plunged deeper into the pit of depravity, I reflected as the lads trembled and breathed heavily. How much deeper would I fall? Was the pit bottomless?

My mouth flooding with a double helping of fresh spunk, I sucked and repeatedly swallowed hard. Wanking their cocks, sucking and tonguing their orgasming sex globes, I moaned softly through my nose as they towered over me and swayed on their trembling legs. Out of the corner of my eye I saw Tracey sucking on the other lads' cocks, their swollen knobs bloating her pretty mouth as she knelt in front of them. The sixth-formers would never forget their visit to my sex den. Even when they were old men they'd recall the dirty nurse, the wicked governess and the double mouth-fuckings. But I hadn't finished with them yet. I'd barely started.

'*Naughty* boys,' I said, slipping their deflating plums out of my mouth and rising to my feet. 'You are *not* allowed to fuck the governess's mouth. Both of you bend over the table.'

My heart raced as they leaned over the table and jutted out their naked buttocks. I eyed their balls hanging invitingly between their thighs. I could hear Tracey gulping down her double cream as her lads orgasmed. She'd had more to drink than I had, I reflected enviously. But the evening was far from over. Kneeling behind my randy pair, I weighed their balls in my hands. Their cock shafts inflating yet again, I stood up and spanked their bare bottoms with the palm of my hand. Again and again I spanked them, watching as their bum cheeks tensed and turned red as my palm repeatedly spanked them.

'Naughty boys,' I admonished them again, spanking their beautifully firm buttocks in turn. 'How *dare* you spunk my mouth like that?'

'May I help you, governess?' Tracey asked me, wiping her sperm-glossed lips as she stood beside me.

'Yes, nurse, you may. I want you to bend over the end of the table with your feet wide apart. You're going to be fucked by four schoolboys.'

Pulling the lads upright as Tracey took her position over the end of the table, I ordered the first one to slide his cock deep into the nurse's gaping pussy hole and fuck her. Helping the youngster, guiding his swollen plum between the girl's inner lips, I grinned as he rammed his knob fully home and impaled her completely on his fleshy rod. The other lads gasped, staring wide-eyed as he began his fucking motions. That was one less virgin, I mused in my wickedness, watching his pussy-slimed shaft appearing and disappearing as he fucked the whimpering girl. One down, three to go.

Clambering onto the table with my thighs either side of Tracey's head, I lay back and ordered her to lick my sex crack. I was sex-crazed, behaving like a nymphomaniac, but I couldn't help myself. I wanted crude sex, hard sex, and I was going to get it. Lifting her head, Tracey obediently complied and began licking and mouthing the hairless outer lips of my vagina. I shuddered as her tongue entered my cream-drenched sex hole and caressed the inner walls of my pussy. She was a good girl, I thought as the lad behind her gasped and increased his fucking rhythm. She'd played her role very well, and was sure to be a valuable asset to the business.

Moving up to my solid clitoris, she sucked the pink protrusion into her pretty mouth and snaked her tongue over its sensitive tip. Had she had lesbian sex before? I wondered. Working for her mother, she might well have done. Slurping and gobbling as her young body rocked with the sixth-former fucking, she took me quickly to a mind-blowing climax. I could feel my pussy milk spurting from my gaping vaginal entrance, my womb rhythmically contracting, my clitoris pulsating in orgasm . . . I'd found my sexual heaven. Squelching sounds resounded around the room and the young guy gasped – I knew that he was pumping his spunk deep into the girl's tight vagina. He was a man now, I thought happily as my orgasm peaked. He'd never forget his first time. His first fuck, in a den of iniquity.

The next lad took his place and rammed his virgin cock deep into Tracey's spermed sex sheath and began his shafting motions. Lifting my head, I watched as the girl sucked and mouthed on my pulsing clitoris. Her eyes closed, her face flushed, her young body rocking, I knew that she was revelling in the debauched act as she sustained my multiple orgasm with her snaking tongue. She was a dirty girl, I thought happily, opening my thighs further as another gush of orgasmic milk spewed from my contracting vaginal sheath and flooded her face. She

179

loved knob-gobbling and drinking fresh sperm, she revelled in having the boys fuck her tight little pussy, and she obviously delighted in her lesbian licking.

Resting my head on the table as my orgasm waned, I breathed in the scent of sex, listened to the sounds of wet flesh meeting flesh. Tracey continued to lick and tongue fervently between my puffy vaginal lips, deftly pleasuring me in the grip of my lesbian desire. Lapping up my spilled cream as the youth behind her announced his coming, she shuddered violently. I knew that she too had reached her well-deserved climax as she bit and nibbled on my inner folds. Her whimpering and gasping echoing around the den, her hot breath playing on my inner lips, she thrust several fingers deep into my contracting love sheath and kneaded my cream-drenched inner flesh.

The second lad reached his coming, pumping Tracey's teenage vagina full of sperm, and I cried out as my clitoris erupted in another incredible orgasm. Again, my orgasmic milk spewed from my fingered vaginal duct and splattered my inner thighs. Shaking fiercely, crying out as my pleasure gripped me, I wondered how many times I could come in one session of illicit sex. There were two more virgin penises waiting to fuck Tracey. Would I come in unison with their sperming?

'God, no more,' Tracey murmured as her young body rocked back and forth. 'I can't take any more.'

'Don't stop,' I gasped, again grinding my gaping sex valley hard against her flushed face. 'Finger-fuck my cunt, suck my clitoris.'

My crude words heightening my pleasure, I yanked my dress down, eased out my full breasts and ordered the two waiting youths to squeeze my tits and suck hard on my erect nipples. Standing either side of the table, they leaned forward and sucked my milk teats into their hot mouths. A female tongue working between my puffy vaginal lips, sustaining my massive orgasm, two boys sucking and biting on my nipples, I writhed and whimpered on the table in the grip of my new-found ecstasy. Slurping, nibbling, licking, sucking, gasping . . . The sounds of illicit sex filled my ears as my aching clitoris pumped out its pleasure.

As I began to drift down from my climax, I thought how amazing it was that I was being paid to be brought such fantastic sexual pleasure. I was deriving as much satisfaction from the crude sexual acts as were my clients, and they were paying for it. Wondering what Sally and Caroline were up to as the lads changed places, I heard Tracey let out a cry as the third boy rammed his cock deep into her sperm-dripping vagina. Only one more lad to break in, I mused as hands wandered over the firm mounds of my breasts and hot mouths enveloped my erect nipples.

'I can't take any more,' Tracey complained again through a mouthful of my creamed vaginal flesh as the boy found his shafting rhythm. 'God, my pussy is aching.'

'Only one more to go,' I breathed, turning my head and focusing on a lad's erect penis. 'Come here,' I ordered him. 'I need your cock in my mouth.'

Sucking on his sperm-slimed knob, I made my plans for the sixth-formers' next visit. I'd have one teenage cock sliding in and out of my hot pussy, another shafting my tight bum, and two bloating my mouth. Sheer sexual bliss, I mused, sucking hard on my lad's cock-head in the hope that he'd be able to furnish me with another load of sperm. In my sexual delirium, I wasn't sure how many times each boy had spunked. There was only one virgin left in the room, but I'd no idea how many times each fellow had shot his load. The lad's knob swelling within my mouth, my nipples sucked into two hot mouths, my clitoris inflating within Tracey's wet mouth . . . I'd discovered paradise.

The youth shafting Tracey's vagina announced his imminent spurting and I gobbled on my lad's knob as he trembled and gasped. Sperm finally gushing from his orgasming glans and bathing my tongue, I swallowed hard as my clitoris again exploded in orgasm beneath Tracey's sweeping tongue. My young body shaking violently, my clitoris pulsating, my cheeks filling with teenage spunk, I thought I was going to pass out. Dizzy in my coming, my mind blown away on clouds of orgasm, I thought I was leaving my body.

Somewhere in the mists of my mind I heard Tracey protesting again and assumed that the fourth and final virgin male was shafting her abused vagina. In a dreamlike state, I suckled on my youth's deflating knob, drawing out the remnants of his fresh cream and swallowing hard. Shaking uncontrollably, breathing heavily through my nose, wallowing in my debauchery, I was oblivious to my surroundings. I didn't know who was coming, who was fucking, who was biting my nipples . . . I was lost in my debauchery, in my sexual delirium.

I finally came to as if awaking from sleep and lifted my head. Tracey was alone, the sixth-formers had gone. Had I passed out? I wondered. Sperm streaming down my chin, my nipples aching, my clitoris inflamed, I finally managed to clamber off the table. I felt drunk in the aftermath of my coming, dizzy with sex, physically exhausted. I needed to wash, to sleep. Tracey held my hand and asked me whether I was all right as I swayed on my sagging legs.

'I think so,' I breathed. 'What the hell happened?'

'You had a million orgasms,' she replied with a giggle.

'The young guys . . .'

'They've gone, thank God.' Looking down at her legs, she sighed. 'I'm full of spunk,' she breathed. 'The stuff's pouring out of me.'

'You did very well, Tracey. I'm very pleased with you. Especially the way you attended my needs.'

'I've never been with another girl. I didn't know what I was missing. Are you sure you're all right?'

'If I can make it up the stairs, I think I'll get into bed and rest. I'm totally fucked.'

'I know the feeling. Here, I'll help you.'

Tracey managed to get me up to my room and onto my bed. Removing my dress as I lay quivering on the bed, she covered me with the quilt and left. I was still dizzy, my clitoris aching, my mind drifting. But I'd had the most wonderful experience ever, and made a lot of money. Sleep finally took me and I dreamed my dreams of teenage males' cocks, their spunking knobs. In my dreams, I swam in rivers of sperm.

Ten

I was up early the following morning. Leaving Sally sleeping, I took a shower, dressed in a miniskirt and T-shirt and enjoyed a light breakfast. The house was quiet, peaceful, after the orgasmic cries and debauchery of the previous evening. Wandering out into the back garden, breathing in the morning air, I felt good, alive. The sun shone, the birds sang, and I felt relaxed, at one with myself. The countryside was wonderful, far removed from the hassles and noise of the town.

I remembered my rented flat. I still found it difficult to believe that I now owned a country house. My life had changed dramatically since moving into Juniper House. Never in a million years would I have dreamed that I'd own a beautiful home in the country. Never would I have believed that I'd own and run a successful brothel.

'You never know what's around the next corner,' I said softly to myself.

'That's true,' Jim said, wandering around the side of the house. 'How are you this morning?'

'Jim, it's great to see you,' I trilled. 'I'm fine. I was just mumbling to myself.'

'I often talk to myself,' he said with a chuckle. 'It's the first sign of madness, so they say. I'm out for my morning walk and I thought I'd call in to say hello. I like to take a walk before opening the shop. By the way, the bureau . . .'

'I think I'll hang on to it, Jim. My finances aren't so bad now, so I'd like to keep it.'

'OK, whatever. We must get together one evening. I keep meaning to ring you or call in. But things crop up all the time. Are you free this evening?'

'Er . . . yes, I think so.'

'OK, my place at seven o'clock?'

'Yes, I'll look forward to it. If anything crops up, as you put it, I'll let you know. I'd better wake Caroline soon. We don't want her to be late for work.'

'Is Caroline all right? The reason I ask is . . . I'm not sure what it is, but she seems different.'

'Different?'

'We chat in the shop and . . . She's been talking about sex. She suddenly seems overly interested in sex.'

'It's her age, Jim,' I said, wondering what on earth the girl had been saying. 'Hormones and all that.'

'I suppose so. I like the idea of her living with you and working in the shop. I feel that she's safe in the village. There are no sex-crazed boys around trying to get their grubby hands on her. I believe she's a virgin, and I'd like her to stay that way for a while longer.'

'Yes, she . . . she did mention that she was a virgin. I wouldn't worry about it, Jim. I'll talk to her, if you'd like me to?'

'That might be a good idea. I'm probably fussing too much, being overly protective. It's just that I feel responsible for her. Right, I'd better get going.'

'OK, Jim. Hopefully, I'll see you this evening.'

'Yes, I'd, er . . . I'd like to spend some time with you, Alison. Apart from our first evening together,

185

we've hardly seen each other. OK, I hope to see you later.'

'Right. And don't worry about Caroline. She's safe with me.'

Shit, I thought as he walked away. Caroline had obviously been blabbing. But what the hell had she said? I decided to talk to her about yesterday evening. I went back into the kitchen and made myself a cup of coffee. I was going to have to lay down some rules, I mused. If Jim found out that his sweet little virgin niece was working for me as a prostitute, he'd go mad. But she hadn't yet lost her virginity, I reflected. She'd sucked cocks, but she hadn't been shafted and spunked.

The girls were banging about upstairs as the front doorbell rang. I knew that a busy day was about to begin. But I'd slept well and was ready for anything. Ready for a good fucking? I thought in my wicked-ness. My pussy naked beneath my miniskirt, the hairless lips of my vulva swelling as I imagined a solid cock shafting my tight vagina, I knew that I'd become a whore. Walking through the hall, I hoped that we had an early-morning client. I wanted a cock, any cock. Two cocks, three cocks, wet cunts . . .

'Sorry to disturb you,' David said as I opened the door. 'I thought you might be able to give me an early-morning milking?'

'Well, I . . . I might be able to,' I breathed. It was an early-morning fucking that I craved 'The thing is, the girls are up and about. Caroline has to go out and . . . Would you like a cup of coffee?'

'Thanks,' he said, stepping into the hall and following me into the kitchen. 'After my last visit, I'm desperate for another milking. You were amazing.'

'I really haven't got time,' I said apologetically. Why didn't he want my pussy?

'What about one of your girls?'

'I'm not sure what's happening yet. It's rather early and I haven't planned the day. By the way, you'll be able to meet Tracey in a minute. The living Tracey, that is. I think you must have mixed two girls up yesterday.'

'I was talking about Alison's daughter,' David said, sitting at the table as I poured him some coffee. 'The old lady's daughter.'

'David, I have the old lady's daughter living here with me.'

'You can't have. Tracey died.'

'There's one way to sort this out. When she comes down, you can see for yourself. Presumably she'll recognise you?'

'I came here often enough – of course she'll recognise me. Tracey never milked me but she knows me, all right. This girl, your Tracey, has she said that she's Alison's daughter?'

'Yes, she has. She said that she left home and moved into the village with a friend. She remembers the house, her old bedroom. You've made a mistake, David.'

'The Tracey I'm talking about is dead. I don't know who this girl is, but it's not Alison's daughter.'

I chatted to David over coffee for about ten minutes, and he was adamant that he hadn't made a mistake. In which case, the girl upstairs was either a ghost or an impostor. If she was an impostor, then how did she know the house so well? She must have been into the place, lurking, spying. None of it made sense, but I was determined to discover the truth. One thing was certain, Tracey wasn't a ghost. While David talked about the old days, I knew that I didn't have time to milk him. Although I'd have loved to feel the hardness of his cock in my hand and wank him to orgasm, there was too much going on to play at farms.

Caroline came into the kitchen and grabbed a sandwich before leaving for the shop. I wanted to talk to her, to tell her not to go blabbing to her uncle about sex. But not in front of David. I'd talk to her that evening, I decided as Sally went down to the sex den to clear up in readiness for the day's business. Tracey finally wandered into the kitchen, wearing a short skirt and a loose-fitting blouse. She was a beautiful girl, sexual, sensual, alluring. But who the hell was she?

'This is David,' I said.

'Oh, hi,' she breathed, obviously not recognising him. She filled the kettle.

'So, you used to live here?' David asked.

'Yes, my mother once owned this house.'

'I knew your mother. She was a lovely lady.'

'Yes, yes, she was.'

'I remember her talking about you. She often mentioned you.'

'Er ... I'd better go and make my bed,' Tracey murmured. 'If you'll excuse me?'

Waiting until the girl had scurried off, David frowned at me. 'That is *not* Alison's daughter,' he stated firmly.

'Are you sure? If you haven't seen her for a while ... She might have changed.'

'Of course I'm sure. She looks similar, same build, same height and hair, but ...'

'In that case, she's an impostor,' I breathed.

'The Tracey I knew –'

'Look, I have things to do, David.'

'Oh, I'm sorry. I shouldn't have called so early.'

'No, no. I'm glad you did. Call round later in the day, if you can.'

'Later this morning?'

'That's fine. I'm sure I have time to fit in a quick milking.'

'Now that *does* sound good.'

'And I won't charge you. I'll give you a free milking, OK?'

'That sounds even better. Right, I'll see you later.'

Fuming as David left, I wondered what the hell Tracey was up to. If that was her real name, of course. How the hell did she know so much about the house? I wondered again. The hole in the bedroom ceiling, the basement sex den . . . She must have done her homework, I thought angrily. She'd said that she'd been talking to Sally. Perhaps that was where she'd got her information, and she might have been sneaking around the house. But what was she after? Money? She'd said that her brother had sold the house and she should have had half the money. How could he have given half the cash to his dead sister? I didn't like her game, whatever it was. I'd had enough of ghosts and weird coincidences. The last thing I needed was a bloody impostor.

I walked down to the den and ordered Sally to send Tracey to see me. I was determined to get to the bottom of this. When I'd first met the girl in the woods I'd believed her to be a ghost. I'd thought then that David had been mistaken . . . The little bitch had been lying to me all along, and she was going to pay dearly for her crime. I concealed my anger as she trotted down the basement steps. I wondered what she'd done with her pink dress as she stood in front of me. More to the point, where had she got that dress in the first place? She'd said that it was her mother's, which was obviously a lie.

'I know that you had a hard time last night,' I said, smiling sweetly at her. 'And I'm giving you the day off.'

'Thank you, madam,' she said softly, returning my smile.

'Before you go, I'd like you to lie on the table.'

'But –'

'It won't take a minute, and then you can enjoy your day off. I'm making a modification to the table and I'd like you to test it for me.'

'Yes, of course.'

'Take your clothes off first.'

Slipping her blouse off her shoulders, Tracey lowered her short skirt and kicked it aside. She wasn't wearing a bra or panties, and I cast my gaze over the beautiful curves and mounds of her teenage body. She was a beautiful girl, young, attractive, sexy . . . But she was also a little bitch. As she lay on the table, I cuffed her wrists to the steel ring behind her head. Her breasts were petite and firm, her nipples becoming erect in the relatively cool air of the basement. I'd had high hopes for her, but now? Hanging her feet down either side of the table and cuffing her ankles, I glimpsed a leather strap lying ominously on the shelf. I'd get the truth out of her, I knew as she asked me what I was going to do.

'We need to have a little chat,' I said, tweaking the ripe teats of her brown nipples. 'Let's start with you telling me your real name.'

'My name?' she breathed, frowning at me. 'I'm Tracey. My name's Tracey.'

'The old lady's daughter?'

'Yes, madam. I've told you about –'

'You lied to me, you mean?'

'Lied, madam?'

'The old lady's daughter is dead. So you're either a ghost or . . .'

'That . . . that was my sister,' she stammered. 'I wasn't going to mention it because I find it difficult to talk about. My sister . . . Sadly, she died.'

'Alison didn't have two daughters. And that chap you met in the kitchen – David – was a very good friend of Tracey's. He's never seen you before. You, young lady, are an impostor.'

'No, no, I . . . My sister lived in the village with me. She knew some of the men. That man must have met my sister. He's never met me.'

'No more lies, *please*. You must have been to this house before. You knew about the bedroom and the basement. You knew that the old lady's son had sold the place to me. You've obviously done your homework. But, why? What is it you're after? Is it money?'

'No, I . . . I'm telling you the truth.'

'I reckon that you thought you could move in here and make some money. I reckon that you planned to rob me.'

'No, I didn't plan anything. Alison was my mother.'

'You're a persistent little bitch, I'll give you that. Where did you get the pink dress from?'

'It was my mother's.'

'Yes, I believe that. You'd been into the house, hadn't you? You'd been sneaking around, you stole the dress, and then you thought that you'd learned enough to meet me and play the role of Tracey.'

'You're wrong. You'd better let me go or . . .'

'Or what?'

'Or I'll . . .'

'I will let you go – once you've told me the truth.'

'I *have* told you the fucking truth,' she hissed.

'Oh, bad language now, is it? What happened to the timid little Tracey?'

Taking the leather strap, I ran it over the hairless flesh of her puffy vaginal lips. Her sex crack was tightly closed, alluring, inviting, and I imagined her masturbating. Did she finger the tight sheath of her young vagina? Did she massage her hard clitoris to massive orgasms? She lifted her head and gazed in horror at the strap as I dragged it over the smooth plateau of her stomach to the firm mounds of her petite breasts. Her nipples were long, beautiful, suckable. Thrashable? Although my anger was out-weighed by my desire for her young body, I knew that I had to punish her most severely. I wanted to masturbate her, lick and suck her clitoris and . . . But she had to be punished.

The first lash of the leather strap landed across her firm young breasts with a loud crack. She let out a high-pitched yelp, begged for mercy and cried out again as the strap once more swished through the air and lashed her teenage tits. One thing was certain, I mused, bringing the leather strap down again. Tracey – or whatever her name was – was no ghost. Pulling against her bonds, she squirmed on the table as the strap bit into the sensitive brown teats of her nipples. Ghosts don't feel pain, do they? She was a bitch, a lying little bitch.

'Please, no more,' she cried.

'You don't want your tits thrashed?' I asked her, eyeing her crimsoned mammary spheres.

'No, no . . .'

'In that case, I'll thrash your pretty little cunt lips.'

'Please, I'll do anything . . .'

'Such as tell me the truth?'

'I *have* told you the truth.'

I rather enjoyed watching the lying little slut writhe and squirm like a snake in agony as the strap came down across the glowing flesh of her puffy outer lips. Again and again I brought the leather length down across her reddening sex cushions, each time with a deafening crack. The strap caught the smooth, un-blemished flesh of her inner thigh and she yelped again, begging me to stop. But her yelping and pleading only served to drive me on, and I repeatedly lashed her vulval flesh, the gentle rise of her mons, her inner thighs. Her inner lips were beginning to protrude from her sex valley. I chuckled wickedly as the strap flailed her delicate sex petals.

To my surprise, a trickle of vaginal milk oozed from Tracey's inflamed sex crack. Was she enjoying the vulval lashing? I wondered. Her outer lips had puffed up beautifully – her sex crack was opening, fully exposing the pink petals of her wet inner folds. Globules of sex milk were clinging to the unfurling flesh of her inner lips and I had to fight an over-whelming desire to suck on her petals and taste her. Finally halting the thrashing as her milk flowed freely from her yawning girl-slit, I stood at the foot of the table and leaned over. I'd lost my battle, I knew as I pushed my tongue out and licked her unfurling inner lips and tasted her teenage juices of desire. Savouring her sex juices, I felt my womb contract, my clitoris swell. I was supposed to be punishing her – but I had no power to resist her sweet little cunt.

Tracey was a little bitch, a lying slut, but she was also beautiful, sexy, horny . . . Peeling her fleshy outer lips apart with my thumbs, exposing the pink cone of wet flesh surrounding the entrance to her young vagina, I pushed my tongue deep into her hot sex sheath. She writhed and whimpered, obviously revel-ling in my intimate lesbian attention as I breathed in her girl scent and savoured her milk of desire. But I was supposed to be punishing her, I reminded myself again. She'd lied to me, she'd tried to con me . . . But I couldn't resist temptation. Pressing my lips to her open hole, I sucked hard and brought out her lubricious cream. Tonguing her dripping love sheath, I finally moved up to the solid bulb of her clitoris and massaged its sensitive tip with my wet tongue. She whimpered and writhed as I forced her pussy lips open to the extreme and sucked her clitoris into my hot mouth. She was a sweet little thing. Better than Caroline? I wondered as she neared her orgasm. I had no need to choose – I had both girls.

Tracey came with a scream of orgasmic pleasure. Her pussy milk splattered my chin and neck as I sucked her pleasure from her pulsating clitoris. Then she shook violently and pumped out another deluge of cream. Ramming two fingers into her spasming vagina, I finger-fucked her hard and sustained her climax with my mouth and tongue. Again she screamed out, arching her back as I sucked really hard on her sweet clitoris. It was a shame that she was a lying little bitch, I reflected again. Lying little bitches needed to be punished, I thought as her orgasm began to recede.

My fingers leaving the wet heat of her vagina, I pulled the chains down from the ceiling and secured her ankles to the straps fixed to the chains' ends. Moving to the wall and tugging on the pulleys, I raised her feet high above her head. Her legs opened wide and her sex holes became fully exposed, completely defenceless. I secured the chains to the hook on the wall and took a speculum from the trolley. Tracey protested, pleading with me for her freedom as I stood at the foot of the table and ran my fingertip over the delicate brown tissue surrounding her anal inlet. She knew how to halt the imminent violation of her rectal duct, she knew that all she had to do was tell the truth and she'd be given her freedom.

'What are you doing?' she asked as I smeared Vaseline over the brown eye of her tightly closed anus. 'Please, I . . .'

'The truth, Tracey,' I breathed. 'I want the truth.'

'I've told you the truth,' she persisted. 'My sister . . .'

'Your mother had one son and one daughter. Sadly, her daughter is no longer with us.'

'We were twins. All you have to do is check and you'll find out that my mother had twin girls.'

'I've heard it all now,' I retorted with a mocking giggle. 'Twins?'

'It's true.'

'What's your name, then? If your twin was called Tracey, what's *your* name?'

'Tracey – we were both named Tracey.'

'You lying little bitch,' I hissed. 'Right, you've asked for it. And you're going to get it.'

Easing the steel wings of the speculum past Tracey's anal sphincter muscles, I pushed the instrument deep into her tight rectal sheath. She protested again and swore blind that she'd had a twin sister. I squeezed the levers and began to open her anal canal. The hairless lips of her cream-smeared vulva bulged alluringly between her slender thighs and I decided to attend her teenage vagina once I'd opened her rectum to capacity. She'd tell the truth at some point, I knew as I squeezed again on the steel levers and stretched open her secret passage.

Taking a huge vibrator from the shelf, I eased the rounded end between the gaping inner lips of Tracey's vulva and pushed the plastic shaft deep into her tightening sex duct. Her holes were now bloated and the pink shaft of her clitoris emerged from beneath its pinken bonnet as she let out a rush of breath when I squeezed the speculum levers and opened her rectum further. I asked her again to tell me the truth, but she persisted with her crazy story about twin sisters. Taking two metal clamps from the trolley, I fixed them to the swollen pads of her outer lips. She protested and pulled against her bonds as I fixed chains to the clamps. She'd break at some stage, I was sure. Securing heavy weights to the ends of the chains, I stood back and admired my handiwork.

'What are you doing?' Sally asked as she bounded down the steps and joined me by the table.

'Trying to get the truth out of this little slut,' I replied. 'She reckons that she's not only the old lady's daughter but one of twins.'

'That's right, madam,' Sally said. 'There were twin sisters.'

'What?' I gasped. 'Twin sisters? How the hell do you know that?'

'I thought everyone knew, madam.'

'I knew nothing of the sort. I've had enough of this.'

'You're the outsider here,' Tracey said, lifting her head and smiling at me. 'You're causing problems. And we've had enough of you.'

'You keep quiet,' I retorted.

I knew that something was very wrong as Sally slipped the speculum out of Tracey's anal sheath. Removing the vibrator and the metal clamps, she lowered the other girl's feet and slipped the leather straps off her ankles. What the hell did she think she was doing? I wondered angrily. Did she think she was in charge? Releasing the girl, Sally took her hand and asked her whether she was all right. I was powerless to move and unable to speak as they whispered to each other. Standing either side of me, they pulled my T-shirt over my head and gazed longingly at the mounds of my firm breasts. I could do nothing to halt my disrobing. Tugging my skirt down, exposing the hairless flesh of my vulva, they lifted me onto the table and secured the chains to my ankles. Why couldn't I defend myself? My hands were cuffed to the steel ring in the table behind my head and my feet rose high above me. I wondered what the hell was going on.

I looked up at the low ceiling and wondered about my future as Sally attached metal clamps to my nipples. The clamps bit into the flesh of my sensitive brown teats and I knew that I'd never tame Sally. She was in charge – the old lady was in charge. Wondering again what was going on in Juniper House as Tracey attached thin chains to the clamps, I lifted my head as Caroline came down the steps. Why wasn't she at the shop? Had Jim sent her home? This was a mess, I thought, reckoning that she'd not even been to the shop. The three girls whispered to each other and I grimaced again as Sally ran the chains down either side of the table and attached heavy weights to the ends. My nipples distended painfully, pulling the brown discs of my areolae into taut cones of flesh, and I felt a chill run up my spine. Something was very wrong, something was nearby, a presence or . . .

'No,' Sally said, raising her voice. 'We can't do that.'

'In that case, what do you suggest we do?' Caroline asked her.

'I don't know, but we can't do that.' Turning and facing me, Sally frowned. 'Why do you cause trouble?' she asked me. 'Why not settle down and enjoy the house and the money?'

'I'm trying to,' I shot back. 'I might ask you why I'm kept in the dark all the time. I'm never told anything, I never know what's going on . . . Since the day you moved in, I've felt redundant.'

'Why question Tracey? She's the daughter of Alison, the old lady. Why can't you accept that?'

'Because it's not true. All this crap about twin sisters and –'

'You have a choice,' Tracey said. 'Either you accept who I am, or we –'

'This could be your last chance,' Sally broke in. 'Don't spoil things for yourself. You wouldn't want to find yourself back in a rented flat, would you?'

'Don't threaten me,' I hissed. 'This is *my* house. And I want you to leave – all of you.'

Lowering the end of the table, Sally dragged my naked body forward and positioned my naked buttocks over the leather-topped edge. My feet high above my head, my sex holes exposed, I dreaded the thought of the anal speculum as Tracey grinned at me. Did she intend to get her own back? I thought fearfully. Stroking the firm orbs of my bottom, running her finger up and down my anal groove, she knelt on the floor and pushed her wet tongue into my most private hole. The sensations were heavenly, sending ripples of sex throughout my naked body. I let out a gasp of pleasure as she locked her full lips to my brown ring and her tongue worked deep inside my most secret duct. But my anxiety outweighed my pleasure. What did the girls intend to do with me? Find myself back in a rented flat? What did Sally mean?

'We need to get things straight,' Sally said as Tracey continued to tongue my tight bottom-hole.

'Damned right we do,' I retorted.

'Firstly, I'm in charge.'

'You're bloody not. *I* own this house, Sally. I said that you could move in as a lodger. I said that you could –'

'You don't understand, do you?'

'No, I don't. Why don't you tell me what you're up to? You and the others – what are you up to?'

'We're living here, running the business, enjoying our work . . . We thought you were the right one. We thought you were ideal for the role, but obviously you're not.'

'What role? What the fuck are you talking about?'

'Shall I explain?' Tracey said, her tongue leaving my tight bottom-hole. Standing by my side, she stroked the ripe teats of my nipples. 'My mother ran the business for years, decades. We didn't get on very well, which was a shame. My sister and I moved out and, sadly, my sister died. I'd always hoped to move back and take over the running of the business. As my mother aged, I thought I'd soon be home, and be in charge. My brother was out of the way, and I assumed that the house would go to me. He was never interested in us, the family. But he certainly became interested when my mother passed on. So much so, in fact, that he sold the house and kept the money.'

'So where do I fit into all this? What's my role, as you put it?'

'I wanted to rebuild the business, re-create the business just as it used to be. There was a girl called Caroline who worked here. So I found a suitable girl with the right name and organised things.'

'And here I am,' Caroline chipped in.

'There was a girl named Sally. Again, I orchestrated things and –'

'But I've known Sally for years,' I said. 'She moved in because I asked her to. It had nothing to do with you.'

'Didn't it? Where do you think the money came from – the money that appeared in your bank account? Why do you think you bought this particular house? I arranged everything.'

'That's ridiculous,' I breathed.

'You have the same Christian name as my mother. I've re-created the business. Girls with the same names, the old customers coming back . . .'

'So, you put four hundred thousand pounds into my bank account? Where the hell did you get that kind of money from? You're a bloody liar.'

'I had a little help,' Tracey said, grinning at me.

'You *need* a little help. Help with your mental state.'

'We'll have to tell her,' Caroline cut in.

'No,' Sally shot back. 'I don't want that. Alison, why can't you accept things? We're all happy here, we're building up our clients, we're making money – why can't you just accept the way things are and enjoy yourself?'

'Because I don't *know* how things are, the way things are. There's been talk of my role here, money was put into my bank account ... There are too many unanswered questions.'

'*I* accepted things,' Caroline said. 'Initially I was against the idea. But I soon calmed down and accepted the fact that I was Caroline.'

'What are you talking about? You've always been Caroline.'

'Not this Caroline. I was led here and –'

'Enough,' Sally hissed. 'Keep your bloody mouth shut, Caroline. Unless you want the chair?'

'No, please ... I'm sorry.'

'What's *the chair*?' I asked.

'You don't want to know,' Tracey replied.

'Alison, are you prepared to accept –' Sally began.

'No, I am not.'

'All right, have it your way.'

The three girls stood around my tethered body, their fresh faces looking sullen. I wondered what the hell they were going to do to me. I still hadn't discovered the truth, I mused fearfully as Sally ordered Tracey to grease my bottom-hole with Vaseline. Play my role? I reflected. Play my role as what?

My thoughts turned to the old lady as Tracey massaged the cooling grease into the delicate brown tissue surrounding my anal inlet. The money had been put into my bank account, Tracey had arranged things, orchestrated things ... Was the old lady behind this?

I couldn't simply accept things, I thought, recalling Sally's words. I couldn't accept what I didn't understand. I didn't know who was in charge, I didn't know who Tracey was ... And I didn't know what the old lady's involvement was. What the hell had Caroline been talking about? I wondered. *We'll have to tell her*. Tell me *what*? Although I was naked and cuffed to the table, I knew that I'd be released at some point. And, once I'd been given my freedom, I'd find out exactly what was going on.

Perhaps I should make out that I was accepting things, I mused as a well-greased finger entered my tight bottom-hole and drove deep into my hot rectum. That was the best way, I decided. Make out that I'd accepted everything and ask no more questions. Go with the flow, I thought as a second finger forced its way into the very core of my naked body. The fingers belonged to Caroline, and I wondered whether she was really the little virgin girl she'd said she was. Had Sally known Tracey and Caroline before? I wondered. Had she met them before she'd moved in with me? Perhaps she had planned this with the girls and ... I had to stop thinking so hard. My head was beginning to ache with the barrage of questions battering my mind.

My feet in the air, hanging from the chains, my nipples distended, the clamps biting into my sensitive teats, I let out a gasp as the fingers slipped out of my anal sheath with a loud sucking sound. The girls were muttering, whispering. What were they planning? I asked myself. I didn't want to announce my agreement to accept the situation too soon because they'd think that I was agreeing for the sake of it. I was going to have to wait a while and endure whatever sexual acts they committed.

'This will prepare you,' Tracey said, forcing a huge vibrator deep into my well-greased rectum.

'Prepare me for what?' I dared to ask her, my face grimacing as the plastic shaft stretched me open to capacity.

'The men, of course. We have two clients booked. Two men who are heavily into anal sex.'

'I knew nothing about . . .' My words tailed off as I decided to stick to my plan and not argue or question the girls. I smiled. 'I knew nothing about two men with lovely hard cocks coming to see me,' I breathed. 'I hope they're paying enough to enjoy my bum?'

'Of course they are,' Sally said. 'I wonder whether you'll enjoy the whip? They're into whipping young girls' bottoms and . . .'

'I love the whip,' I lied. 'A good anal fucking followed by a thrashing – sheer bliss. I think the business will do well with you in charge, Sally.'

'You've changed your tune,' she said, frowning at me.

'You're right, I should accept things. I have a lovely house, money coming in . . . What more could I ask for? Besides, it doesn't matter who's in charge. As long as the money rolls in, what the hell?'

'I'm pleased to hear that,' Caroline said. 'We want you to be one of the team. It would be a shame to lose you.'

'We need to talk this over,' Tracey muttered, walking towards the steps. 'We'll have some coffee and discuss this.'

As the girls left the basement, I squeezed my anal muscles and ejected the vibrator from my rectum. Two men? I mused, imagining them taking turns to shaft my rectal duct and spunk my bowels. I rather liked the idea and hoped that it wasn't just some idle threat. But I couldn't think about cocks: I had plans to make. How the hell was I going to discover the truth? I could do nothing until I was released. What were the girls talking about? Were they making plans? All I could do was bide my time.

Eleven

The girls seemed to believe that I was happy with the way things were and they finally released me. I dressed in my skirt and blouse and wandered out into the garden as they tidied up the sex den. The men they'd said were calling, the anal-sex men, never did turn up. Perhaps the girls were trying to worry me, but I'd been rather looking forward to a couple of hard anal shaftings. I breathed in the summer air and made my plans to discover the truth. Someone in the village would know whether or not there were twin sisters, I was sure. Perhaps Jim knew? I wondered as I ambled down the garden to the woods.

Perhaps I *should* accept things, I reflected, leaning against a pine tree. As the girls had said, I had a nice home and plenty of money. Perhaps I should stop worrying and enjoy my new life. But thoughts nagged me continually. I was the curious type: I couldn't just let things be and get on with my life. I had to know what was going on, and why. I'd been the same at school, always asking why, why. The other girls had got fed up with me and become pissed off with my questioning.

Did it matter where the four hundred thousand pounds had come from? Everything had happened so quickly since I'd got the money. I'd moved into

Juniper House, Sally had moved in and then Caroline
. . . Orchestrated or not, did it matter? Concluding
that the girls were right and that I shouldn't question
everything, I decided to walk into the village and see
Jim. I'd arranged to meet him several times but things
had got in the way and I was feeling guilty. I also
wanted to see what he had to say about Caroline,
particularly since she hadn't gone to the shop that
morning.

I walked into the village and watched Jim through
the shop window for a while. He was talking to a
customer, showing him an old cabinet. I knew that
there was money in antiques but nowhere near as
much as I was earning. I had a thriving business,
though it was nice to be out of the house for a while.
As the customer left I wandered into the shop and
smiled at Jim. Little did he know that I wasn't
wearing any panties. Would he ask me where Caroline was? I wondered. What could I say?

'Lovely to see you, Alison,' he said, returning my
smile. 'Come to spend some money?'

'No, sorry,' I said. 'As it is, I have a house full of
furniture. Did Caroline . . .'

'She rang earlier. Is she feeling any better?'

'Er . . . yes, yes, she is.'

'Probably a bug going round. She'll be OK in a day
or so. By the way, I was talking about you this
morning.'

'To Caroline?'

'No, to the chap who owns the little hardware shop
down the road.'

'Oh?' I felt my stomach churn. Had someone
discovered something about me? 'Er . . . nothing bad,
I hope?'

'It wasn't so much about you as about Juniper
House. I happened to mention that my niece had

205

moved in with you. We got chatting and he said that the woman who used to live there was psychic.'

'What, a medium?'

'Yes, that's right. She used to hold séances. He went along to one or two and found it was very interesting.'

'Talking to dead people?' I breathed, my mind flooding with a thousand thoughts.

'Yes, I suppose so. I don't believe in it myself. It's a load of rubbish if you ask me. But he said that it had worked and he'd communicated with his grandmother who'd passed away years before. I reckon it's easy for charlatans to con people by asking a few tentative questions. They pick up on the odd thing and then –'.

'Jim, did the old lady have twin girls?'

'Twins? No – why do you ask?'

'Are you sure?'

'I never went up to the house so I don't know much about it. But I do know that she had a son and a daughter. Tracey and . . . Ian, I think. Tracey came to live in the village after a row with her mother and the son lives abroad.'

'I wish I'd asked you about Tracey before,' I sighed. 'Where is she now?'

'She died. Had some illness or other and –'

'She died and there was no twin sister?'

'That's right.'

'Shit. Did you know her? I mean, you saw her out and about?'

'No, I didn't. Bit of a recluse, apparently. What's all this about?'

'I dread to think,' I muttered, heading for the door. 'I'll talk to you later, Jim. Thanks.'

As I walked along the lane to the house I didn't know what to think about Tracey. She was a liar, I already knew that. And she wasn't a ghost. So who the hell was she? Turning my thoughts to the old lady, I wondered whether her psychic powers were still with her. Perhaps from her world, wherever it was, she was able to communicate with us. That would explain her influence, I thought. Taking a short cut through the woods, I decided to slip into the house through the kitchen and eavesdrop. With any luck, the girls would be talking, planning, and I might learn something.

I was about to emerge from the woods into the back garden when I noticed two ropes tied to the trunk of a pine tree. One was fastened around the base of the trunk and the other about five feet up. I hadn't noticed them before, which I thought was odd because they were clearly visible. Turning, I noticed two more ropes tied to another tree about six feet away. They definitely hadn't been there before, I was sure of it. There was no way I could have missed them. Probably kids messing about making a rope swing or something, I mused, heading for the house.

'Oh – who are you?' I asked a scruffy middle-aged man as he rounded the corner of the house. 'What are you –'

'I'm the gardener, miss,' he replied matter-of-factly.

'But . . . I don't have a gardener.'

'I've worked here for twenty years or more,' he said with a chuckle. 'Mistress Tracey rang me and . . .'

'Mistress Tracey?'

'The lady of the house. I haven't been here since her mother passed on and the garden's become quite a mess. She called me and . . . well, here I am.'

'Oh, I see,' I sighed. 'OK, that's fine.'

As I slipped into the kitchen and listened out for the girls, I decided that I was pleased to have a gardener. But *I* was the lady of the house, I thought. Not Mistress fucking Tracey. Hearing nothing, I wondered whether the girls might be upstairs or in the den. Mistress fucking Tracey, I thought again angrily. Sally was trying to take over and run the business and now Tracey was taking liberties. I crept into the hall, jumping as I bumped into Caroline. She seemed normal enough, chatty, and I said that I'd been out for a walk. I then told her about the ropes and she asked me to show her. I thought it odd that she should be interested as she followed me into the back garden. But then she said that someone had been hanging around outside.

'That's the gardener,' I said as we neared the woods. 'Mistress fucking Tracey rang him and he's back in his old job. It'll be nice having him here because he'll be able to keep an eye on things. I don't want any more intruders.' Pointing to the ropes, I sighed. 'We'll have to keep the back door closed in future.'

'Yes, madam,' Caroline breathed, gazing at the ropes.

'I called in to see your uncle, by the way.'

'Oh, right. I phoned him and said I wouldn't be in today.'

'Why?'

'It's boring, standing in the shop all day, madam. I'd rather be here.'

'Yes, I suppose it must be pretty boring surrounded by old furniture. He was telling me about the old days, Juniper House and . . . Apparently, the old lady was psychic, a medium.'

'Yes, that's right.'

'You knew?'

'Yes, she –'

'What are you doing here, Caroline?' Sally asked accusingly as she approached with Tracey in tow.

'We were chatting,' I said. 'Enjoying the sunshine and chatting. And I was showing Caroline those ropes,' I added, pointing to the trees. 'They weren't there before, I'm sure of it.'

'*I* put them there,' Sally enlightened me.

'You? Why?'

'I'll show you.'

As Sally and Tracey grabbed my hands, I realised what the ropes were for. After pulling my arms out and tying the ropes to my wrists, they dropped to their knees and yanked my feet to each side. Sally had obviously planned this, I thought as they bound my ankles. I'd thought that they'd accepted me, had believed me when I'd said that I was happy with the way things were. I was obviously wrong. Standing with my arms outstretched, my feet wide apart, I wondered what the hell they were going to do to me. I'd learned one thing, I thought fearfully as Tracey stood in front of me and grinned. The old lady had influence over us even when we were out of the house.

By the look on Tracey's face she took great delight in tearing my blouse open. Wrenching the garment from my tethered body, exposing the firm mounds of my breasts, she knelt on the ground and ripped my skirt open. Naked apart from my shoes, completely defenceless, I said nothing, did nothing, as the three girls stood in a row, looking me up and down. There was nothing I could do, nothing I could say to convince them that I'd accepted things. Why did they want me in the woods? I wondered. Why not the basement?

'So,' Sally breathed, running the back of her hand over the erect teats of my nipples. 'Been into the village snooping around, have you? Been asking questions, yet again?'

'I went to see Caroline's uncle,' I sighed, pulling on the ropes. 'Surely that's not against your rules?'

'Seeing her uncle is one thing. But asking questions is another. It's a shame because we'd thought that you'd come to terms with things. We were hoping that you'd play your role properly and –'

'As I've said before,' I cut in angrily, 'I don't know what role I'm supposed to be playing.'

'Your role is to fit in with us, Alison. All you had to do was fit in with us, become part of the team. But you wouldn't do that, would you? You had to pry, ask questions . . .'

'The old lady was a psychic medium,' I said. 'Is she telling you what to do?'

'You're sure everything's arranged?' Sally asked, turning to Caroline.

'Yes, yes, it is. Nothing can go wrong, I'm sure.'

'Good. I don't want any last-minute cock-ups.'

Watching Sally snap a branch off a nearby bush, I feared the worst as she stood behind me. As she ran the branch up and down my inner thighs, the rough leaves scraping my smooth flesh, I knew what I was in for. The leaves grazed the swollen pads of my hairless vaginal lips and I pulled frantically on the ropes. But I knew that there was no escape. Tracey and Caroline stood in front of me, their young faces displaying admiration as they looked my naked body up and down. Why tie me up in the woods? I wondered again. Why not the sex den?

The branch swished through the air and the rough leaves swiped the tensed cheeks of my naked bottom. I let out a scream. The birds fluttered from the trees as the branch again lashed my stinging buttocks. My naked body jolting with every lash, the wicked girls giggling, I knew that I couldn't take this. A gush of golden liquid spurted from my gaping sex valley, streaming down my legs as the leaves bit into the burning flesh of my bottom. I cried out and begged for my freedom. Swamped with humiliation, degraded beyond belief as the clear warm fluid splashed on the ground between my parted feet, I knew that Sally would show no compassion. She was a bitch, and was undoubtedly revelling in my pain and embarrassment.

I had no idea what Sally was trying to achieve as she stood in front of me with the branch at her side. She obviously loved thrashing my naked buttocks, but what was she after? As she ordered the girls to get 'the equipment', I wondered what on earth she had planned for me. The equipment? She ran the branch over the erect teats of my breasts, the leaves scraping my sensitive protrusions, leaned forward and locked her lips to mine in a passionate kiss.

'You're beautiful,' she breathed as her lips left mine.

'Sally, what's this all about?' I asked her. 'We were friends. We've been friends for years. Why are you doing this to me? What's going on?'

'We're still friends, Alison,' she said, kissing me again. 'It's just that . . .'

'Just that what?'

'I don't know, I . . .' she stammered, holding her hand to her head. 'It's just that I . . .'

'Are you all right?'

'Yes, I think so. When you suggested that I move in with you, I didn't want to. I had plans and . . . It was as if I had no choice.'

'Release me,' I said, reckoning that the old lady was losing her grip on her.

'No, no – I can't do that.'

'You must, Sally. You must let me go before it's too late.'

'I can't, it's not allowed.'

'Why was I brought here? The money, the house . . . What's the connection between Caroline and Tracey and us? Why us four?'

211

'The village is the connection,' Sally replied.

'How? We'd never been here before, so what's the connection?'

'Caroline came here because her uncle has a shop in the village, and a cottage. That's her connection. I came here because you invited me. Tracey has always been in the village and . . .'

'But why was *I* drawn here?'

'Your name, your age, your looks. You're perfect, Alison.'

'Perfect for what? Look, you must release me. Can't you see that the old lady is trying to possess us? She's already got you and the others in her clutches. Maybe I'm too strong-willed for her. Maybe she can't . . . What is it that's keeping her here?'

'The business. She has to run the business.'

'*I* can run the business. I don't need her, for God's sake. Why can't she move on? Hasn't she got her own world to go to?'

'She's looking for Tracey.'

'But Tracey is here. What do you mean?'

'Her little Tracey.'

'Little Tracey? What the hell are you talking about, Sally?'

'The twin sister. She's lost somewhere and Alison is trying to find her to take her home.'

'There *is* no twin sister.'

'Yes, there is. No one knew about her. She should be in the other world with her mother, but she's lost. Alison must find her and take her home.'

As Tracey and Caroline returned, I began to piece the jigsaw together. If there had been a twin sister and she'd passed on, if there was another world, an unseen world . . . then the girl should be with her mother. That was why her mother was unable to escape from this world, from Juniper House. She was hoping that her daughter would find her way here, and then she'd be able to show her the way to the other world. Although it all sounded fantastic, unbelievable, it made some kind of sense.

As Caroline fixed metal clamps to my erect nipples, I wondered again why they were doing this to me. How would this help the old lady to find her lost daughter? Jim didn't know that there were twin sisters, I reflected as Caroline hooked two chains onto the nipple clamps. He'd said that Tracey had died, so where had the living sister been hiding out? If the villagers thought that there was only one girl, and she'd died, then where had the living Tracey been? She'd said that she'd often been to the woods, to the back garden, looking at the house. But where had she been living?

Grimacing as Caroline attached two heavy weights to the thin chains, I looked down at my abused breasts. My milk teats were distended, pulling my areolae into taut cones of dark brown flesh, and I knew that this was only the beginning of my ordeal. Tracey knelt in front of me and clamped my outer lips as Sally moved behind me. Heavy weights hanging between my parted legs, my outer labia stretched, my nipples painfully distended, I let out a rush of breath as Sally drove something deep into my rectal duct. Guessing that it was a vibrator, I winced as the weights between my legs swung from side to side and stretched my outer labia further.

'They should be here soon,' Tracey said, turning to Caroline.

'I just hope this works,' Caroline murmured.

'It will,' Sally said, moving behind my tethered body. 'I'll give her another thrashing.'

'No, please . . .' I cried as she ran the branch over the stinging orbs of my bottom.

'Harder this time,' Tracey said.

The branch swished through the air, landed squarely across my clenched bum cheeks and I screamed out and pleaded again for my release. The four weights swinging, distending my aching nipples, painfully stretching my swollen outer lips, I knew that they'd show me no mercy, no compassion. Again a gush of hot liquid left my yawning vaginal entrance and splashed loudly on the ground between my feet. Never had I been so humiliated, so degraded. *Who* would be here soon? I wondered fearfully, yelping as the rough leaves bit again into the burning flesh of my buttocks. *They should be here soon.* What the hell did *they* have in store for me?

As Sally halted the gruelling thrashing of my fiery buttocks, I heard twigs cracking underfoot. People were approaching from behind. *They*, whoever *they* were, had arrived. Tracey blindfolded me, plunging me into darkness, into the depths of fear. There were no words, no conversation, as people moved about behind me. I still couldn't understand why the girls were doing this to me. Then someone yanked the vibrator out of my tight rectal duct. How would this help a lost soul to find its way home?

As fingers pulled my buttocks wide apart, I knew that it was a man's swollen knob pressing hard against my anal ring when I heard heavy breathing behind me. The huge bulb entered, stretching my anal duct, and I squeezed my eyes shut. The man's penis was huge, his shaft opening the delicate sheath of my rectal channel to capacity as his knob made its way deep into the dank heat of my bowels. How many more men were waiting to force their cocks into my bottom-hole? I wondered anxiously. How much sperm was to be pumped into the cavern of my hot bowels?

Withdrawing his penile shaft, the man held my hips as he drove his knob back deep into the very core of my young body. He withdrew again, until my anal ring hugged the rim of his helmet. Holding his knob there, obviously enjoying the tightness of my anus, he thrust back into me once more. Eventually finding his shafting rhythm, his lower belly slapping my buttocks as he arse-fucked me, he let out a grunt with each push of his huge cock. My tethered body rocking back and forth, my head hung low, I bit my lip and squeezed my eyes shut as I endured the crude anal abuse.

I couldn't stop thinking about the old lady as my anal ring rolled back and forth along the man's slimed shaft. In a way, I felt sorry for her. Searching for her lost daughter, trying to re-create scenes from the past in an effort to guide her back to Juniper House . . . It wouldn't work, I was sure. Where was the girl? I wondered as the four weights swung from my nipples and my elongated vaginal lips. Roaming somewhere in the blackness of an unseen world? Perhaps the old lady had hoped that Juniper House would be like a beacon, a guiding light in the darkness. Would the girl see it and come home?

I could feel the man's creamy sperm lubricating his crude pistoning of my rectum as he gasped and clung to my naked body. His swinging balls battering my distended vaginal lips, he repeatedly rammed his orgasming knob deep into my spunk-flooded bowels. I could feel the nub of my clitoris swelling as I swung back and forth like a rag doll. I was amazed by the height of my arousal as my vaginal milk streamed down my inner thighs. My naked body tied with rope, my nipples and vaginal lips stretched painfully, my naked buttocks thrashed with a branch . . . And now a man I couldn't see was pumping his creamy sperm deep into my bottom-hole.

I'd changed beyond belief, I realised. From a relatively shy little thing living in a rented flat and with no money, I'd become a sex-crazed wanton whore. Did I have the old lady to thank or blame for that? I wondered. Was this what I wanted? Crude sex, cocks shafting my bottom, my pussy and my mouth, girls tonguing my vagina, my clitoris ... Given a choice, I might not have sought this way of life, I thought. But now that I'd experienced the crudest sex imaginable I couldn't contemplate life without it.

The man's deflating cock left my sperm-drenched rectum and I leaned forward to hang from the ropes as my pussy milk decanted. I was exhausted, but I knew that I had to endure more cocks, more anal shafting, more spunk. One of the girls knelt in front of me and removed the metal clamps biting into my outer lips. Breathing a sigh of relief, I hoped that she'd remove the nipple clamps and allow my tits to resume their original shape. I needed to rest, to sleep and regain my strength. Would she take my blindfold off?

I protested as the clamps were fixed to the delicate wings of my inner lips and the heavy weights allowed to swing freely between my thighs. I couldn't believe what the girls were doing to me as another man pressed his bulbous knob hard against my sperm-oozing anus. I could feel his shaft entering me, opening me as his swollen knob journeyed along my inflamed duct to the heat of my bowels. How would the abuse of my young body help anyone? I wondered again as the man grabbed my hips and rammed his cock fully home.

My body aching, the sperm within my rectum squelching as the man began fucking me there, I hoped that the old lady and her daughter would find each other before long. What would happen once they'd returned to their world? What would happen to the girls and to me? Would I keep the house? Sally had said that she hadn't wanted to live with me. She'd had other plans but had seemed to have had no choice about moving in. Would she leave once the old lady had gone? Where would Caroline go? More to the point, what would Tracey do?

Since she was the old lady's daughter, Tracey would probably want to stay at the house. What was I thinking? I wondered as my naked body jolted with the second anal fucking. No one was going anywhere. The old lady, if she really was a ghost, would haunt Juniper House until the end of time. Possessing or at least influencing the girls, she'd never move on. And if she did find her lost daughter they'd both haunt the house. I didn't know what to do. There was nothing I *could* do, I knew as the man behind me increased his thrusting rhythm. At least outside the house, in the woods, Sally had almost slipped out of the old lady's grip. If I could get the girls away from the house . . .

'Caroline, go and get a chair,' Sally said.

'What's that for?' Tracey asked as I heard Caroline run back to the house.

'You'll see in a minute,' Sally replied with a giggle. 'This has to be as depraved and debauched as possible if it's going to work.'

Her words echoed around the wreckage of my mind as I wondered what on earth she was talking about. *As depraved and debauched as possible if it's going to work*. Did she mean that the old lady's daughter would be attracted by the presence of debased sex? But why in the woods? The man behind me let out a low moan of pleasure and began pumping his sperm deep into my rectal sheath. What was it about the woods? What had happened there in the past?

217

My anal duct flooding with sperm, lubricating the pistoning cock, I wondered again how many men were waiting to shaft my bottom-hole. How much more could I take? I asked myself anxiously as I heard Caroline return. My body rocked with the enforced anal spunking as I heard movements in front of me. In the darkness of my blindfold I couldn't imagine what was going on, what they planned to do. One of the girls held my head and told me to open my mouth as the man behind slipped his spent penis out of my inflamed rectal sheath. Realising what the chair was for, I knew that I was about to be mouth-fucked.

'Open wide,' Tracey said. 'You're going to have a drink.'

Another solid knob slid past my defeated anal sphincter muscles and drove deep into the sperm-flooded cavern of my bowels. I breathed in the heady scent of pubic curls as a bulbous knob slipped into my mouth. As I tasted the salty glans, I wondered who the men were. Were they from the village? I asked myself as the swollen knob slipped to the back of my throat. My lips stretched tautly around the base of the rock-hard cock, pubic curls tickling my nose, my body was jolted repeatedly with the double fucking. As fingers parted my distended inner lips and entered the drenched sheath of my vagina, massaging my inner flesh, all I could do was endure the crude sexual acts and pray for my freedom.

The fingers slipped out of my dripping vaginal sheath and I jumped as the huge shaft of a buzzing vibrator sank deep into my tight sex duct. The rounded end pressed hard against my cervix, the vibrations transmitting deep into my contracting womb, and I felt my clitoris swell. I was going to come, I knew as my vaginal muscles tightened around the plastic shaft. The weights pulled on my inner lips, my nipples throbbed painfully, and I breathed heavily through my nose as my naked body began to shake uncontrollably.

Would the old lady's daughter arrive? How would the girls know when she was here? Was the old lady herself nearby? My rectum flooded with another deluge of creamy sperm as I simultaneously felt the knob within my mouth swell. The man looming over me on the chair began gasping, and I knew that he was about to shoot his sperm down my throat. I really couldn't endure much more, I thought as my clitoris began to pulsate. The vibrator buzzing within my tightening vaginal duct, my naked body rocking, the weights pulling hard on my nipples . . . Was there no end to the crude abuse? My mouth flooded with creaming sperm, the male liquid bathing my tongue and filling my cheeks as I swallowed hard and prayed again for my ordeal to end.

My clitoris exploded in orgasm as someone repeatedly thrust the vibrator deep into my spasming vagina and I felt another stream of hot liquid pouring down my inner thighs. The golden rain splashed over the ground as my clitoris pumped wave after wave of pure bliss throughout my trembling body. I fell into a dreamlike state. Was I leaving my body? I wondered fearfully as I became oblivious to my surroundings. Drifting on clouds of orgasm, my mind blown away by blasts of lust, I thought that the old lady was trying to possess me.

I had no idea how long I'd been lying on the ground as I opened my eyes and looked up at the trees. The sky was black and it was raining hard. Managing to prop myself up on my elbow, I looked around me. The girls had gone and I was alone in the woods. Was I alive? I wondered, looking at my naked body. My nipples were three times their normal size and my inner lips protruded from my inflamed vulval crack – I knew that I was still in the land of the living. Wondering what had happened, I managed to climb to my feet and stagger down the garden to the house. A streak of lightning shot from the heavy clouds as I made it to the kitchen and closed the door behind me.

Where the hell was everyone? I thought as I slipped into the hall. There were no sounds, no signs of life, and I wondered whether the girls and the old lady had completed their task and finally left Juniper House. I was too exhausted, both physically and mentally, to worry any more. Climbing the stairs, I knew that I needed to wash. But I had no energy. I needed sleep, I decided, wandering into my bedroom and flopping down onto the bed. Pulling the quilt over my naked body, closing my eyes, I tried not to think about my horrendous ordeal. Thunder shook the house. I could still taste sperm on my lips, creamy liquid oozed from the inflamed eye of my anus, my nipples ached . . . stark reminders of my nightmare. I had no idea what time it was as I curled up into a ball. But I didn't care. All I wanted was for sleep to engulf me.

Twelve

I woke with a start and gazed at the window. The sun was shining – morning had come. Thoughts of my ordeal in the woods filtered into my mind and I wondered whether I'd been dreaming. My nipples still ached, my inner lips were sticky and inflamed, so I knew that it had been no dream. Had the girls returned? I wondered as I slipped out of my bed. Or was I still alone in the house? Was the old lady nearby? Grabbing my dressing gown, I decided to take a shower and wash away the blend of sperm and vaginal cream. My thighs were sticky, my hair was dishevelled . . . Looking in the dressing-table mirror, I realised that I was a mess.

'Tracey,' I breathed, turning as I saw the girl's reflection in the mirror. 'So you are here? Are the others downstairs?' She said nothing, her pretty face smiling as she stood by the bed in her pink dress, admiring my naked body. What was she planning? Were the other girls waiting downstairs for me? 'What's the matter with you?' I asked her, heading for the landing. 'I'm going to have a shower. After that I want to talk to you. I want to talk to all of you.'

After what had happened in the woods, I reckoned that the stupid girl didn't know what to say. What *could* she say? I asked myself as I stepped into the shower. The way she'd treated me, the way they'd *all* treated me . . . One thing was for sure, I decided, lathering shampoo into my tangled and matted hair. They weren't going to drag me back to the woods. All that nonsense about a twin sister lost in some unseen world, I thought. The old lady wanted to find the girl and take her home? It was rubbish.

When I'd been in the woods talking to Sally I'd thought that there really had been a twin sister, a little girl lost. It made some sense: the old lady haunting the house, trying to find her daughter. But now the fact as I saw it was that the girls had sold me for sex. They'd taken money from the men and allowed them to use and abuse me to satisfy their craving for crude sexual acts.

Washing the dried vaginal cream from my vulval crack, the starched sperm from the gully between my stinging buttocks, I knew that I could never wash away the memories of my time in the woods. At least I'd survived, I thought, gazing at the elongated teats of my firm breasts. Survived to fight another day. The girls were going to pay for what they'd done, I decided. They were probably downstairs, preparing the sex den. Or planning to get me into the woods again and sell me for sex, take money from men who craved to abuse a young girl's body. Rinsing away the soap, I stepped out of the shower and wrapped a towel around my naked body. The girls worked for *me*, I thought angrily as I returned to my room.

Tracey had probably gone downstairs to join the other sluts, I reckoned as I walked across the room and gazed out of the window. The gardener was working, pushing a wheelbarrow across the lawn. Had he been aware of the debauchery in the woods? I wondered. Was he part of the plan, whatever it was? Tossing the towel onto the bed, I dressed in a miniskirt and blouse and slipped my shoes on. While brushing my hair, I decided to round the girls up and order them out of the house. Juniper House belonged to me, the business was mine . . . I wasn't prepared to take any more nonsense from a bunch of conniving little bitches.

I bounded down the stairs to the kitchen and filled the kettle. I wondered where the sluts were. They were probably in the sex den, I concluded as I grabbed a cup. They wouldn't want to leave the house, I knew that. But I was determined to be rid of them. They'd argue, call on the old lady or whoever to help them, possibly try to drag me down to the basement . . . But I was in charge and I'd use force to throw them out if necessary. Taking my coffee into the lounge, I sat at the bureau and made my plans. I'd need to employ new girls. I had no idea where to find girls who were willing to work for me as prostitutes, but I'd succeed. New girls, fresh young girls, obedient teenage girls . . . And I'd keep one sweet little beauty purely for my own pleasure.

Caroline would have to live with her uncle. If there wasn't room in his cottage, then that was his problem, not mine. Wondering why Sally's parents hadn't been to see her, I thought that the old lady might have kept them away. I'd have thought that her father would have been only too willing to come and see me after I'd sucked the spunk from his beautiful cock. I'd have thought that he'd be down to see me every day so that he could slip his knob into my wet mouth. There were plenty of other men, I thought happily. Sally would have to go home to her parents, Caroline to her uncle's cottage, and Tracey . . . Where the hell would she go?

'Not my problem,' I breathed, looking forward to having the house to myself. Noticing Tracey standing in the doorway, I scowled at her. 'Go and get the others,' I said sternly. 'You'll be pleased to hear that I'm throwing you all out. After the way you treated me yesterday, I'm going to make you all homeless. Now fucking well get those slags in here.'

I was fuming as she ambled out of the room. 'Fucking little sluts,' I breathed, aware of my aching nipples brushing against the thin material of my blouse as I paced the lounge floor. Until I'd found new girls to work for me I could deal with the clients myself, I decided. Suck their swollen knobs and swallow their creamy spunk, play farms and milk them, take an anal shafting or a vaginal fucking . . . I'd have no problem satisfying several clients each day. My clitoris swelled and my pussy-milk seeped between the abused lips of my pussy as I imagined six teenage lads lining up, each one awaiting his turn to fuck me. I'd manage perfectly without those lying little sluts.

Gazing out of the window at the gardener, I wondered whether he was married. I needed a housekeeper, I thought. If he had a wife she might agree to call in for an hour or two now and then and clean the house. Things would work out all right, I concluded, wondering where the hell Tracey had got to. I wouldn't be able to tell Jim the truth, but I might be lucky enough to keep him as a friend. Spinning round on my heels as Sally walked into the room, I scowled at her.

'Where are the others?' I asked her.

'In the sex den, madam,' she replied softly. 'They're preparing the den for our client.'

'Client? What fucking client? What the hell have you arranged now?'

'He's due any time now, madam.'

'You listen to me, Sally,' I hissed. 'You and the

others have behaved despicably. What you did to me in the woods yesterday was –'

'But, madam . . .'

'Shut up. I invited you here to live with me and work for me. Since the day you moved in, you've been nothing but trouble. Trying to take charge, pushing me out of the way so that you can run the business . . .'

'Madam, I –'

'I don't want to hear any more of your crap about ghosts and lost souls, do you understand? You took money from those men, you sold me for sex and . . . I've had enough of it. You'd better answer the door,' I ordered her as the bell rang. 'I'll talk to you and the others later.'

I decided to throw them out once they'd dealt with the client. I made my way down to the den as Sally opened the front door. Tracey and Caroline were naked, and I feasted my eyes on their pert little tits, their hard nipples. Their hairless pussy lips rising alluringly at either side of their sweet cracks, I thought it would be a shame to have to throw them out. But I'd made my decision and was determined to stick to it. There were plenty of teenage girls in the world, I thought. I only wanted three or four little beauties. That shouldn't present a problem.

Saying nothing, the girls seemed to be rather sheepish as I grabbed the leather strap from the hook on the wall. They probably thought that they were in for a thrashing after the way they'd behaved in the woods. It was no good showing remorse now, I thought, deciding to lash their naked bottoms once the client had left. It was too late – they couldn't turn the clock back. They were in line for a severe thrashing. Their sweet little bottoms, their firm breasts, the hairless lips of their vulvas . . . Thrashed severely.

225

'I'll deal with you two later,' I whispered through gritted teeth as Sally showed a young man into the den.

'This is Rob,' Sally said as he gazed longingly at the naked girls.

'Hi,' he breathed, unable to drag his stare away from Caroline's young body.

'Hi, Rob,' I said. 'You'd better get stripped off.'

'Yes, yes, of course.'

'He wants all of us,' Sally said, smiling at me. 'He's eighteen and he wants our pussies, our mouths, our bums . . .'

'Not Caroline,' I cut in. 'She's not for sale. You must be quite a virile young man,' I said, frowning at him as he slipped his trousers off. 'You want all of us?'

'I can last for ages,' he replied proudly.

'I'm pleased to hear it. OK, let's see just how good you are. Tracey, bend over the table.'

'Yes, madam.'

I thought how well behaved the girls were as Tracey took her position, bent over the end of the table. Her feet wide apart, her rounded buttocks jutting out, her vaginal lips bulged beautifully between her slender thighs. I imagined that after the incident in the woods the girls probably thought they'd better try to make up for it. But it was too late, I mused, gazing wide-eyed at the young man's huge cock. His foreskin fully retracted, his purple knob glistening in the light, he was more than ready to sink his beautiful organ deep into Tracey's tight little vagina.

Sally peeled the girl's dripping inner lips apart as the teenage male grabbed his cock by the base and moved in. Watching closely, I felt my womb contract as his knob slipped between Tracey's wet pink petals and disappeared deep inside her sweet cunt. She was a beautiful girl. They were all beautiful, and I was going be sad to see them go. But I had no choice, I knew as I watched the young man push his thumb into Tracey's tight anus. My clitoris swelling, my vaginal milk seeping between my engorged love lips, I knew that I'd miss the lesbian sex. But there'd be other girls, I tried again to console myself.

Moving behind the young man as he grabbed Tracey's hips and increased his shafting rhythm, I watched his full balls swinging between his firm thighs. Kneeling to cup these rounded prizes in the palm of my hand, I looked up at his pussy-wet shaft emerging from and thrusting back deep into the girl's vaginal sheath. I could see her clitoris, its pinken tip massaged by the lad's solid cock shaft, and I wondered whether she'd come. The sight turned me on, sending my libido sky high, and I left his balls and stood up.

Ordering Caroline to kneel in front of me, I lifted up my short skirt and stood with my feet apart. Peeling the crimsoned cushions of my outer labia wide apart, exposing the dripping entrance to my tight vagina, the nub of my solid clitoris, I instructed her to lick me there. She obeyed and ran her pink tongue over my wet flesh, my unfurling inner lips. I thought of keeping Caroline on at the house as her tongue entered my vaginal hole and caressed the creamy walls of my love sheath. Sally was the ringleader and Tracey was her accomplice. Perhaps I'd allow Caroline to stay.

Clutching her head, tufts of her long blonde hair, I ground my open cunt flesh hard against her pretty face as my womb contracted and my juices of desire flowed in torrents from my tightening vagina. I could hear her slurping, sucking and licking. The teenage male breathed heavily, moaning softly as his lower belly slapped the flesh of Tracey's firm buttocks. I knew that I couldn't survive without crude sex. Sally knelt behind me and parted my buttocks, running her tongue up and down my anal valley as Caroline attended my swollen clitoris with her wet mouth. I was in my sexual heaven – I'd found my niche in life.

The boy announced his coming as Tracey lifted her head off the table and let out a rush of breath. Her face flushed, her eyes wide, I knew that she too was about to reach her climax. As Sally's wet tongue entered my anal hole, delving deep into the dank heat of my rectum, my clitoris swelled and pulsated within Caroline's hot mouth. Both girls licked and mouthed, sucked and gobbled, and I shuddered and gasped in the grip of my lesbian pleasure. My obedient sex slaves, I mused dreamily as I teetered on the verge of ecstasy. My disobedient little sluts.

My orgasm erupted within the pulsating bulb of my clitoris. I shook uncontrollably as my girl milk spewed from my rhythmically contracting vagina and flooded Caroline's face. Looking down at her as she slurped and gobbled, I thought again how beautiful she was. My orgasm peaking, another deluge of sex milk smothering her face, I shuddered once more in my sexual delirium. Two female tongues attending my holes, licking, lapping, tasting . . . Whimpering, I clung to Caroline's head as my legs sagged beneath me and my rectal duct tightened around Sally's wet tongue.

Never had I known such ecstasy, an orgasm of such strength and duration. Crying out as my orgasm rocked my young body, I could feel Sally's full lips pressing hard against my anal ring, her tongue darting in and out of my rectum. In the mist of my mind, I could hear the sounds of sex in the distance.

Whimpering, squelching, the sounds of wet flesh meeting flesh. The boy was still shafting Tracey's pussy, pumping his spunk into her teenage body. Perhaps he was as virile as he'd said, I thought as I shuddered again in the grip of my incredible coming. Dizzy, drunk on sex, I hoped to feel his hard cock gliding in and out of my yearning cunt – and the tight tube of my rectum. Would he last long enough to spunk my cervix and my bowels?

'God, no more,' I finally managed to gasp as my orgasm began to recede.

'Was that all right for you, madam?' Caroline asked me, her pussy-wet face smiling as she looked up at me.

'Yes, yes, it was . . . God, it was amazing.'

'You taste like heaven,' Sally said, her tongue leaving my bottom-hole as she rose to her feet. 'Did I do all right?'

'You both did. I've never known anything like it.'

'Who's next?' the young man said, smiling at me. Withdrawing his sperm-dripping penis from Tracey's sweet vagina, he helped her up. 'You were good,' he praised her. 'So, who's next?'

'You'll need a minute to stiffen again,' I breathed. 'In the meantime, Caroline can clean Tracey. Suck the spunk out of her pussy, Caroline,' I ordered the girl. 'Clean her up in readiness for another fucking.'

The boy stood back and watched as Tracey once more leaned over the table and Caroline knelt behind her beautiful body and parted the swell of her spunk-smeared vulval lips. Caroline was a sweet little thing, I mused, watching her lock her lips to the pink cone of flesh surrounding the other girl's vaginal inlet. I could hear her sucking, gulping down the cocktail of sperm and girl-juice, and my clitoris swelled again and my own juices of desire flooded down my inner thighs in rivers of milk. My sex den, I mused as I plummeted deeper into the pit of depravity. My brothel, my den of iniquity – my life.

'You can take his cock next,' I said to Sally as she watched Caroline drinking from Tracey's hot vagina. 'You'll take him up your arse, do you understand?'

'Yes, madam,' she replied.

'When this is over, when our client has gone, I'll be talking to you and the others about the future.'

'Yes, madam.'

'And you can cut out the madam crap, Sally. You don't fool me with your false obedience. "Yes, madam, no, madam." After what happened yesterday, I'm surprised that you're still here. After the way you treated me . . .'

'Yesterday, madam?' she murmured, frowning at me.

'In the woods. The things you did to me in the woods.'

'I wasn't in the woods, madam.'

'Sally . . . For fuck's sake, don't make out you can't remember.'

'It's my turn, madam,' she said, watching Caroline help Tracey off the table. 'I'd better take my place and –'

'Not until I've finished talking to you. When that young buck has gone, I want you to pack your things and leave.'

'Leave, madam? Leave the house?'

'Yes. What did you expect? Did you think that I'd beg you to stay on after yesterday?'

'I . . . I don't understand, madam.'

'You're a fucking little bitch, Sally. But you're not stupid. Why have you done all this? Since the day you moved in, you've been trying to push me out. And, as I said to you earlier, don't start that crap about ghosts and lost souls.'

'I don't know what's been happening, madam. I didn't want to live here, I didn't want to ... I had other plans. Since I moved in, I've not been able to ... I do and say things that I don't want to do or say. I have no control over my actions.'

'That's your excuse, is it? You're trying to make out that you've been possessed or whatever by that old lady. It won't work, Sally. I almost believed you yesterday when you talked about Tracey the twin sister, how she was lost in some other world and her mother was trying to rescue her. I *did* believe you – for a while. But, now, I can see that it was all crap. It was all designed to –'

'God, you're a tight little bitch,' the lad gasped.

'No,' I cried, turning and staring in horror as he sank his solid cock deep into Caroline's virgin pussy. 'I told you not to ...'

'She'll be all right, madam,' Tracey said as she stood next to Sally. 'Let her have some pleasure.'

'I didn't want her to ... It's too late now,' I sighed dolefully. 'This was *your* doing, Tracey. You knew damned well that I didn't want Caroline fucked. All along, I've made it quite clear that I didn't want her to get fucked.'

'Shall I go, madam?' Sally asked as the doorbell rang.

'You're naked, you stupid bitch. You can't answer the door ... I'll go. You stay down here and entertain our client.'

I was fuming again as I climbed the basement steps to the dining room. Caroline, my sweet little virgin, had been sullied, soiled – fucked. At least a young man was enjoying her teenage body, I mused. The thought of some old pervert fucking her ... It was no good complaining, I thought as I walked through the hall to the door. What was done was done.

Straightening my clothes, running my fingers through my hair, I composed myself and opened the front door to find Jim standing on the step.

'Hi,' he said, smiling at me. 'Not interrupting anything, am I?'

'Er . . . well, no,' I muttered. God, his niece was being fucked in the basement. 'It's all right. Come into the lounge. What about the shop? Who's running it?'

'I'm not opening today,' he replied, following me into the lounge. 'A village antiques shop is quiet at the best of times. I don't think I'll be losing a great deal of money just because it's closed for one day. Is Caroline feeling any better?'

'Er . . . yes, yes, she is.' Guilt swamped me as Jim gazed at me. She would be feeling much better, I thought. After all, she was being fucked senseless. 'She's sleeping at the moment so I won't disturb her.'

'That's good, let her sleep. Anyway, it's you I've come to see.'

'Oh?'

'I went to the pub last night and had rather too many beers. That's one of the reasons I didn't open the shop this morning.'

'You came here to tell me that?'

'No, no. I got talking to one of the locals. He's an old boy in his late seventies and he's lived in the village all his life. I asked him about Juniper House and the old lady.'

'And?'

'Apparently, there *were* twin sisters.'

'But . . .'

'The old lady called them by the same name: Tracey. God knows why, it seems pretty daft to me. Anyway, she kept one of them under wraps. No one knew that there were two girls. I have no idea why she did that but she obviously had her reasons.'

'So, one of them died?'

'Yes, that's right. The living one moved away and, obviously, everyone thought there was no more Tracey. The old lady started the séance rubbish, presumably in an effort to communicate with the dead girl.'

'So what else did this man say?'

'His wife knew the old lady fairly well. She never came up to the house, but she did meet her now and then. It seems that the old lady had about half a million in cash stashed away.'

'In the house?'

'Yes. The living Tracey knew about it –'

'I know about the money,' I breathed, fitting the puzzle together. 'What else did he say?'

'Oh,' he sighed. 'You've spoiled my fun. I was hoping it would be news to you and you'd search for the cash and find it.'

'No, no. Did he say anything else?'

'That's all he said. So, this money . . .'

'It's a long story, Jim. I'll tell you about it one day.'

'OK, well . . . I suppose I'll head for home.'

'Thanks, Jim. You've been a great help.'

'I can't see how.'

'I'll tell you one day, OK?'

Seeing him out, I realised that the living Tracey had put the money into my bank account. Perhaps Sally hadn't been lying, I reflected. The lost soul, the old lady trying to guide the girl to the house . . . If it was true, then had it worked? Had the girl's mother found her and taken her home? Wherever home was. My head spinning, I didn't know what to think. Had all this been orchestrated by Tracey to help her mother find her lost sister? I had to believe it, I decided, flopping down into the armchair. Fantastic though it was, it explained just about everything.

'Excuse me, madam,' Tracey said as she appeared in the doorway. 'About us leaving . . .'

'Sit down, Tracey,' I invited her, eyeing her naked body as she made herself comfortable on the sofa. 'I know about the money. The money you put into my bank account.'

'Oh, that,' she sighed.

'Yes, that. Did you have a twin sister or not?'

'Yes, it's true.'

'I see. And your mother has been searching for her?'

'Yes.'

'Crazy though it is, I believe you.'

'There's more money, madam,' she told me. 'Under the floorboards in my mother's . . . in *your* bedroom.'

'By rights, the money belongs to you.'

'No, I want you to have it.'

'Well, I . . . I don't know what to say. I was going to throw you out but . . . This plan to lure your twin sister here. The episode in the woods – did it work?'

'Yes, it did.'

'Why the woods? I mean, why not use the sex den?'

'Tracey died in the woods. She fell out of a tree.'

'Oh. So, your mother is no longer hanging around the house?'

'It's over – my mother succeeded. You will now be left in peace.'

'I'm pleased to hear it,' I said, forcing a giggle. 'And I'm in charge?'

'Yes, madam.'

'In that case, you may stay on at the house. You can all stay here. Have they finished with the young guy?'

'Yes, madam. He's about to leave.'

'Right. Well, I'll go and tell the girls the good news.'

'I'll stay up here and see the lad out, madam.'

'OK. I'll send him up.'

Leaving the room, I still thought that the story was too fantastic to be true. But there was no other explanation. The money in my bank account, the old lady influencing me to buy Juniper House ... It certainly added up. Ghosts, I mused, crossing the dining room. So they really did exist. At least I'd now be left alone to run the business. I'd earn myself a small fortune, and there was more cash beneath the floorboards in my bedroom. But I felt uneasy about the whole thing. I couldn't believe that it was over. Was this another of the girls' tricks? If so, what was it they wanted?

'Everything all right?' I asked the young man as he emerged from the basement.

'Never been better,' he replied, his fresh face grinning. 'I'll be back for more, if that's OK?'

'Of course,' I said. 'We'll be only too pleased to accommodate you.'

'Right – thanks very much. I'll see you soon. Oh, do I need to make an appointment?'

'I don't think so. You call in as and when and I'm sure we'll be able to fit you in.'

'OK, thanks. Bye.'

As he headed for the hall, I gazed out of the dining-room window at the back garden, the woods at the end of the lawn. The girl must have climbed a tree and ... Again, I thought that it made sense. It was incredibly difficult to comprehend, but it made sense. I didn't want any more hauntings, any more ghosts roaming the house and influencing the girls and me. Was it really over? I'd soon find out, I thought, descending the steps to the basement sex den.

'So,' I said, meeting Sally at the bottom of the steps. 'Another satisfied customer.'

'Yes, madam,' she said softly. 'We'll tidy up down here and then pack our things.'

'I've had a change of mind,' I announced, watching Caroline wiping away the sperm and girl milk from the leather-topped table. 'You may stay – all of you.'

'Oh, thank you, madam.'

'But, Sally, I'm in charge. One step out of line, and you'll all have to leave. Do I make myself clear?'

'Yes, madam,' Caroline said as she joined us.

'You've lost your virginity, Caroline. How does it feel? Did you enjoy having your sweet little pussy fucked by a hard cock?'

'Very much, madam. I had the biggest orgasm . . .'

'I didn't see you come down,' I said, gazing at Tracey as she emerged from the corner of the room.

'I've been here all along,' she said.

'Did you see the young man to the front door?'

'No, I've been down here, madam.'

'She hasn't left the basement,' Sally confirmed.

Staring at the girls as they frowned at me, I was speechless. Tracey had been in the lounge, she'd spoken to me and . . . Bounding up the steps and dashing across the dining room, I felt my heart banging hard against my chest. I was wrong, I had to be, I thought fearfully as I headed for the lounge. Stopping in the doorway, frozen to the spot, I stared at Tracey. She was standing by the window next to an old woman. This could not be, I thought anxiously. The hairs on the back of my neck stood up as the old lady took Tracey's hand and I clearly saw her mouth the words 'Thank you.' They both smiled at me – and then they faded, disappearing into thin air.

236

nexus

The leading publisher of fetish and adult fiction

TELL US WHAT YOU THINK!

Readers' ideas and opinions matter to us. Take a few minutes to fill in the questionnaire below and you'll be entered into a prize draw to win a year's worth of Nexus books (36 titles)

Terms and conditions apply – see end of questionnaire.

1. Sex: Are you male ☐   female ☐   a couple ☐?

2. Age: Under 21 ☐   21–30 ☐   31–40 ☐   41–50 ☐   51–60 ☐   over 60 ☐

3. Where do you buy your Nexus books from?

☐ A chain book shop. If so, which one(s)?

_____

☐ An independent book shop. If so, which one(s)?

_____

☐ A used book shop/charity shop

☐ Online book store. If so, which one(s)?

_____

4. How did you find out about Nexus books?

☐ Browsing in a book shop

☐ A review in a magazine

☐ Online

☐ Recommendation

☐ Other _____

5. In terms of settings, which do you prefer? (Tick as many as you like)

☐ Down to earth and as realistic as possible

☐ Historical settings. If so, which period do you prefer?

_____

☐ Fantasy settings – barbarian worlds

- ☐ Completely escapist/surreal fantasy
- ☐ Institutional or secret academy
- ☐ Futuristic/sci fi
- ☐ Escapist but still believable
- ☐ Any settings you dislike?

_____

- ☐ Where would you like to see an adult novel set?

_____

6. In terms of storylines, would you prefer:

- ☐ Simple stories that concentrate on adult interests?
- ☐ More plot and character-driven stories with less explicit adult activity?
- ☐ We value your ideas, so give us your opinion of this book:

_____

_____

_____

7. In terms of your adult interests, what do you like to read about? (Tick as many as you like)

- ☐ Traditional corporal punishment (CP)
- ☐ Modern corporal punishment
- ☐ Spanking
- ☐ Restraint/bondage
- ☐ Rope bondage
- ☐ Latex/rubber
- ☐ Leather
- ☐ Female domination and male submission
- ☐ Female domination and female submission
- ☐ Male domination and female submission
- ☐ Willing captivity
- ☐ Uniforms
- ☐ Lingerie/underwear/hosiery/footwear (boots and high heels)
- ☐ Sex rituals
- ☐ Vanilla sex
- ☐ Swinging
- ☐ Cross-dressing/TV

☐ Enforced feminisation
☐ Others – tell us what you don't see enough of in adult fiction:

_____

_____

_____

8. Would you prefer books with a more specialised approach to your interests, i.e. a novel specifically about uniforms? If so, which subject(s) would you like to read a Nexus novel about?

_____

_____

_____

9. Would you like to read true stories in Nexus books? For instance, the true story of a submissive woman, or a male slave? Tell us which true revelations you would most like to read about:

_____

_____

_____

10. What do you like best about Nexus books?

_____

_____

11. What do you like least about Nexus books?

_____

_____

12. Which are your favourite titles?

_____

_____

13. Who are your favourite authors?

_____

_____

14. **Which covers do you prefer? Those featuring:**
    (tick as many as you like)

☐ Fetish outfits

☐ More nudity

☐ Two models

☐ Unusual models or settings

☐ Classic erotic photography

☐ More contemporary images and poses

☐ A blank/non-erotic cover

☐ What would your ideal cover look like?

_____

15. **Describe your ideal Nexus novel in the space provided:**

_____

_____

_____

_____

16. **Which celebrity would feature in one of your Nexus-style fantasies?**
    We'll post the best suggestions on our website – anonymously!

_____

THANKS FOR YOUR TIME

Now simply write the title of this book in the space below and cut out the
questionnaire pages. Post to: Nexus, Marketing Dept., Thames Wharf Studios,
Rainville Rd, London W6 9HA

Book title: _____

TERMS AND CONDITIONS

NEXUS NEW BOOKS

To be published in July 2006

FRESH FLESH
Wendy Swanscombe

Out of the shadows of myth an ancient horror invades lesbian Europe, seeking fresh female flesh with which to fulfil his dark dreams of dominance and empire.

Only a handful of women stand between the monster and his final victory, and as time runs short they must risk all in a desperate game with their own bodies for dice. Dracula rises again, and again, in Wendy Swanscombe's *Fresh Flesh*.

£6.99   ISBN 0 352 34041 X

MANSLAVE
J D Jensen

Endowed with the magnificence of a Golden God, Shane is saved by his mistress from *The Ceremony of Glorious Transformation*. Yet, torn by so many conflicting emotions; his devotion to her; his fascination for her . . . there is also his love for maidservant Li-Me; and not least his own fearful degradation.

So deceptive is the opulent tranquillity of The Pavilion of The Divine Orchard Ladies and how fragile must his pathway be through the turmoil of petty jealousies and cruel perversities. Escape is impossible; survival an ever tenuous state.

Ruled by the devious Grand Lady, the Pavilion is a dangerous place for servants and royal concubines alike. Even so, neglected by the ageing emperor, The Honourable Sisters resort to alternative but forbidden pleasures. Resented and shunned by his fellow Novice-Eunuchs, can Shani rise above his unwilling role of a freak plaything to Their Royal Ladyships?

£6.99   ISBN 0 352 34040 1

UNDER MY MASTER'S WINGS
Lauren Wissot

Under My Master's Wings is the true story of a French-Canadian master and his American slave girl and how they navigate the fine line separating reality and fantasy, love and lies in Manhattan.

Lauren Wissot is an extraordinary and beautiful young woman. Her book begins at a Times Square strip club where she meets David – a beautiful male dancer – and ends on New Year's day after exploring and documenting their numerous orgies and S&M rituals in midtown Manhattan motels.

The content is very strong and explicit. The insights into Manhattan urban sleaze are raw and vivid.

£6.99   ISBN 0 352 34042 8

If you would like more information about Nexus titles, please visit our website at www.nexus-books.co.uk, or send a large stamped addressed envelope to:
Nexus, Thames Wharf Studios,
Rainville Road, London W6 9HA

NEXUS BACKLIST

This information is correct at time of printing. For up-to-date information, please visit our website at www.nexus-books.co.uk

All books are priced at £6.99 unless another price is given.

---✂--------------------------

Please send me the books I have ticked above.

Name   ....

Address   ....

              ....

              ....

              .... Post code ....

Send to: **Virgin Books Cash Sales, Thames Wharf Studios, Rainville Road, London W6 9HA**

US customers: for prices and details of how to order books for delivery by mail, call 888-330-8477.

Please enclose a cheque or postal order, made payable to **Nexus Books Ltd**, to the value of the books you have ordered plus postage and packing costs as follows:

UK and BFPO – £1.00 for the first book, 50p for each subsequent book.

Overseas (including Republic of Ireland) – £2.00 for the first book, £1.00 for each subsequent book.

If you would prefer to pay by VISA, ACCESS/MASTERCARD, AMEX, DINERS CLUB or SWITCH, please write your card number and expiry date here:

....

Please allow up to 28 days for delivery.

Signature ....

Our privacy policy

We will not disclose information you supply us to any other parties. We will not disclose any information which identifies you personally to any person without your express consent.

From time to time we may send out information about Nexus books and special offers. Please tick here if you do *not* wish to receive Nexus information. ☐

------✂--------------------------